SURVIVAL IN STALIN'S RUSSIA

THE STORY OF IVAN IVANOV

* * * *

A TALE OF HUMAN METAMORPHOSES

BY

JOHN TOMIKEL

* * * *

The story of Ivan Ivanov is based on interviews with many Russian people. It is the story of heroic adventure and romance.

For the convenience of American readers, conventional English measurements such as distances, temperatures and weights are used rather than the metric system.

Theme
　　　"Yet in these thoughts myself almost despising
Haply, I think on thee, and then my state
Like lark at break of day arising From sullen earth,
sings hymns at heaven's gate.

　　　　　　　　　　　　from a Shakespeare sonnet

The material on the Battle of Voronezh and the conditions of the Siberian labor camp are based on eyewitness interviews. with participants in those events.
ISBN 978 1484122150 and 1484122151

ISBN 978-0-910042-99-4 Copyright 2008 John Tomikel
Printed in the United States of America
on recycled paper

1. Igor Mikovich and the NKVD

Igor Mikovich lived in the city of Voronezh in the Soviet Union Federation of Russia. He lived in an apartment next to that of his friend Dimitri Stepanovich. The two apartments consisted of two rooms each, with a shared kitchen and toilet. Igor lived with his mother-in-law and his daughter Anya. His wife, mother and father had passed away in the great flu epidemic

Igor, Dimitri and Dimitri's wife, Tanya, had been friends since childhood and they considered themselves one big family. Dimitri and Tanya had a son Ilych whom they called Ilya. Tanya's mother, Olga Ivanov, lived in another part of Voronezh in an apartment assigned by the government. All apartments were assigned by the local government housing agent.

Ivan Ivanov was the brother of Tanya and son of Olga Ivanov. Ivan finished college studies at the University of Voronezh in 1938. On the advice of his mentor, he was enrolled in graduate studies at the university. He lived in a room just off the university grounds.

Igor Mikovich was employed as a junior clerk with the NKVD, often referred to as the secret police. The acronym stood for Narodny Komisariat Vnutrennykh Del, which translated was the People's Commissariat for Internal Affairs. He was a member of the communist party. His job in the local NKVD office was to type reports and file papers created by those in a superior capacity. He did not want any promotion, since the execution rate for crimes against the state among government workers was actually higher than in the general population.

No one in Igor's apartment was supposed to know that he worked for the NKVD. However, due to the friendship with Tanya and Dimitri, he often described his work, and some of the documents he had transferred and filed.

Stalin had been in absolute power for eight years and in 1934 members of the Communist Party leadership began to question his role in the economy and the collapse of farm production due to collectivization. This was unfortunate for those party members, since Stalin was perhaps the most ruthless tyrant ever to walk the face of the earth.

In 1932 Stalin had ordered the confiscation of all crops produced in the Ukraine. Agents were sent there to "steal" this production and insure that collectivization was in progress. This resulted in one of the worst famines ever recorded in human history.

The immediate superior of Igor Mikovich was sent to Ukraine to record the grain harvest as well as document the animal harvest. Igor had to accompany him, since he was good at taking notes and recording. Stalin was said to want the grain and meat in order to exchange it for industrial machines, since he remarked that the Soviet Union was fifty years behind the west, and he wanted to catch up in ten years.

In November 1932, Stalin's second wife, Nadezhda Allilueva, chastised him about the famine in front of guests and he insulted her with the bitterest words imaginable. She went upstairs to her bedroom and shot herself. People said Stalin never recovered from this. In the next few years, he was often seen at her gravesite.

When Igor returned from the farmlands of the Ukraine he had a lot to tell his friends Tanya and Dimitri. He waited until the children and grandmother were in bed before he began his tale.

"You wouldn't believe what I had seen. Our agents actually went into every home and removed all the food. Winter was coming and everyone said, 'What will we eat?' The reply was to eat each other if you had to. When people resisted, they were bashed in the head. When large supplies were discovered hidden in underground caches, the people who hid them were exiled to Siberia. Wagon load after wagon load of starving people were transported eastward out of the region."

Igor went on to say that people dug their own graves and waited on the mounds of earth to die with the hope that someone would push them in once they expired. He saw a young child on his dead mother's breast. He thought the woman was alive and the child was suckling. When he got closer, he saw that the mother had been dead for a few days and the child was actually eating the breast. He said he cried at that.

When he and his supervisor were walking to the center of a

village, a hysterical woman came running at them. She said "I ate my son Petrov last week and this week I will eat my daughter Anna." The supervisor pulled out his pistol and was going to shoot her. He changed his mind and kept walking.

In another incident, his supervisor was about to exile a man dressed in rags, who was apprehended hiding grain. The man said out loud to the group standing around "Adam and Eve were the first communists. They had no clothes, had to steal their food, and they thought they were living in Paradise." His supervisor decided to shoot the man.

Igor referred to the Ukrainians as those poor bastards. He said the countryside was devastated and there was no hope for them. When his supervisor gave him the report to type he said there was an estimate that twenty million people had died from the famine. From what he read and knew, Igor's estimate was that about fourteen million people had died. Another six million had been sent into exile in Central Asia and Siberia.

On December 1, 1934 a gunman shot and killed Sergei Kirov, the popular mayor of Leningrad. Stalin used this as an excuse to get rid of more members of the Politburo who had been part of the original government under Lenin. He claimed that the popular Kirov was a great communist and his death should be avenged. There were enemies of the people everywhere, and they had to be rooted out and punished.

Kirov had called his bodyguard on that fateful day, to tell the guard that he would not be going to the office. However, he decided to go to the office anyway, only to be gunned down. The next day, the bodyguard, Borisov, died under mysterious circumstances. There was reason to suspect some sort of conspiracy. Heading the list of suspects were priests, kulaks, the intelligentsia, exploiters and wreckers.

The Kirov affair gave the NKVD authority to start a campaign of mass arrests and executions. Communist leaders Zinoviev, Kamenev and other lesser figures in the Leningrad area were charged with complicity in the murder. Six hundred and sixty three people who had known Zinoviev were exiled from Leningrad. The key figures were eventually executed.

What became known as the show trials were key events in

5

the terror that was the trademark of Stalin. When the accused were brought before Judge Andre Vishinsky he used endless vicious phrases about them. He was in inquisitor, not a judge.

It was in the show trials of 1937 that Igor had to participate. His supervisor asked Igor the age of his daughter. Igor said that she was ten years old. The supervisor said that the city of Voronezh was sending a delegation of children to Moscow to protest in the streets about the show trails.

Everyone in authority knew that the trials were a travesty of justice. Defendants were accused of impossible crimes. Officials were accused of being spies for Germany and Japan. Worse yet, many of them were accused of being Trotskyites. Trotsky was the founder of the Red Army and was a challenge to Stalin as leader of the government. Eventually, Stalin won out and Trotsky sought refuge in Paris. His son stayed in Paris while he went on to live in Mexico. Stalin had a death contract out on both of them.

Igor had no choice, but to permit ten year old Anya to go on the mission to Moscow. Her group stayed eight days and marched in the streets every day. However, it was not to protest the lewdness of the show trials, but to carry banners asking for the death penalty for the traitors and wreckers of society.

When Anya got back to the apartment, she told in great detail how there were enemies of the people that had to be shot. The people on trial deserved to die. Indeed, they had confessed to all kinds of crimes.

In Moscow, the Voronezh bus load of children had an audience with Stalin. One of the children had been selected to present the general secretary with a bouquet of flowers and deliver a speech. The speech was printed out and each member of the entourage was given a copy of it for their memoirs of the historic moment.

Anya gave the copy to her father who later brought it to the Stepanovich apartment and read it to them. It started out "To our glorious, honorable, loving, dedicated, sacred leader of the common people." Igor stopped and scratched his head. Dimitri said that the language used to be reserved for people like Buddha or other divinity. Igor said that they had a divine figure for a leader and observant people were aware of this. It was unfortunate for anyone who didn't recognize divinity in its human form.

Nicolai Ezhov was head of the NKVD at the time of the show trials. The public perception was that Ezhov was cleaning up the country on behalf of Stalin, and the general secretary had too many other duties to bother himself with the trials. Actually Stalin attended the trials from a secret booth he had built high in the back of the courtroom. He was very interested and involved with the trials.

Along with the show trials, Ezhov was busy getting rid of some members of the communist party which he described as routine house cleaning. His reasons for expulsions and executions of party members were that they might be spies, Trotskyites or former members of the White Army, that is, those who were still loyal to the Czar. Other reasons for expulsion were that some persons were classed as swindlers, wreckers and scoundrels.

Igor escaped expulsion from the party, probably due to his innocuous position and partly due to the fact he lived nowhere near Moscow. When asked why he didn't seek a higher level position in the party, he answered with an old Russian proverb, "If you fear the wolf, you shouldn't go into the forest."

One of the important leaders of the communist movement was Nikolai Bukharin, one time confident of Josef Stalin. Bukharin had given great service to the party At his trial he said "Why did I do this (traitor things) if I am a wrecker and if I hate Comrade Stalin, whom I in fact love, if I hate the leadership of the party, which I in fact love."

Bukharin went on to defend his record. In prison he dictated a book to his wife to commit to memory, which she did. In exchange for his family's lives, he agreed to confess to ridiculous crimes. He was executed. Later his wife would publish his memoirs.

In the second trial of January 1937, the leader Piatakov and several of his associates were convicted of wrecking in conjunction with spying for Germany and Japan. Piatakov was given the death penalty. One of the accused, Radak, received ten years in prison. There were many protests in the street calling for the death penalty for Radak. No one dared carry a banner asking for leniency. Piatakov confessed to carrying out sabotage on Trotsky's orders as well as wrecking production across the country.

7

Under Ezhov's direction, prisoners were severely beaten to obtain testimony. The celebrated case was General Tukhachevskii, commander of the Red Army. Eventually, even the general confessed and was executed. His forged signature on documents captured from the Germans was entered as evidence. Actually, in many speeches the general had warned the government about the growing power of Germany.

With this execution, the Red Army became suspect and Stalin ordered a thorough house cleaning. This meant many executions which would serve to terrorize the survivors.

The list of class enemies began to expand to include members of nationalist movements and people who had traveled abroad. Accused were divided into two categories, those to be executed and those to be sent to prison camps. There was no escaping these fates once one was accused.

In January 1938, Stalin approved of 48,000 executions of Armenians, give or take a few hundred. In December of that same year, Stalin and Molotov signed documents approving the execution of 3,167 detainees. They did not see a need for a trial. After signing the documents, the men sat down and ordered a lunch..

Between January 1937 and December 1938, Stalin ordered 38,679 military personnel to be shot. There were also 24,624 air force officers who disappeared at the same time period. There was no trace of what had happened to them.

There was no publicity accompanying the executions. They appeared in official documents and were bandied about by word of mouth. When Igor told Dimiti about this, he added a statement by Stalin who said that if you kill one or two people that is a tragedy, but if you kill two thousand, that is a statistic.

If you define a group of people by a category and that category is not an accepted part of humanity, then there are no moral restraints against killing those people. So it has been throughout history and ever shall be. We must dehumanize the enemy, or at least, make him subhuman before we kill him.

So it was in the publicity campaign of the Soviets. Everyone who questioned the leadership of Stalin did not have the welfare of the people at heart. Questioning Stalin was equivalent to aiding the enemy and that of course was treason. Traitors were also those workers who did not meet their production quotas. Uneducated people, in the name of a classless society, were appointed to key positions of leadership. Two thirds of the people associated with the judicial system had no legal training. Their job was to get wreckers and anti-socials off the streets by any means necessary. People denounced each other and a culture of suspicion invaded all aspects of life.

Igor reported that the system was now burdened by inefficiency. The large number of arrests in 1937, as well as the executions, was staggering burdens to those who worked in records and archives. He often worked twelve to sixteen hours at his clerking job. A few times, he was sent to Moscow with secret documents that were destined for the archival tombs.

In many cases, the police knew they were arresting innocent people. But, quotas had to be filled. When these people came to trial, the police created fictitious cases against them. One good accusation was that of wrecking. Their argument was that the enemies had to be unmasked. In many areas, Stalin set quotas for arrests. If the police did not meet these quotas, they might be accused of being in league with the criminals that were out there waiting to be unmasked. Because suspects would not confess voluntarily to their horrible crimes, police saw torture as a proper way to gather evidence.

As Germany increased its military strength the Soviet military leadership began to panic. Stalin seemed oblivious to this build up and did not move to encourage a similar build up. Germany, under the Versailles treaty, kept its army at the agreed numbers and trained them to be officers. When the time came to enlarge the army, they had leadership in place. It was just a matter of supplying this leadership with soldiers. In contrast, Stalin looked upon leadership as a threat to his position.

2. Factory Life and Dimitri Stepanovich

City dwellers were the factory workers. After Stalin came to power there was an emphasis on industrial production. Workers were in short supply and peasants were induced to come to the city. This migration of peasants from the farm to the city lowered the level of skill, as well as, the average age of workers. There was a dramatic decrease in literacy and many of the peasants were unable to read the signs posted around factory walls.

Dimitri Stepanovich, the brother-in-law of Ivan Ivanov, was a worker in the Peter the Great Shipyard near the harbor of Voronezh. When Peter became Czar he had already been interested in building a huge navy to attack the Turks, who were rulers of the Black Sea. The Don River runs into the Black Sea, so it was Peter's idea to construct a navy at Voronezh, which was on a tributary to the Don, and sail down to the Sea of Azov and attack Turkish forts there. He did this, and was able to hold onto a port on the Sea of Azov for three years before his army had to retreat back north. The present ship building facility was a descendant of those early shipyards.

Dimitri worked at stamping out plates for the interiors of the hulls of ships. His plates were put against steel joints and riveted to hold these areas together.

In the 1930s, there were industries dominated by women, such as textiles, and those dominated by men, such as metallurgy. All factories contained strong Communist Party organizations which held regular meetings to discuss working conditions and the norms of production expected of the workers. Dimitri was not a member of the Communist Party. All workers had to attend these open meetings where they were given the latest laws and news concerning factory work. Communist party members had the best jobs and most of the foreman and yard bosses were party members.

Workers were supposed to be the rulers of the country under the communist system. These workers sometimes enjoyed input into the running of the factories. However, even in a classless society, they were of secondary importance. First came the intelligentsia, which were the more educated white collar workers. At the bottom of the classless social ladder were the peasants who produced the food.

Peasants were too scattered to have any political influence. They were also locally oriented and bound to the land. They were no threat to the ruling class. However, factory workers could unite and have an effect on their conditions. In the early years, factories had no cafeterias, no showers and little safety regulations. The worker's meetings began to change all that. It was in the best interest of management to listen to worker's gripes and try to do something about them. There was a shortage of workers and more illiterate peasants were beginning to move into the city and work in the factories in large numbers.

Very few people in the Soviet Union lived well during the 30s. In 1931 their real wages were fourteen percent above the levels of the last years of the Czar. But in 1937, their real wages were only sixty six percent of the 1913 rate. This caused much unrest and the view that sacrifices had to be made for the new state was beginning to wear thin.

The statistics on wages in the 30s might not be accurate, since workers were able to eat their main meal at the factory. If they lived in the suburbs, they were able to raise a vegetable garden. Also, more family members were employed under the communists than under the Czar.

A persistent problem with Russia has always been housing. Once the communists became organized, housing was issued on a priority basis. Workers were given two rooms and shared baths to house their families. People with political pull might be given three rooms which included a kitchen. Factory managers had preference when housing was assigned.

The family of Dimitri Stepanovich consisted of his wife Tanya and their son Ilya. They shared a kitchen and toilet with their good friend Igor Mikovich who also had a two room apartment. Igor lived with his daughter Anya and his mother-in-law Gemma, the grandmother of Anya on her mother's side.

It was possible for Igor, even in his low level job with the NKVD, to get a better apartment. However, he, his deceased wife, Dimitri and Tanya had been very close friends from childhood and they looked after each other and thought of themselves as one unit. Igor told his supervisors, it was good for him to live in the apartment, because he could keep an eye on the four hundred, or so, people who lived there. His superior's accepted this explanation. The supervisors didn't want the hassle of adjusting apartments when they didn't have to do it.

The Igor and Dimitri apartments were not a bad deal considering the severe housing shortage that always existed in Russia. In the smaller cities, cities around two hundred thousand in

11

population, people might have one toilet for as many as ten apartments. When new housing was built, there was an attempt to get one toilet for every two apartments.

The city offered upward mobility to the peasants. By manipulating their circumstances, it was possible for peasants to achieve better living conditions than they had back on the farm. They could work their way up the economic ladder. Once new factories were built, peasants migrated to work in them. This caused shortages of labor on farms and in the 1930s farm production diminished. The reduction of the farm labor force, coupled with the terror of collectivization, wrecked havoc with food supplies.

In some factories, workers became scarce, and the supervisors, who were obliged to meet quotas of production, often made special deals to retain workers. Workers could get extra income by a variety of schemes. The communist members in the factory did not like the bribing of peasants, but they could do little about it, since their positions depended on meeting production quotas.

Dimitri was a highly prized employee, since he could read blueprints and literature concerned with production. He was often asked by his immediate supervisor to translate some document into understandable language in order for the supervisor to pass this on to the other workers. It would have been easy for Dimitri to advance in pay and prestige, but with advancement came responsibility. The communist system did not like those in responsible positions to fail in their assignments.

There were dormitories in the shipyard and two nights a week Dimitri would sleep there. Often on these workdays, he would work overtime. When he slept at the shipyard, the immediate supervisor would let Dimitri go home early the following day. He liked having Dimitri around to let him know when things were not going well.

Up until 1935, clothing and food rationing was in effect. At this time, rationing was removed, but, there was a shift in emphasis toward the military. Japanese were moving slowly into Manchuria and spreading over into what was deemed Soviet territory. This had to be stopped. Thus, even without rationing, food and consumer goods were in short supply and would remain that way indefinitely.

Construction of new industry was at a break-neck pace in the Urals where most of the metals of modern civilization could be found. In these new plants, many workers slept on the floors at night, since the work day stretched from dawn to dusk. In that rapid construction, there was no housing and the peasant workers made temporary living quarters by burrowing into the sides of the mountains they were exploiting.

Housing for workers improved in 1937, but it still was inadequate. It seemed worker-management confrontations over housing would continue into eternity.

In order to keep workers tied to their jobs a 1932 statute declared workers could be denied housing and their ration cards could be withdrawn if they had unexcused absences from their jobs. Local housing assignments became tied to local factory work. If a worker quit his job, he was immediately asked to vacate his housing assignment. With shortages of skilled labor, many of these workers found it easy to move to another factory and get a new housing assignment. Later laws were passed to make it illegal for a worker to quit his job without permission of the director of the factory.

On the night of August 30, 1935 a coal miner, Alexsei Stakhanov, cut 102 tons of coal in one shift at a Donbas mine in Ukraine. This was fourteen times his assigned norm. Publicity of his achievement spread across the country. He was removed from his two room apartment and given a five room apartment. This publicity prompted a new movement called the Stakhanovite Movement where workers tried to outdo the norms set for them in order to get better living conditions.

All producers tried to become Stakhanovites. Many foremen fudged production levels in order to have a Stakhanovite recognized in his area of the factory. As a result, the norms kept rising until they were so high that it was impossible for anyone to meet them. Thus, workers were often accused of slacking off in their duties.

In worse shape than the workers, were the supervisors. If production schedules were not met, then the supervisor might be accused of being a "wrecker." These were people who purposely did not want the communists to succeed. In many cases, those accused of wrecking were put to death. Usually, the punishment was exile to a labor camp in Siberia.

Workers recognized as Stakhanovites were given an increase in pay, if not an increase in apartment space. However, the increase in pay did not do them much good, since there were no consumer goods, such as bicycles, to be purchased.

When factory workers realized that their complaints to the party organization were given an ear, the complaints increased. Supervisors became afraid of offending workers, even though they might not be chastised for their treatment of the worker, but, their names were kept at the forefront of the organization meetings and this was not good.

In many instances, it was not good to criticize management because management was in a position to put pressure on employees. Keeping quiet was always a good option. However, the injustice and irritation would never be rectified for many employees.

The director of the shipyard, Mr. Ivan Vikhanch, was king over a considerable domain. He was a personable fellow who kept his door open to anyone connected with the shipyard. He often went out onto the factory floor to consult with even the lowliest of workers. Their suggestions and complaints almost always received a follow-up investigation. Workers were aware of this and trusted Vikhanch..

There were four Stakhanovites recognized at the Peter the Great Shipyard in November of 1935. Two of them were later killed in accidents at the shipyard. The rumor was that people who wanted their apartments arranged these accidents. The high accident rate and deaths of Stakhanovites did not go unrecognized by the Central Committee for Internal Affairs.

One of the suspects in the accidents was Georgi Kamholz who worked diligently at his lathe job. His production always exceeded the norms set for him. When he outdid himself on one occasion, after the deaths of the two Stakhanovites, he was given a four volume set of the collected works of Lenin rather than a new apartment.

As a group, workers did not like the Stakhanovite Movement, since it put too much pressure on them to exceed norms. Many were content to work within the norms. After Georgi Kamholz exceeded his norms, the norms were raised and an extra effort had to be made every work day to reach the norms.

Finally, Georgi complained to Mr. Vikhanch that his lathe was made in France and was of inferior quality to those made in Russia and it was dangerous. It was obviously purchased by wreckers. Mr. Vikhanch lowered the norms for Georgi's lathe. The man on the second shift also appreciated that. When Georgi was first assigned to the lathe, he was so enamored of it, he arrived at work early every day and had to be kicked off the machine by the man on the second shift.

Central Committees in industrial districts welcomed letters and criticism from workers who need not identify themselves. It was a check on the behavior of management officials and it was a reliable way of getting information on performance. It also gave workers a feeling that they were participating in the system.

Once the barriers to communication were lifted for workers, there was an increase in arrests of foreman and lower level managers for wrecking. Since Mr. Vikhanch was accessible to his employees at the shipyard, he was seldom criticized by them. They regarded their plights as that of the system, rather than any fault of Mr. Vikhanch. However, yard bosses and floor managers were not immune from criticism and investigation.

The Peter the Great Shipyard had a dormitory for men without families. Many of these were peasants who had come to Voronezh from the surrounding farms. Their complaints centered on such things as bedbugs in the dormitories and lack of radios for entertainment. Complaints for the factory itself included a shortage of toilets, no snack bars, poor food in the cafeteria and improper ventilation.

When a worker complained to the wrong supervisor, about such things as the shift he was working, he might be arrested and temporarily held in custody. He would be released later with a reduction in wages. Once this technique was publicized, there was a reluctance to criticize certain supervisors. If the worker resisted this mild penalty, he could find himself on a train to Siberia.

Dimitri worked a twelve hour shift in the shipyard, six days a week with one day off. He chose Tuesday as his day off. On Mondays and Thursdays he would sleep at the shipyard in one of the rooms and cots provided for exceptional workers there.

On Mondays and Thursdays son Ilych would sleep in the

apartment of Igor. The grandmother of Anya would watch over them and go over school homework with both Ilych and Anya while Igor was presumably working at the office as he called it.

It was on a Thursday when Ilych forgot his satchel of homework. Without the knowledge of Anya or her grandmother Ilych left the apartment and went to his own apartment to fetch the satchel. When the grandmother missed him she assumed Ilych had gone to use the toilet.

When Ilych got to his apartment he thought he would be cautious, sneak in, get the satchel and not disturb his mother's sleep. When he passed the low room divider he looked at the sleeping cot on the other side since noise was coming from that direction. His mother was naked and a naked Igor was on top of her pumping away. Ilya tried to be discreet and slowly moved to the door. It made a noise when he closed it.

Tanya broke the cadence of intercourse "The door made a noise, didn't you lock it?"

"No, I thought you did."

"No, I didn't. Go and make sure it's locked."

Igor rose and headed toward the door "I hope I can continue when I get back."

"Oh, I don't doubt you will continue, long into the night."

When Ilych returned to Anya and the grandmother, he was visible shaken. The grandmother asked if anything was wrong.

"I got dizzy when I went to the toilet. Maybe I better just go to sleep, and I will feel better in the morning."

On Friday, Dimitri returned home and embraced Tanya and Ilych. At supper he noticed Ilych not eating with his usual gusto. He recognized a problem and wondered how it could be handled. "My son, why don't we go out under the street light and kick some football."

Ilych jumped at the idea. "Yes let's do that. I will get the ball."

The lights were bright and the ball was kicked back and forth a couple of times. Dimitri ran the ball around Ilych a few times. The twelve year old finally got the ball and elbowed his father to the ground, or at least he thought he had made a score.

Dimitri laughed "You're getting bigger and soon I won't be

able to keep up with you. Let's sit on the bench and rest a while."

Over at the bench, Dimitri said something was bothering Ilych and would he like to talk about it.

Ilych offered "You know I love you and mother."

"Yes I know that."

"And also Anya and Uncle Igor, Uncle Ivan and our babushkas."

"Yes I know that"

"Last night I went back to our apartment to get my satchel and I saw mother and Uncle Igor on the sleeping cot without clothes on either of them. You won't kill Uncle Igor will you, or tell him what I saw?"

"No I won't kill Uncle Igor. Let me tell you a story about your Uncle Igor, me and your mother. Do you remember Anya's, mother Elana?"

"Yes I do, she had long yellow hair that was soft and she fluffed it in my face."

"Well, your mother, Elana, Igor and I were the very best of friends. It was only a matter of time when Elana and Igor would be married and I would marry your mother. We planned on having children at the same time so that our children would be the best of friends, just like we were. That is why you and Anya were born at pretty much the same time."

"Why didn't you have more children?"

"I will come to that. Life is short sometimes and we made a vow to each other. If one of us died, me or Igor, the other one would take care of both families. The same pact was made between your mother and Elana. When you and Anya were six years old, Elana became ill with tuberculosis. We were afraid that all of us, including you children, would get it. Igor's mother got it and died along with Elana."

"I remember the sadness of it all."

"So, Elana is dead and your mother is taking care of both families from a wife's point of view. For all purposes, she is married to both me and Igor. If something should happen to me, Igor will take care of you and mother, and if something should happen to Igor I will take care of Anya and her grandmother. Do you understand that?"

17

"Yes I do. I have always thought of Uncle Igor as a substitute father, when you are not around."

"Your Uncle Igor loves you very much and would do anything for you and the rest of our family. He is my blood brother. When we were your age, we cut our finger tips and pushed them together and made a blood oath as our blood was exchanged through our cuts. We have the same blood within us."

Ilych seemed satisfied. "Let's go back to the house and I will finish my supper. I am hungry now. Kicking the ball has given me an appetite."

Igor, as a worker for the new KGB, was sent as a field agent on special occasions. His usual job was to certify papers and file them. He had some clout in his division, but was still a junior member. People in the apartment were told that he was employed as an accountant in an import firm. He kept regular office hours and appeared in a business suit. People in the apartment accepted this, since a KGB agent would have a grand apartment of more than two rooms and a shared bath. Of course, Tanya and Dimitri knew his real occupation.

Dimitri, as a laborer in the shipyard, was an excellent hard worker and the administration appreciated him. His supervisors didn't recommend him too highly, since a good recommendation would get him transferred to another division and they would lose a valuable worker. They usually recommended their third line workers for promotion. Dimitri understood this and appreciated it. He was content to stay where he was.

In order to comply with the present five-year-plan the administrators of the shipyard would falsify documents. It was common practice to falsify production documents or figure out some way to justify just meeting quotas without showing improvement.

One Saturday, after their combined family supper, Dimitri said he would like to talk to Igor about a problem. The two went outside and strolled, since one never knew if an apartment had been bugged with electronic surveillance devices.

Dimitri explained that Boris, his department supervisor at the shipyard, had been transferred to a better position somewhere along the Oka River, which was to the north. The high supervisor had approached Dimitri and offered him the job as department supervisor if he wanted it. This came with a bigger apartment and a raise in salary.

Igor looked straight ahead. "Boris has been transferred to Hell. He was executed two days ago for falsifying production figures. Actually it was his supervisor that falsified the figures, but Boris was the one to get the blame. Don't take the job. Say that you are not qualified because you are poor in mathematics. You never finished high school. You were born to be a worker, nothing more. If you didn't approach me I would have told you this before it was too late."

Dimitri winced. "I thank my stars that we had this talk. Is everyone adjusting the production figures."

"I would say yes. Remember Stakhanov."

"How could I not remember Stakhanov? He is going around the country making speeches about stepping up production and giving extra effort. He spent three days at our shipyard."

"He got credit for cutting 120 tons of coal in one twelve hour shift and he became a public hero. Rumor is that there were 30 tons of coal left over from the previous shift, and that every coal cutter in his crew worked on his coal seam to make this astounding production. He got a five room apartment and a city named after him. Not bad. Sometimes a little deceit pays off, but most often it ends with a head rolling in the street."

A few days later Dimitri burst through the door of the apartment and took off his coat, and rather than hang it up, put it on the kitchen chair and sat on it. The time was seven o'clock and Dimitri usually was home by six thirty. Tanya began putting out the dinner for him that she had warming over the gas heater. She sensed something wrong, but she didn't want to encroach on her husband's mood even though Dimitri never got angry at her.

He looked over at Tanya as she separated some forks from entanglement. "Sasha has been arrested."

"Arrested, for what, what did he do?"

"Nobody knows for sure and most of the crew did not want to discuss it. Something about being an enemy of the people."

"That's ridiculous, Sasha is a super-patriot. He is the number one socialist we know. When was he arrested?"

Dimitri put the fork of macaroni away from his mouth. "About a week ago. I thought he was sick and that's why I never saw him at the dock. Someone else was running his crane. No one has seen him since."

"That's the third person we know who has been arrested since Kirov was assassinated. We were warned that there was a vast underground conspiracy trying to overthrow the government."

"Yes, there are conspirators, I'm sure of that. There must be some mistake. Sasha couldn't possibly be mixed up with anything like that."

Tanya tried to understand. "You don't know what he does in his private life. He must have done something or he wouldn't have been arrested. People are not arrested for no reason."

Dimitri put his fork down and rubbed his eyes. "No, I will never understand his arrest, it makes no sense. We should call on his wife."

"Are you crazy, when they see us with his wife, they will think we are a part of his plot or his underground contacts. No keep away from his wife. She will probably be arrested too, since it seems improbable that a man could be involved in underground activities without his wife knowing it."

" Logic tells you that he couldn't have done anything. We work twelve hours a day and sometimes eighteen, he wouldn't have time to do anything."

"Just the same, keep your distance from this situation. Don't even discuss it with your crew. You never know who they talk to about you."

And so it was that the arrests of enemies of the people were getting closer to home. Everyone began to keep a closed mouth, since no one knew the identify of informers. What was particularly bad was that informers had a quota of information to maintain and if there was nothing to report, perhaps, they invented something. After all, if they were being paid, they had to show something for their money or benefits.

Enemies of the people seemed all around the shipyard. Foremen who didn't meet some exaggerated quota were chastised and demoted. Soon apartments started opening up in the October House on Petro Street.. New people were moved into these openings. One was a three room apartment and Tanya thought she might talk to the building supervisor about getting it. Dimitri put a stop to that by saying "We have a good deal here with Igor, only our two families with our own toilet and kitchen. If we go up to the next floor we will be in strange company and maybe that is why the apartment is open at this time."

A word to the wise was sufficient and Tanya made no attempt to get more room for her family. She stopped being friendly to people on other floors and made herself scarce to people on her own floor.

Sasha's wife lost her job at the library and she confined herself to the little patch of garden in the vacant lot between her building and the next. Her two daughters, aged six and ten, were never out of her sight. People shunned her, and she didn't blame them. About a month after her husband's arrest, she was next. They came after midnight and she had to leave the children with a neighbor who didn't want them. She assured the neighbor, it was just for the night, and the daughters would walk the three miles to her mother's apartment and stay with her until the mistake had been corrected.

The instinct of self-preservation ruled the day. People became introverted. Everyone was anxious to assure others they had no connection with the newly discovered criminals. The family was contaminated by the arrest and it spread to all members and even strangers that happened to have the same last name.. The other aspect of the situation was that people had a natural impulse to turn away from the cruelty and suffering that was the order of the day.

Arrests were being made all over the country and especially in Moscow where traitors and saboteurs were suspected to have headquarters. The government led people to believe there was a counter-revolutionary web spreading throughout the country.

Most people arrested were never heard from again. Some of those that were sent east to work in Siberia somehow got word to their relatives that they were alive, not doing well, but at least alive. Military personnel who fell under the blanket of suspicion were shot outright. Stalin purged seventeen thousand army officers with one stroke of his pen.

When Igor came for one of his nightly stints with Tanya, she asked him about Sasha. He said that Sasha was shot for being a traitor and he was afraid to discuss the crime. He admitted later that he had no idea of the nature of the crime. What about Sasha's wife? She was sent to a farm in Kazakhstan. Her sentence was five years for aiding and assisting Sasha.

Later into the night, and after the second intercourse, Igor said that the government was trying to change the nomadic life of the Kazaks by introducing farming on their rangelands. In order to get the farms going, the government decided to send petty Russian criminals to work the farms.

Tanya said that she thought perhaps the government wanted workers for the farms and so they arrested a number of people on trumped-up charges. Sasha was probably shot because he didn't want to abandon his family. Igor said he couldn't argue with that.

Tanya questioned Igor further. She wanted to know what would happen if she and Dimitri were arrested on some ridiculous charge. Igor said "Dimitri and I both love you Tanya and I would sacrifice my own life, if ever you should be threatened."

It was hard to understand how a government dedicated to the highest welfare for the greatest number of people could be involved in a conspiracy against the people. Rumors that the starvation of people in Ukraine was the deliberate act of government were quickly squelched. The rich peasants, the kulaks, were reluctant to give their goods and farms to the new collectives, and when they finally did this, or were executed, or sent to labor camps in Siberia, there was no one to run the farms. The average person thought that the kulaks should have stayed on the land even though they were no longer its owners. Most people were unaware that the kulaks had no choice.

When it came to courage in those days, the award must go to those who befriended the families of the accused, and gave them a helping hand. Children who were left stranded when their parents were arrested, either went to the home of a relative, or were sent to one of the hastily created state orphanages. The orphanage business was booming and housewives looking for employment had merely to approach the orphanage. Many of the local orphanages were staffed by young girls coming to Voronezh from the steppes of the Ukraine.

It was early summer when Ivan was arrested at the university. He did not have the luxury of going to his dormitory room for personal items. He was advised to put his parcel of books in a locker and accompany the arresting agents. There were always two of them sent for each individual arrest.

Ivan was arrested because someone had informed on Professor Arcada, a Jew. The professor was accused of sedation, since he often wrote letters to relatives living in the Middle East and Germany. Even though Russia had the Molotov-Ribbentroff Pact with Germany, there was no doubt that Germany was to be suspected. Each country had hundreds of spies in the other. People receiving voluminous mail from Germany were definitely suspect and Arcada fit the profile.

Ivan could not understand the connection between him and his professor. As it turned out, Ivan's name appeared on a list of students who were to be recommended as teaching assistants in biology for the fall session. These were top students who did research on genetics, most of which concerned insects, since entomology was the specialty of the accused professor.

Ivan's questioning lasted for five hours without a break. When one inquisitor became tired, another stepped in to relieve him. It was decided to keep Ivan overnight. The records were sent to a file clerk for documentation and security. The clerk receiving Ivan's file was Igor Mikovich.

When Igor got to the apartment that night, he went straight to Tanya and Dimitri. "Ivan's been arrested."

There was a flurry of questions and Tanya had to be seated to collect her wits. Dimitri was strong and questioned Igor about the entire affair. Igor related all he knew, as well as the high secrecy of the files. If it got out that he was discussing a case with an outsider, he would have been executed, no questions asked. Dimitri wanted to know if there was any hope?

Igor said that he knows the main interrogator on the case and he could possibly be bought off. What would it cost? Igor thought that fifty rubles would be sufficient, but if this got out, both he and the interrogator would suffer, not just execution but torture as well. He was taking a chance just approaching the interrogator.

Between the three of them, Tanya, Dimitri and Igor, they were able to scrape together fifty rubles which was about two weeks wages for Dimitri. The bribe was successful and Ivan was free to go back to the university.

However, it was just a matter of time until just about everyone connected with the university was considered leeches on society. The university was no longer recognizable. Its foreign language staff was expanded and government workers were enrolled in six week courses in German and English. Military instructors took the place of seasoned faculty.

Ivan and most of his male classmates were arrested again. This time there were serious charges. A connection had been made between the University at Leningrad and Voronezh. Kirov was the popular mayor of Leningrad and his assassination must have some connection to intellectuals. People remembered what happened when the intellectuals called the Decembrists had free rein in St. Petersburg, which was the old name for Leningrad. In World War I the name had been changed to Petrograd to dispel the German connotation. Later it was changed to Leningrad since it was the city of his Revolution.

The Decembrists were a group of educated men, mostly military leaders, who had fought in the war against Napoleon. When the French army retreated from Moscow, they were followed all the way to France by the Russians. When the Russians returned, they liked the idea of getting rid of the "king" and having free elections. They were easily captured by the Czar's military. Since the revolutionaries were all from prominent families, only five of them were executed. The rest were packed off to the Siberian city of Irkutsk, some forty miles from Lake Baikal.

Igor went to Dimitri and Tanya and said that there was no use in bribing any more officials. Ivan would not be shot but he was doomed. He would keep being arrested until he was shipped off somewhere. However, there was something he could do.

Since Igor had access to the petty criminal cases and was in charge of typing up orders and documents, he might be able to get Ivan a good deal. Most of the false sedation charges resulted in the defendant being sent to the mineral mines of Siberia, to the canal projects north of Moscow, or to hydropower projects. These were twenty year sentences and Igor doubted if there would be any survivors. He said that when you consider the Revolution was less than twenty years old, a twenty year sentence was pretty stiff.

However, there were also several prisoner road projects going on around the country. . The interrogators had quotas for each of the projects. All he had to do was switch Ivan's name from the twenty year list to one of the road projects which carried a ten year sentence.   "Actually," he said "this might be a good deal when you consider we might be going to war soon. That is if rumors have any foundation. The war would probably not last ten years and if Ivan could hang on, he will ride out the war building a road

somewhere."

Tanya warmed up to the idea. "But, what if they decide to put prisoners in the army and on the front lines?"

Igor said "We just have to take our chances on that. I'll have to change the nature of the crime and rearrange the books, but I think I can pull it off."

Dimitri embraced Igor. Tanya sat down.

Igor offered "If war does begin, both Dimitri and I will probably be forced into military duty somewhere, so let us live for today, the best we can."

3. The Sentence

Judge Primakov looked out over the courtroom and beyond Ivan who was standing between two brown uniformed guards. "Ivan Ivanov, you have been charged with crimes against the state, how do you plead?"

"Will you identify the charges against me your honor, so that I may determine if I have committed these crimes or not."

"Do you mean that you have not consulted with your legal advisor about the charges against you?

"No your honor. As far as I know, I do not have a legal advisor."

The judge looked at a desk clerk seated off to one side who was recording the proceedings. "When he returns to his room, see that he gets to talk to his legal adviser." Then to the guards "Please escort Mr. Ivanov back to his lodgings."

Ivan had no lodgings. The guards each placed an arm on Ivan and escorted him from the courtroom. They released their grip on him when they reached the hall and the three of them walked briskly. They led him back through the corridor from which they had come and down a flight of stairs to the basement and the holding cells. With blunt force, they pushed him through one door, and as it slammed into place, it locked.

The cell was made of cinder block, a type of cement block that used sinter from the steel making process instead of gravel. It was made of sinter, sand and cement and was not very sturdy, but good enough to keep a prisoner from breaking out. It was about eight feet square.

On the floor, in the corner was a bucket, presumably to be used as a toilet. On the floor, and against one wall, was a mattress made from blankets sewn together and stuffed with straw. There was a newspaper next to the bucket. Ivan went to the mattress and lay down. He had expected something like this, but it was still unreal. The only light came through the window in the barred door. It was produced by a single light bulb a few feet down the hall. The light swung haphazardly as the bulb on a strand of wire and small chain was jostled with every footstep above it.

Ivan lost all track of time as he lay in a trance, partially hypnotized by the light dancing against the opposite wall and reflecting into the room. How had he gotten into this state. He had applied for membership in the communist party, but was rejected because he was a university student. His family had no connections. His father was wounded fighting for the winning side in the revolution and yet he was here. At least there was natural gas heat in the building and it filtered down the corridors and into the cells.

Sometime, many hours later, there was a rumbling in the hall. It sounded like a cart with uneven wheels. A small door at the bottom of the cell door was pushed open and a bowl of food was placed inside by some mysterious hand. The rumbling continued beyond the cell door.

Ivan looked at the bowl full of kasha. It was a gruel mix of grains and milk. It was very runny and Ivan was used to kasha that had more body to it, more grain and less milk. He wasn't sure he wanted to consume it, but prudence told him that he couldn't be sure there would be any more food for him that day. There was no spoon or other utensil, so he slurped up the milk and with his index finger managed to get the contents of the bowl into his mouth. He set the bowl down and sat on the mattress.

Ivan was about to go back into his state of stupor when a hand reached into the food door and felt around. A voice with the hand said "Give me your bowl. When you are finished, put your bowl back where I can reach it."

Ivan picked up the bowl and moved on his knees to the door and placed the bowl within reach of the hand. "I am sorry comrade. I do not know the rules here. Please, accept my apologies."

The bowl was quickly taken and the rumbling in the hall continued, stopped, continued, stopped, continued until it was heard no more.

About two hours after the bowl incident, the door was opened. Outside stood a brown suited guard and a man who looked like he had just crawled from the gutter. Without a word the disheveled man came in took the bucket and looked at it. "You should use this for a toilet. I will collect it once a day. I empty it into my holding cart." He pointed at the door where a 30 gallon oil drum was mounted on wheels. "See you tomorrow" He turned and went to the outside where the door was slammed and the guard and "honey" gatherer moved down the corridor.

This scene was repeated for two days and Ivan did not know how long it would last or how long he could last. He looked for a place in the wall where he might tie his belt or trousers or something and hang himself. But there was none. There was the barred door window but he thought he needed more height to hang. He settled for eating the gruel and using the shit bucket. He wiped himself with the newspaper. He had tried reading the newspaper, but the light was not strong enough for that.

By now, he was disheveled and wished he had a job dishing

out food or even wheeling the slop bucket to its final destination. His beard had grown. He often took his clothes off and spread them on the floor in order to dispel the body odor that was accumulating in them. He assumed the mattress was full of lice, but apparently it wasn't. He would have welcomed a mouse for company. Perhaps the authorities would spray the cell with insecticide after each occupant departed.

When Ivan moved his mattress to plump it up, he noticed a black beetle scampering toward the wall. Apparently spraying for lice did not get the beetle. He cornered it and picked it up. He was able to identify its type as an elator, since he was a biology major and his favorite professor was an entomologist. He considered the beetle as a friend, another living creature in the ecosystem. When he put the beetle back under the mattress, he noticed that there were others.

On the fourth day, the cell door opened and a guard said, "Come and talk to your legal advisor." Ivan rose and had difficulty straightening up. He wished he had done exercises or something, other than just lay around.

The guard led him to another cell which had its own light bulb and a table with chairs on opposite sides. A man in a brown business suit sat in one chair and motioned Ivan to sit in the other.

The man spoke. "I am Lev Lefkovich, your legal advisor. I have a law degree from Moscow University where I studied under Andre Vishinsky. I might say you look like shit."

"I feel like shit" mumbled Ivan. "What am I charged with? I have done nothing wrong." His voice rose. "I am not an enemy of the state."

"That's what all you criminals say" said Lev with a slight laugh. Ivan frowned.

"Come on Ivan, lighten up. I am here to get you a good deal for your crimes."

"Again I say, what crimes?"

"It doesn't matter, you will be found guilty of whatever they charged you with." He looked at the paper in front of him as if he hadn't seen it before. "It says here you have been disrespectful to the state. That is a high crime. Probably get you twenty years."

"Who said that I was disrespectful."

28

"We never know, probably no one, but they had to charge you with something." Lev looked at the paper. "Hey Ivan you must have friends in high places."

"Why? Am I getting out of here?"

"No, you will have to be sent away. You are down for ten years, and on a road crew, no less. That's a lot better than digging canals or building a dam for electric power."

"What does that mean?"

"It means that someone has pulled strings for you, and instead of going to the mineral mines in Siberia for twenty years, most people don't last twenty years, you will be going to a road crew in Siberia."

"But I haven't done anything."

"That's what all you criminals say." This time Lev did not laugh.

Ivan looked at him. "Can't you defend me? Really, I have never criticized the state or any of its officers."

"No. If I defend you too vigorously my own ass would be in jeopardy and we wouldn't want that, would we?"

"I guess not. Is there anything you can do?"

"Since everyone here is presumed guilty, my job here is to determine the level of guilt and make recommendations for your rehabilitation. I might be able to get you on the road gang near Krasnoyarsk. Compared to Norilsk, Krasnoyarsk is considered in the tropics. You are part of the doomed. However, if you do the ten years, you will be rehabilitated and released. You would still be a young man, in your early thirties. Not too bad considering the present situation."

"What has to be done then?"

Lev became businesslike. "First we must get you a bath and shave. As soon as that is done, we will go into the judge's chambers and plead guilty. He will sentence you and you will be on your way to Siberia."

"Just like that!"

"Just like that." echoed Lev.

"What if I don't plead guilty?'

"Oh, you will plead guilty without doubt. If not today, then tomorrow, or the day after." Lev scribbled something on a piece of paper which he handed to Ivan. "You will plead guilty." On the paper was written "through missing teeth."

Ivan read it and shook his head. "I will plead guilty"

Lev took the paper from Ivan's hand and tore it in half and stuffed half of it in his mouth and chewed and swallowed it. He gave the other half to Ivan who followed his example.

"One of my criminals decided not to plead guilty. He was taken out of the chambers for interrogation and two hours later brought back. He would have pleaded guilty to any crime. He was given the maximum of twenty years in a diamond mine. It was a death sentence."

Ivan was taken to a shower and another apparent prisoner shaved him with a straight razor in the presence of a guard. He looked at the guard and the razor "What would you do if I should grab the razor and cut my throat comrade?"

The guard looked at him "You are not permitted to speak. If you do, I will have to bash you with my truncheon." He patted his billy club.

"Okay, okay, I speak no more."

"To answer your question, I would let you bleed to death and kill the man shaving you and accuse him of being your accomplice."

The toilet procedures over, Ivan was taken back to Lev and the two of them escorted by two guards made their way to the courtroom where the same judge Primakov in the same clothing looked at him.

"How do you plead now comrade Ivanov? The charge is crimes against the state."

Ivan wanted to show his mettle and say again he didn't commit any crimes but Lev's counsel seemed genuine. "I am guilty as charged your honor and I apologize to you and to my countryman for having committed these crimes. I ask for your mercy.

The judge did not seem to want to waste time. "I sentence you to ten years at hard labor at a place specified in the legal document before you and on file in the district office." Apparently the sentence was previously decided somewhere, and just waiting for the guilty plea. Lev had little influence on it except to change the destination..

Ivan was led back to the same holding cell where he would spend eight more days. He knew the routine. This time, he would exercise and prepare himself mentally for whatever lay ahead.

He was permitted to take a cold shower in tight security. While he showered a team of two prisoners sprayed his cell with insecticide and the smell was obvious to Ivan when he returned. When the guard set him into the cell, he said that Ivan should be grateful since his hotel room was fumigated.

When everyone was gone Ivan settled onto the mattress. After a few minutes he rose with a jerk and turned the mattress over to see if the beetles were still alive. They were alive and well and scurrying about some serious beetle business.

The days dragged on and Ivan played with the beetles. He inadvertently broke the wings off of one of them. He looked at the light tan thorax and wondered if it was edible. He did not like the gruel diet and would have traded his soul for a piece of meat. In an instant, he put the beetle between his teeth and squashed and chewed on it. It had a pleasant taste and he swallowed it. He thought, why not eat the beetles, they are protein. Don't the monkeys in Africa groom each other and eat the fleas and lice they find?

In the days ahead Ivan searched out insect life in the cell. If the beetles survived, then there might be other insects. The limited light made intense exploration difficult. There might even be mice lurking around and he was prepared to eat mice if he could catch them. There were no mice in evidence.

On the sixth day of Ivan's confinement two guards came to the door and opened it. One had a tightly wrapped bundle.
He spoke "You have friends somewhere. They have sent you some clothing."

Ivan squinted as more light was let into the room. "Who sent me some clothing?"

"We don't know. The bundle arrived at the hotel entrance and it had your name on it. We checked the contents and these are things you are permitted to have in your possession. So here they are." The door was slammed.

Ivan opened the shoe laces which held the bundle together. It contained a pair of trousers, a heavy jacket, a hat with flaps and a pair of shoes. These were his clothing and apparently someone who knew him and his sentence had gathered these possessions and dropped them off anonymously at the prison door.

There was something in the lining of the jacket. It felt like a small stone, but it was softer than a stone. He held the jacket up to the light and looked at the inside. A small slit was made in the lining and he worked the stone over to the slit and slid it out. It was a piece of hard cheese with the letter B scratched on it. Perhaps it was from his university friend Boris. Perhaps not. Ivan felt it was not good to speculate on such things, as he might be tortured and have to reveal his speculations. It was best to consume the welcome contraband as quickly as possible.

Olga Tries To Get Some Answers.

This was the second time Ivan had been picked up, since he was not married and a student at the Voronezh University, which was no longer high on the priority list of sacred institutions. Voro U, as the students called it, was an institution that was destined for oblivion until the government decided to use it for military housing and classrooms. A smattering of non-military classes were still on the schedule and degrees in engineering, hard sciences, and teaching were still being offered. Most of the new students were the offspring of government officials and this was another reason Ivan was vulnerable. He did not have the necessary connections to escape his destiny.

Ivan reviewed his arrests and tried to find some reason to feel confident. When the first arrest was made, the case was still in a district office. He reasoned that Igor, NKVD agent and friend of his sister Tanya's family, effected a well placed bribe. But the second arrest was in the hands of a higher court and it would not be prudent for a low ranking NKVD agent to try to interfere. He would probably be sent to some work camp with a big project like a dam or a road. Actually it might be better for him, since it was obvious there would be a war, possibly with Germany, Poland or England, or a revolt in the Caucasus and the incarceration would prevent him from having to serve in the military.

Tanya and Dimitri accepted this. Igor assured them that they would be better off not making a fuss and the fact that their last name was different than Ivan's would not make them suspect, or be questioned. He pointed out that, in many instances, a family was designated as subversive and eventually the entire lot was transferred to some remote area such as Uzbekistan.

Olga, mother of Ivan and militant force in the family did not accept that Ivan was a criminal. Her last name was Ivanova and she lived in old people's housing. She had survived for sixty- four years under the most trying conditions and she was not to be dismayed. She would go to the district court and complain that there was some mistake. Ivan was not a criminal and the only evidence against him was some unknown source who said that Ivan agreed with his professor Arcada that acquired physical characteristics could not be transmitted to the offspring. Lysenko was becoming the chief philosophical biologist in the Soviet Union and it was his contention that acquired characteristics could be transmitted to offspring along with genetic characteristics. He had fed chickens food dyed red, as well as iodine laced pellets, and the chickens eventually laid red colored eggs. He had little success with mice that had their tails decapitated. Lysenko had connections and Arcada did not.

Arcada had been accused of making the statement that Stalin was not a biologist which was blasphemy to the worshippers. He was immediately removed from his chair at the university and disappeared in the bureaucracy. Since an unknown informant said Ivan agreed with Arcada, then Ivan must agree that Stalin had no knowledge of biology. In the eyes of many, Stalin could perform brain surgery, if he wanted to, and had the time to do it. Stalin was no longer considered an ordinary being.

Grandmother Olga arrived at the district court at six in the morning and the line was already a block long waiting for the opening at eight. She took her place at the end of the line.

Waiting in line was as common to Russians as getting up in the morning. Most of the people in line were women who did not speak to each other, except to comment about the weather. A light covering of snow was on the street and the roofs of buildings.

A stout old lady in robust health pushed ahead of two people who had lined up behind Olga and said, "You look to be about my age, why are you here?"

Olga said "My son was arrested and I want to get the facts. He is not guilty of any crime."

The stout lady looked at her and said "My son was arrested too and he is not guilty either."

Olga looked at the lady suspiciously. She was brazen and if her son was anything like her then he was guilty. Most people were in line to protest the most recent group of arrests. Some were there concerning their apartments and others for licenses of one form or another. Most people assumed that if you were arrested you had committed some crime or else you would not have been arrested. Most everyone pleaded guilty which was affirmation that some crime had really been committed. Of course, everyone protested that their relative was innocent, which they probably were.

One of the ladies behind Olga tapped the stout lady on the shoulder and told her to get back two places where she belonged. If she didn't, she would call one of the several uniformed policemen who were standing around watching the crowd.

The stout lady moved back under protest, bumping into the two that were ahead of her. She stood there muttering under her breath and stamping her feet into the light covering of snow.

The lady behind the stout one said "If Comrade Stalin knew what was going on here, things would change in a hurry."

The stout lady turned around and said in a raised voice "Are you crazy? Who do you think is responsible for all this confusion? We are all being sacrificed for industrialization. There is no more leisure or pleasure in this city. All our wealth is being taken to Moscow." With that said, she turned back to face the front of the line. It was getting near the opening time of eight o'clock. You could count on punctuality where the district court was concerned.

The stout lady's comments did not go unnoticed. A man in dark clothing standing next to a uniformed policeman came toward the stout woman and said "Babushka, you seem to be in an extra hurry today."

"I am. There is shopping I must do and if you have any influence, you can get this line moving as fast as possible."

"If you will come with me, you will be placed at the head of the line."

The man smiled, motioned her forward. The stout lady

34

grinned and followed him. As she departed, she smiled at Olga and said, "The squeaky wheel gets the grease."

Snow melted and the line moved slowly as Olga progressed to about twentieth in line. A lady with a broom, sack and dust pan came past her. It was the stout lady and her eye was swollen and there was blood coming from the corner of her mouth. She moved to the gutter and began sweeping objects into the dust pan which she emptied into a sack.

As people came out of the district court office, they passed the line and someone would ask them how it went. "Not good" was the usual reply, but mostly there was no reply at all. The looks on their faces were upsetting. One man mumbled as he passed Olga "They put your name on a complainer list."

Olga thought about it as she moved closer to the entrance door. She could see people inside lined up on the stairs. She was a lot further back in line than she previously thought. The looks on the faces of those coming out were frightening. She decided to get out of line and go back to her apartment where she could cry in privacy.

As she stepped out of line and headed back, a policeman said "Babushka, you are so close, why not stay in line?"

Olga bit her lip "I have to start getting dinner ready for my family. It will take me almost all evening today."

As she moved down the street, Olga passed the stout lady with her sweeping equipment. Neither spoke.

4. The Train Ride

There was no exercise yard in Ivan's prison, only the cells. Exercise was not required. Ivan started doing push-ups and knee bends and his body was responding by toughening. The food was always some form of boiled grain or boiled potato.. A couple of times, there was a spongy tomato, and at other times a half cucumber. There was a chunk of bread at least once a day, as well as a bottle of water to wash it down, and this was welcome.

Ivan started looking again at the possibility of committing suicide. He could hang himself by attaching one of his package shoelaces to a jutting piece of cinder block high in the cell. All it would take would be a short fall and a quick snap and it would all be over. However, he thought of the promised road work and the fresh air that went with it. He could handle cold weather, but did not like hot weather. Of course, he had never worked outside in very cold weather, so he had no way to judge his ability to handle working outside in the cold for a long period of time. These were just some of the thoughts that went through his mind.

On the eighth day after his trial and confession, he was awakened at 3 a.m. by a clanking noise. A voice came through the door. "You have fifteen minutes to get yourself ready for travel. Take only the clothes you wear. You will be issued new winter clothing when you arrive at your destination."

Ivan hurried to put on two shirts and a jacket. He wore his cap with the flaps. His shoes were adequate, but they were not his felt boots which would have been ideal in most freezing weather.

The door opened and two uniformed men stood in the hallway. One asked, "Are you Ivan Ivanov?"

"Yes I am Ivan Ivanov."

"Take this card and guard it with your life. If you are found without it, or you cannot produce it, you will be shot on the spot."

Ivan looked at the card. It had Ivan Ivanov printed in bold letters and the designation V dash 22 under it. He put it in his front pocket.

Ivan knew what to do and took a place near the guards and one of them turned him in the desired direction and pushed him forward. At an intersection in the hall, he was advised to turn right and then later left until they reached a guarded door. The guard opened the door and Ivan passed through it to the outside where prisoners were forming into lines of four. One of his guards said "Do not talk to anyone."

Ivan was handcuffed to a man forming a new line and another man was handcuffed to his other hand. There were twenty such lines, a total of 80 men. Many of them had black eyes and swollen faces. Ivan assumed they refused to immediately plead guilty. Lev had given Ivan good advice.

A man in uniform moved to the head of the line and three guards moved to each side of the line and another guard brought up the rear. "Follow me." He set a brisk pace walking down the middle of the street.

The march lasted about forty five minutes when they reached a railroad station where they were told to sit on a platform covered with two inches of snow. In front of them were two railroad box cars with their central doors open.

Four men were asked to come forward and their handcuffs were removed. Each in turn showed their identify card as a uniformed man checked off their names. They stepped on the box in front of the first box car door and climbed in. When forty men were in the box car, the step box was put inside and the door was closed. A large padlock was snapped onto it. The same procedure was used to fill the second box car.

In front of the line was a single coal fired engine with a coal tender car behind it. Behind the coal tender was a passenger car. Behind that was a sleeping car for the guards.

The sleeping car was standard for the military and others who had a long journey. It had one aisle near the row of windows. The rest of the car consisted of bunks, three tiers high, with a small standing area between the bunks. Anyone sleeping on them would have to crawl up and insert himself at an angle The person on the top bunk would be able to sit up if he so desired.

Ivan was in the first car. It had a small window with bars in each end. One could see the military sleeping car in front and the prisoner car behind, but there was no side view. The roof was at least eight feet high, so there was plenty of standing room. Sitting or lying down would be a problem when the car was fully loaded. The men still observed the no talking rule, even though there seemed to be no one present to enforce it..

Finally, one man said "Break the glass in the window so we can get some fresh air. If we are in here for any long time we will die from each other's breath."

Someone answered "Don't break the glass until we are under way. We don't want to attract too much attention to this car."

Another said "How are we going to break the glass? Did anyone bring a hammer with them?" A few muffled chuckles rose up.

Ivan offered "We better find a place to lie down. Only hope the floor is decent. What is that smell in here anyway?"

Someone piped in. "I think it's tomato. They must have used this car to ship tomatoes this past summer." Others agreed that the smell was that of musty tomatoes.

"Does anyone have a watch?" came another voice.

"What do you care what time it is, you need a calendar not a watch." At least they were able to muster up some humor in what was a grave situation. "Let's just relax. Is there any water barrel in here." No one responded. "Think we will get any breakfast?"

As the windows began to let in a little daylight the train rumbled backward. After a hundred yards or more it rumbled forward. "Look's like we are on our way."

The ride was slow with many stops. A small man was lifted to the windows which he kicked out and cold winter air filtered into the car. "Oh, that is great" "Notice how it is getting warmer, spring will soon be here."

"At least we won't spend our first six months in the dead of winter."

"No matter, I should live to see twenty winters where I am going." With that statement Ivan felt like he indeed had friends in high places.

A voice rose up "I have to piss." An answer came "Go piss at the door, since it is loose and the piss will go out under it." "What if we have to shit?" "That will be a problem. Nobody shit until we can figure out what to do about it."

There was a lunch break and the men were let out along the tracks with an open field on both sides. A mobile kitchen dispensed hot tea, bread, the usual boiled potato and boiled grain. The guards seemed to be doubled and the prisoners were lined along the track.

One man from Ivan's car asked the guard "Are we supposed to shit on the floor of the car?" This was overheard by a plain clothed man who was obviously in charge. "Don't you have a shit bucket in your car.?" "No comrade we do not."

The plain clothed man barked a couple of orders to a guard who hurriedly went to a car further down the line and came back with an empty five gallon paint can. The PC, as he came to be known, said "Now you can shit in comfort. He handed the bucket to one of Ivan's car mates and a small bundle of newspapers to another. "Do not burn the paper for heat, use it for your toilet." Someone blurted out "We have no matches." The PC said "You are not supposed to talk unless I ask you a question or give you permission to talk. That better be understood. You have ten minutes more and then you must load up. I will blow a whistle to let you know when you are to load up."

Prisoners began to get up and stamp their feet and many moved them up and down in piston fashion. The whistle blew and they moved to the door with double armed guards on each side of the step box. About halfway through the loading, a prisoner in the rear began coughing and hacking. The guards looked toward him. As they looked back, a man about to step on the box ducked around it and disappeared under the car.

One of the guards yelled, "Get him. Do not shoot him." Two guards moved under the car and chased the man into an open field. They easily caught up with him and both guards clubbed him with their rifle butts. The man fell and both guards kicked him in the ribs and stomach. They got on each side of the prisoner and carried him under the arms. The prisoner's head and nose were bleeding and he was gasping for air. Ivan thought perhaps his ribs had also been smashed..

They dragged the half-conscious man back under the tracks and bodily threw him inside the car. The car finished loading. Ivan had purposely hung back until he was next to last to load. He didn't want to be last, since often in his experience, the last in line was given some job to do. In this case there was no job to do. The door was shut and the padlock restored to it.

The train rumbled forth and the injured man was still gasping and moaning. The other prisoners made room for him under the rear window. "What is your name?" asked one prisoner. The injured man gasped "Sergei."

The shit bucket was placed near the door and the stack of newspaper placed next to it. There was some argument about the privilege of sitting on the movable step.

Night came and there were no more food stops. Everyone was hungry and thirsty and they settled down to trying to stretch out, but this was frowned upon by the others. The proper position was to sit with one's knees up and rest the head upon those knees.

Bright lights were filtered through the two tiny windows and the train had reached a city where it chugged to a halt. "Where are we?" "Maybe someone could tell somehow by looking through a crack in the wall. You, next to the wall, find a crack and look through it."

"I have a crack here, but all I can see is a loading platform and some guard's heads in front." "Keep looking, maybe a sign will appear." A voice with authority in it said "I think we are probably in Kubyshev, the gateway to Siberia."

"I don't know Kubyshev, never heard of it, is it a big city?"

"It used to be Samara until they changed the name and named it after a general."

"Oh, yes, I know Samara, they make airplanes here."

The man at the crack was fascinated with his view and kept looking as the train belched and rolled forward. As it began to pick up speed, he noticed a sign that said Ryazan Stadium with a pointing arrow. "We are in Ryazan" shouted the viewer.

"What the hell are we doing in Ryazan, it's on the Oka River, north of Voronezh."

The answer would not come quickly. At the next stop the familiar sounds of a boxcar being loaded with prisoners down the line and the usual shouts and whistles occurred. New cars were being added to the train.

"We have been traveling almost a full day and we only made three hundred miles. At this rate we will die of old age in this car."

"Don't be in any hurry to get to a destination."

"Does our time start from the day we were sentenced, or does it start when we get to our work stations?"

"Who the hell knows? We will all probably die before we get out anyway."

Ivan begged their attention. "I think Sergei is dead."

A prisoner felt for a pulse. There was none. "He is dead all right. Let that be a lesson for the rest of us."

"What is the lesson?"

"The lesson is, if you are not a good runner and you can't dodge bullets, you better not be a trouble maker. Unless, of course, you wish to die. Perhaps, in time, we will all wish to die."

The noon stop for lunch was again near an open field and the routine established in the first stop was followed. The same plain clothes man was in charge. He had been riding in the passenger car behind the coal tender. When informed that the prisoner had died, the PC asked for identification of the dead man. He was told the man said his name was Sergei and the PC looked at the list of forty and said, "There are three men named Sergei in this car. Is it Plushna." A voice answered "I am Plushna." Is it Coleno?' There was no answer. "Then it is Sergei Coleno. You will have to keep him in your car until the next stop when we can properly take care of this matter."

Ivan wondered why each of them did not have a tag or a name on their clothing. The PC made no attempt to find the identification card which must be in one of the pockets. Ivan could not imagine this efficient organizer not knowing who was whom. He could have said he was Sergei Coleno and the dead man was Ivan Ivanov and maybe his deception would not be discovered. He thought, if he had a twenty year sentence and a man with a ten year sentence died, then that would have been a good option, just switch cards and keep your head down. However, he had a ten year sentence. There seemed to be no people in the box car with a fifteen year sentence. There was a lot of idle conversation in the car and terms of imprisonment was one of them. When terms came up again, Ivan hinted that he had a twenty year sentence. He didn't want anyone using his ploy and perhaps assisting his demise.

There were several stops just after midnight and the sound of doors opening and closing and people shouting filled the air. The train was loading with human cargo obviously headed for the Trans-Siberian Railroad and Siberia.

Lunch in a lonely area surrounded by fields was the order of the day. There was one meal and it was sufficient. Each man filled himself with as much water as possible, since a twenty four hour hiatus left them quite thirsty by the next lunch. They pissed freely at the sliding door and emptied the shit bucket at each stop. No one argued about the bucket and generally the first man out took the bucket with him and emptied it in the field near the tracks.

There was a long stop at Nizhni Novgorod, the metropolis at the junction of the Oka and Volga Rivers. The hole in the side of the car had been enlarged and it was easier to see station markings. When the train stopped, the hole was stuffed with the piece of wood that was removed to enlarge the hole. Sergei Plushna seemed to be the man in charge of the hole and its reporting.

Someone spoke up "Nizhni Novgorod is too far north for us to be going to Siberia. We must be going to the Urals or the Pecora Basin in the north."

Another voice spoke, "There's a lot of mineral mines in the Urals and that's where we must be going. We should be there by tomorrow."

"Maybe we can get a bath."

On the morrow, they had the usual lunch near open fields and in the distance boat whistles could be heard. They must be along the Volga. Were they going north or south?

It was the fifth night of travel. Beards were growing. Weariness set in and most of the time in travel was spent in a stupor and sleep. Resignation had set in. No one would give the guards any trouble, since they had no energy left for dissent.

On that fifth night, the train stopped at a very large city to load on more cargo. Sergei Plushna said it was Ufa, capital of the Bashkir Republic. "What the hell are we doing in Ufa, why did we skip Kazan?"

"Kazan is nothing but Tatars, Mongolian blood, and they probably didn't want to have riots and sabotage on their hands. They probably just execute the Tatars."

"But the Bashkirs are also Mongolian. Why are we stopping here?"

There was the usual clanking of doors, whistles and yelling and cars jostling back and forth. A couple of gunshots startled the lethargic entourage. Those lying down sat upright. Sergei Plushna said he couldn't tell what was going on.

When things looked like they were settling down, a big searchlight hit the door side of the box car. There was a fumbling of the lock and the doors flew open with a shout for everyone to step to the back of the car. The order was quickly obeyed.

The box step was installed and men started getting into the car. There were sixteen of them. The box step was put back into the crowded car. The door slammed and the padlock returned to its roost.

No one spoke for about ten minutes. Everyone squinted in

the poor light of the car. It was obvious that the car had been filled beyond capacity. The new prisoners looked around in order to claim a little piece of sitting territory.

Ivan asked a new man, "Where are you from?"

"I am from Ufa, but most of my comrades are from the south Volga. In our entire group there are a lot of men who speak nothing but German. They are from Saratov."

"You seem to know a lot, maybe you are an informer."

"I am one who keeps his ears and eyes open. If you do not want my information, then I will shut up and you will hear no more."

"What is your name Mr. Speaker?"

"That's it; just call me Mr. Speaker, since we will all be nameless in a couple of days. We will be known only by a number."

"How do you know that?"

"Let's just say I have had experience in these matters."

Traveling became more depressing as the train rolled on and there was no longer any room for lying down. Men started crying out in the darkness. One man cried "Oh Mutka, oh Mutka." Everyone seemed to echo him with "moya mutka" (my mother).

Chelyabinsk was the next big stop, but no more prisoners were being loaded. Two cars were unloaded and some prisoners were taken from other cars, but none were from Ivan's car. Mr. Speaker had informed them that he counted twenty seven cars from his vantage point on the dock. There were probably more, but he couldn't see them. He knew it was a long train because it had two engines, both belching smoke.

Plushna said, "The second engine must have been added at Ufa."

Mr. Speaker enlightened the crowd. "We are on the Trans-Siberian Railroad and the stops will probably be Kurgan on the Tobol River, Petropavlosk on the Ishim River, Omsk on the Irtysh River and Novosibirsk on the Ob River and Kemerova on the Tom River."

"How do you know all of that Mr. Speaker? Were you a geography teacher?"

"I worked for the Army Map Service. I would advise all of you to start thinking in terms of geography. It is necessary to have a feeling for where you are."

Kurgan was the next 3 a.m. stop as predicted. No one in Car Number One would know that two more cars of prisoners were being removed from the train. The train jostling back and forth on the tracks made Ivan sick to his stomach. He went to the shit bucket and vomited in it. Other prisoners complained of being sick from the jostling, but none vomited.

"Why don't we ask them to give us a bucket of water for our car. That way we can at least have a few mouthfuls when we get really thirsty."

The train pulled out and headed east with its cargo. There were two tracks here and a train moved in the other direction. All of a sudden here was a snapping sound and a loud oomph.

"What was that?"

A man sitting near the rear window said "This man just hung himself."

Sure enough, there was a man hanging from the rear bars of the window. It looked like he used some sort of belt to do the job.

Someone asked the man sitting near the hanged man, "Why didn't you stop him?"

"Why should I stop him, I might want to do that myself. I think I am at my limit right now. He just attached his rope belt and threw his knees up under his chin and hit the floor. He looked like a kid doing a cannonball jump into a creek."

"We better elect someone as spokesman and he can tell the PC what happened and perhaps get us a bucket of water. What do you say Mr. Speaker, do you want to be our spokesman?"

Mr. Speaker was subdued "I don't want to talk to the authorities any more than I have to. Get somebody else to do it."

There was a murmur through the crowd with prisoners asking if someone would do it. The situation was getting desperate. Finally a man said, "What can the bastards do to me that had not already been done. I will do it."

Everyone immediately started giving the leader advice on how to proceed and a list of demands. The man said he was Peter the Great from Ryazan and he had been in charge of a construction crew, so he knew how to talk to authority.

The lunch break was somewhere between Petropavlosk and

Omsk. There was swamp on both sides of the tracks and the men were fed on an artificial island. The armed guards were extra attentive.

When the PC arrived for checking, Peter the Great, moved toward him. A guard aimed his gun at Peter's head who said, "I just want to talk to the man in charge."

The PC observing this said "Let him approach me."

Peter, feeling his courage, stepped to within three feet of the PC. "I am the spokesman for Car One comrade and would like to discuss some matters with you."

"What kind of matters?"

"There is a dead man in our car, he hung himself from the window bars. I wish to report that. And we have a modest request. We would like to have a bucket of water in our car, so that we might drink some water if we get sick to our stomachs, as some of our men did last night."

To a guard, "Find a bucket and fill it with water for Car One."

Peter was feeling some power and a pleased expression came over him. The PC retained his usual stern eye-piercing look.

"How did you get to be in charge of Car One?"

"We had an election and I won."

"Are you used to being in a leadership capacity?"

"Yes, comrade, I was foreman on a construction crew in Ryazan."

"Let me see your card."

Peter reached into his right front pocket, there was no card. Neither was it in the left front pocket. He then remembered it was in his jacket flap. He produced the card.

"I see you are Peter Kolna of Ryazan. Your number is R-64."

Peter was pleased to say that it was all true and he was happy to serve the PC and the motherland, in whatever capacity he could.

"Well Peter we don't like prisoners organizing things behind closed doors. We don't like prisoners forming groups or clubs, since they might organize to revolt or try to escape. We don't like people assuming leadership roles while they are prisoners. Do you understand that?"

"Forgive me comrade, I didn't know, I thought I was doing

everyone a service."

The PC held Peter's card in his left hand and with his right hand reached into his chest flap and produced a revolver. Peter looked puzzled. The PC aimed it at Peter's forehead and pulled the trigger. The blast killed Peter instantly and he slumped to the floor. The PC threw the card on top of the dead man.

"Let that be a reminder to all of you" yelled the PC. "We do not permit elections. When we want someone to be a leader, we will appoint him."

The train was loaded and the next destination was Omsk. At this stop, the door to Car One was opened. Four prisoner's names were called out from behind the searchlight and the men stepped forward and out of the car. The door was slammed and locked again. The remaining prisoners appreciated the extra floor space.

The train chugged along and the distance seemed to stretch forever. It was especially long since there were sidings that had to be navigated. There were long waits at each siding.

After the lunch stop, east of Kemerova, Mr. Speaker pointed out that the train now had one engine and was about half the size that it was at Omsk.

Kraznoyarsk, on the Yenesey River was the destination of Ivan. At the usual 3 a.m. stop his name was read and he stepped toward the lights. On the other side of the lights, he was given a jar of water, which he quickly gulped down. He was then led to a small building with a waiting room and told to go inside. Eleven of his Car One comrades were with him. Guards were everywhere.

5. The Trek North

The waiting room was well lighted. Ivan counted over forty men before he lost track of where he had begun counting. He estimated there were sixty men in the room. A guard stood at each of the corners and one near the door. Everyone looked like they had been dragged through Hell. Dirty hair and unkempt beards were the hallmark of the arduous journey. Most men sat in the traditional survival position with their knees up near their chin and their heads resting on the knees. A bucket of water with a dipper in it was passed around and no one refused to partake of it.

After about an hour, a new plainclothes man came into the room with two guards behind him. He coughed for attention. "Prisoners, when I read your name you will accompany the guards to the outside."

He read the first name. A man got to his feet and followed the guards. As they came to the door two new guards stepped forward. This continued until he came to the name Sergei Colena. No one responded. He read the name again. Sergei Plushna, who was in the room, said that the man had died on the trip. The new PC put an x in front of the name and called out the next name.

It was Ivan's turn and he followed the guards to the outside where he was handcuffed to two other men and placed on the back of a truck. The truck had sideboards and a gate at the back. When the truck seemed full, the gate was locked and the driver headed north into the night.

After about an hour at a very low speed, the truck stopped near an open area. It was dawning now, still an hour before sunrise. The snow reflected light and there was good visibility.

A guard came to the rear and opened the gate. "Come out slowly now."

The men debarked and were escorted off to the side. Their names were called and one at a time they were taken to a long cable with handcuffs attached to it in ladder fashion. The rungs of the ladder were three feet apart and the handcuffs had a chain also three feet long. A handcuff was put on one hand.

Another truck pulled up and the prisoners were again escorted to the long cable with the handcuffs. There were forty sets of handcuffs on each side of the cable for a total of eighty prisoners.

An old chugging army tank appeared and a guard advised the men to pick up the cable between them and the front men were told to approach the tank. The tank had a full track. Once the cable was attached to the tank, it pulled forward and the men followed. Several began to slip on the snow, but soon they learned to walk at the pace set by the tank.

Shortly after noon, the tank came to a series of field kitchens with a staff of servers and a plethora of guards. The tank pulled beyond the kitchens and halted. Ivan thought he would get a chance to walk around, but there was no such luck. Their lunches were brought to them in a metal bucket. It was the usual gruel and boiled potato, topped by a hunk of bread. There was also a jar of warm tea. Ivan recognized several men from his car including Sergei Plushna and Mr. Speaker.

The old PC was still with them. Apparently he was riding in the tank. He came to the line. "If any of you prisoners have to shit, do
it now, because you will not be able to do it on the trail. Just put your ass out as far as you can. When we move again, we will be out of this mess."

Several men took him up on it and a guard handed each of them a bit of newspaper.

Ivan asked, "Can I have some paper in case I have to shit on the trail?" The guard obliged. Others also asked for a bit of newspaper.

Soon the tank started and moved forward. The human centipede had no choice but to follow. There was a break after three hours, and another after two hours, but they had to keep walking. One man fell and couldn't get up and was dragged for several yards.

Finally a guard with a key came up and took him out of the handcuffs. The man was left behind with the guard.

There was no rule about talking, but most prisoners were silent. Ivan was on the right of the cable. The man across from Ivan moved toward the cable, reached down and took it in his right hand and was saving energy by being dragged along. Ivan tried it. He grasped the cable with his left hand and agreed that he was conserving energy by letting the cable pull him forward. Soon the cable was lifted from its position near the ground and was elevated to hip level. Many men preferred to just walk along as others held up the cable.

The centipede stopped at dusk and the men were told to settle down and try to get some sleep. There was snow on the ground and the air temperature was slightly below freezing. Ivan slept in fits and starts with many violent dreams, awakening with a snort or a shout after each one.

The tank cranked up at first light and the noise roused the

men. It moved forward for a half hour and stopped. There was a field kitchen set up and each man was given a slab of bread and a jar of warm tea. Men relieved themselves in the usual manner with one hand in the handcuff.

The next leg of the journey, before a stop, lasted for four hours. Ivan figured they had covered about twelve miles in their dawn to dusk march. He thought perhaps they would cover thirty miles a day, maybe even forty.

At this stop, the prisoners were uncuffed and told to remember their place in line and go to the food line, get their allotment and sit down. It was a remote area and if any prisoner decided to make a run for it, he would be cut down in the time it would take a guard to raise his rifle.

After Ivan received his gruel, boiled potato and tea he noticed Mr. Speaker sitting off by himself. He ventured over to him and sat on the snow beside him. "Hello, Mr. Speaker, I was in Car One with you."

"I know that, I know everyone here who was in that car. You are Ivan. If you had been observant you would know my name. It is important to be observant Ivan. Your life might depend on it."

"Thank you for the advice. Where are we?" asked Ivan.

"We are heading north parallel to the Yenesey River. It's just over there, about a mile, behind you."

"How fast do you think we are walking?"

"I can tell you exactly." Mr. Speaker produced a watch. "The time is 1407 and we have been averaging three miles per hour. We have come about 55 miles since we started."

"How do you know how fast we have been walking?"

"My step is about 30 inches or two and a half feet per step. There is nothing else to do but check the time, count out one mile of steps, and calculate from there."

Ivan shook his head. "That is amazing. So you calculate about 1150 steps per mile."

"I took you for an educated man Ivan and I was right. Probably no other prisoner on this cable could have figured that out as quickly as you. Speaker laughed, "What did you do before you committed your crime."

"I was a graduate student in biology, specializing in entomology."

With that said, the whistle blew, the prisoners moved to the kitchen area, piled up their jars and tin plates and moved to their position on the cable. Someone up front got out of line and a minor adjustment had to be made.

As usual, the trek continued until dusk and the men lay down for a bad night's sleep. Fortunately there had been no wind on this journey and even though there was snow on the ground, it had not been rough going. The prisoners noted a fairly good road under them.

As Ivan lay on the ground he heard the tinkle of a bell. Then there were more bells. Soon a reindeer appeared, followed by a sledge and driver. This was followed by another reindeer, sledge and driver and another. It was the first time Ivan had seen a reindeer, although he had seen many pictures of them and had studied them in classes on mammals. Someone down the line said "That's our food supply for tomorrow." Another voice answered, "I am willing to eat the cattle pulling the sleds."

Dawn brought the usual chunk of bread and jar of warm tea. Men were standing and urinating freely and the warm piss made frosty clouds of steam around them. Many were moaning and complaining about their leg muscles. The guards warned them to quit complaining and be quiet this time.

Ivan spent the next four hours walking along and counting footsteps. With his new found hobby he figured he was taking 3500 steps per hour. It was better counting steps than wondering how his mother, sister and her family were making out. He considered himself lucky for not being married. He heard many men referring to their wives and children. One man said he had absolutely forgotten what his wife looked like and probably would not recognize her if she walked by him.

This lunch had the usual boiled cereal and boiled potato, but it had a surprise, boiled fish. The fish were hacked into three parts. Ivan's part was from the middle of the fish. He thought it was a carp as he picked the scales and skin off. The bones were big and easily discovered. He chewed the welcome change in diet with gusto.

Ivan again sought out Mr. Speaker and asked him where the guards slept when they were not on duty. Speaker said there are trucks and vans behind them and the guards probably slept in the vehicles and rotated from them. They have their own kitchens. At this time of year, the trucks can move freely over the frozen mud, but any day now the mud will start to thaw and it will be very difficult for trucks to move. Speaker said "I told you to be observant. Don't you see a truck coming up behind us and guards shifting positions? Ivan said he only looked forward, since he was near the head of the line and when he did look back, he only saw the men behind him. Speaker said that it was a good time to look when they made a turn. "Then you can see the entire entourage."

The trekkers moved forward at a brisker pace this time. The skies became darker than usual and the wind was picking up. Snow began to fall and the wind hurt Ivan's face even though it was now covered with a beard. He was glad he had his hat with the ear flaps on it and the two layers of clothes underneath. This padding was also comfortable sleeping on the ground. Others were not so fortunate. There were whimpers about the chilling wind.

The tank driver could no longer see his way in the falling snow and there was nothing to do but stop until it blew over. It was near dusk anyway. This type of storm only lasted about a half day and there was never more than three inches of snow from any of them in this location.

The man on the cable next to Ivan was Genedy Ustinov and he and Ivan had become friendly. They were birds of a feather and flocking together, as Genedy called it. As Ivan lay on the ground with the snow shooting over him Genedy said to Ivan "Do you mind if I cross the cable and lie next to you. I am freezing."

Ivan said he didn't mind and Genedy moved over to the other side of the cable and Ivan moved his body next to him. It was warmer that way. Soon the man below Ivan moved into their circle and the three of them clustered on the ground. Others saw this and the cable became a line of small mounds of men clustered together. The guards who were walking their rounds made no attempt to stop this interaction.

Dawn came on with a clear sky. The air was much colder and breathing out produced puffs of frost. The usual warm tea and chunk

51

of bread was there. Although the tea came from boiling pots it cooled very rapidly. However, it still had some warmth as the men drank it.

At lunch, Mr. Speaker figured they had covered about a hundred and ten miles and the Angara River junction with the Yenesey River was either just ahead of them or just behind them. The Angara had the city of Irkutsk on it, about forty miles after it left Lake Baikal. There was a big hydroelectric project to be built at Bratsk, down river from Irkutsk, and many prisoners probably were sent there. Mr. Speaker knew of no project going on in this region and hoped they weren't going to be marched the thousand or more miles to Norilsk, a nickel and copper mining city north of the Arctic Circle.

There was a hurried march and Ivan figured the quicker pace meant something was about to happen. The tank stopped about an hour before sunset. After a pause, the PC stepped from behind the tank and told the men to arrange their cable in a half circle because he wished to speak to them. They obliged and the PC got into the center of the half circle.

"Prisoners of the Soviet, you have been obedient and cooperative and as a reward you will get a ration of barbecued reindeer meat in a short time. You are at your destination and you will remain attached to the cable tonight. But, tomorrow you will be in a warm barracks and you will have a chance to wash up. Those of you who wish to shave will be able to do so, or at least you can trim your beards with scissors. After that, you will begin the tasks assigned to you. This is a good assignment for you and the man in charge of operations, Major Mikoyan, rewards cooperation and punishes non-cooperation. I might add that he punishes non-cooperation severely. So get a good sleep and enjoy the reindeer meat and hot tea that will be served to you shortly."

Meat and tea and a slab of bread arrived shortly. It was served by men of Nentsy heritage. These were Eskimos living on the tundra who make their living by herding reindeer. They sold meat and hides and seldom ventured far from their homeland. These Nentsy were men who took risks and who had a contract with the Soviet military. If a man was lost or escaped, usually it was the Nentsy who went after him. They could survive in this savage environment, but the average Russian could not.

Ivan looked around and for the first time noticed his surroundings. The group was on a river flood plain and in the distance there was forest. He knew this was the Taiga, the largest single expanse of forest in the world. It was a region of dense trees, most of them coniferous and poplar. The taiga is bordered on the north by the tundra, a flat treeless plain, and on the south by mixed forest with broadleaf s dominating.

Taiga is created by a continental climate where winters last from six to seven months. The growing season is short, although summer temperatures north of Krasnoyarsk have often reached 90 degrees Fahrenheit in July and August. Despite these high daytime temperatures, the nights cool off very quickly and frosts in July are common.

The unforested area south of Krasnoyarsk produced, among other crops, wheat and sugar beets. Truck crops such as tomatoes, red beets, carrots, potatoes and cucumbers were common. Most of this produce was sold in the markets at Krasnoyarsk. However, large quantities of wheat from this region, was shipped to Moscow. All roads and railroads eventually led to Moscow.

A good dairy industry thrived around the Krasnoyarsk area. Butter was the main cash product from these ventures and most of this was shipped west to the Moscow region.

The Yenesey River is 2,500 miles long. It begins in the Tuva Republic from streams rising in the Altai Mountains. It flows westward, then turns north where it enters the Kara Sea of the Arctic Ocean. Its main tributary is the Angara River which empties out of Lake Baikal. North of the Angara River is the small Stoney Tunguska and further north is the Lower Tunguska River. All of these major streams join the Yenesey from the east.

Sturgeon and salmon abound in the rivers. Carp is the main fish found in the many swamps created by the Yenesey when its northern waters are dammed by ice as the southern section thaws in spring. The Angara River, 1150 miles long, is the only outlet of Lake Baikal. It flows from the southwest end of the lake.

The largest city on the Yenesey is Krasnoyarsk located where the Trans Siberian Railroad crosses the river. It is halfway between Moscow and Vladivostok on the Pacific Ocean. The double track railroad crosses the Yenesey on two four thousand foot bridges. The Yenesey at the time of Ivan's imprisonment was being connected to the Ob River by a series of small canals.

A mud road parallels the Yenesey for most of its length. There are small villages about every fifty miles along the Yenesey. The road connecting these is impassable in spring and barely passable in summer .When winter arrives, the road becomes available to vehicles. When the river freezes to ice, it becomes an extra driving surface. People in the villages make a living by lumbering and trapping in the long winter and fishing in the short summer.

In the villages, the mud road is paved with logs topped with sawed timbers. There is a constant struggle to keep the boards from coming loose and the village residents are in a constant state of attaching boards to logs. The wooden road was necessary in the mud seasons.

Ivan's prison camp was in the Kraslag District, an administrative area which reached from Mongolia in the south to the Arctic Ocean in the north. The Yenesey River was the common factor in the designation of this area. The total district was commanded by General Mikhail Frunze who made a name for himself by defeating the Muslim tribes to the southwest, when they sought independence, just after the revolution. It was a good time for the Muslims to try to break away and the Uzbeks, Krygyz, Tajiks, Kazaks and Turkmen each made a try for independence. However, they were not only fighting the Red Army, they were fighting among themselves, which worked to their disadvantage. General Frunze, with only a small force of four thousand soldiers, was able to wreck havoc and secure the land for the Soviets. In his honor, the Bolsheviks changed the name of the ancient city of Bishkek to Frunze.

When daylight came, the men were unshackled, four at a time, and marched two miles to the prison complex. The snow on the ground had been trampled and earth was exposed. The prisoners passed through a large guarded gate which had a sign with the number 193 painted on it. They were taken to a room in one corner of the enclosed compound. Their identity cards were checked. A large wood burning stove was in the center of the room and for the first time in three weeks, the men felt real heat.

A soldier wearing the sergeant designation told the prisoners they were about to be sprayed with a lice killing concoction and given a shower. They were to put their clothes in the large basket in the next room and a barber would use scissors to cut their hair and beards. This would facilitate the removal of lice.

There were four barbers in the next room who had no training as barbers. They were prisoners who had drawn this assignment. The hair was removed very quickly from the nude men. Some chest hair was also removed as well as armpit hair of those needing it. The barbers did not speak except to give an instruction to their customers.

When the hair cutting was finished, the men were moved to the next room where two men with canisters of lice killer pumped the containers and sprayed the nude bodies completely. They were told to sit in the next room.

There was a ten minute wait and the deloused men were told to go to the next room station. This room had two windows and a door. The windows were triple glazed and held the heat of the building at a cool but comfortable level.

An attendant in the room pointed out the window. "See that shower out there." He was pointing to a raised pipe where several streams of water poured down from openings. "You are to go out there, find some soap, which is on that low table, wash yourself thoroughly and then come back into the room next to this one. There are towels there and you can dry yourself."

The tallest prisoner said "Won't we die from exposure to the cold air?"

"No, we have done this many times and no one has ever died. Someone in the next room will be watching you and if you do not wash completely you will be sent out again. You are fortunate; today, the temperature is slightly above freezing. When our guests arrived last month, the temperature was twenty degrees below freezing. The water is pumped from a deep well and its temperature is around forty five degrees, maybe even fifty degrees so it should be better than standing in the thirty five degree air."

The men rushed out, grabbed a bar of soap, lathered and showered and hurried into the drying room where towels awaited them. After drying, they were told to go into the accompanying room and have their identification photos taken, then sit and wait for instructions.

In the waiting room the first ID cards were returned. The attendant checked the men against a list. The group of four was told they should go to barracks 14 which was pointed out to them. "There is no need to knock, just walk in and someone will take care of you."

The still nude men hurried across the yard to building 14 and entered the only visible door. A man was waiting for them. In two corners of the room, a guard with a pistol was seated on a chair.

The greeter looked at the first card. "Gregor Mishkov you have been assigned bunk number 37." He waved his hand for Gregor to accompany him to bunk 37. It was the upper bunk in a set of bunks. At its base was a pile of clothing, consisting of three sets of underwear, two pairs of pants, a light tunic jacket, a heavy parka, a light hat, a warm hat with ear flaps, four pairs of socks, two shirts, a belt, a pair of work shoes and a pair of felt boots. The jackets and shirts were greenish blue and each had number 863 painted on them.

"From now on prisoner you will be known as number eight six three and you are never to use your birth name as long as you are here. Is that understood?"

"Yes, I understand."

"Good, dress yourself. Put your extra clothes in the left locker under the bunks. Sit up on the bunk and wait for further instructions."

This was the routine for the prisoners who arrived at Camp 193. This batch of prisoners was evenly divided between barracks 14 and 16. There were seventy eight men. There should have been eighty, but two had died during the trek. Ivan was in barracks 14.

The barracks held one hundred men. There were thirty nine newcomers to Barracks 14. The old timers would introduce them to life in camp.

Camp 193 consisted of ten barracks, each built to house one hundred prisoners. In the center of the barracks was a wood burning stove and a rack to hold fire logs. The fire was going, but at a low rate. Each bunk had its accompanying locker under it with a number that corresponded to the bunk. Gregor Mishkov would be in bunk 37 of barracks number 14 and his official designation would be number

863.

The camp also had a large dining hall which could seat four hundred men under crowded conditions. The prisoners usually ate in three shifts, depending on their duties. The first shift was for the prisoners engaged in service activities and light duties. Second and third shifts were for the menial workers. Which shift one ate depended on his working distance from the compound.

Outside the compound, Camp 193 had other holdings. There was a two story house for the camp commandant Major Gregor Mikoyan and his family. Two lesser buildings housed the captains and their families. Guards were housed in a building in the compound. They had their own dining hall and recreation room. A dog pound was on the outside of the compound. It usually had sixty dogs of various breeds with shepherds and huskies dominant.

Major Mikoyan was responsible for the welcoming routine of the prisoners. He had worked it out from his experiences as a prisoner of the Czar. His philosophy was to work the prisoners hard, but to try to get them adequate food and promote a healthy atmosphere. He felt that this would limit escape and mutinous attempts and the mere threat of being sent to another camp would deter any insubordination of the prison population.

About a mile from the camp there was a pig and goat farm. Prisoners worked this property, but seldom enjoyed its benefits. Goats were milked and eventually slaughtered and fed to the guards and the families of the officers. When a particular item was needed, but not at hand, Major Mikoyan was not above sending someone to Krasnoyarsk to do some bartering with goat milk, butter or meat. The compound received a regular beef allotment from south of Krasnoyarsk. The goat and pig scheme was not widely publicized. Major Mikoyan did not want the authorities at Krasnoyarsk to know about his side business which might lead to a decrease in his meat and fish ration.

6. New In Camp

Camp 193 was located approximately 56 degrees North Latitude. At this location there would be seventeen hours of daylight in June and seven hours of daylight in December. Work was still long and hard in the winter months since there was actually about an hour of light before sunrise and an hour of light after sunrise.

Around four o'clock in the afternoon the men were all processed and dressed in new outfits. Ivan was prisoner number four four one. Since there were always slightly less than a thousand prisoners, the numbers were recycled as names were deleted from the list and others added. Major Mikoyan figured a three digit number was easier to recognize and report than four or more digit numbers.

Guards went to barracks number 14 and 16 and told the men to assemble in the dining hall. Once there, their numbers were called and they responded. They then went to the food line, picked up a metal tray and a metal cup and moved through the line. It was a familiar meal of boiled grain, this time it was barley, boiled potato, a slab of bread and hot tea. There was also a third of a fish. Ivan got the tail on this draw. He was surprised to find a lot of flesh in the tail. He believed it to be some sort of pike and its actual length must have been about sixteen inches which fed three or four men if this was a good division of the fish.

After eating, the trays and cups were put onto a counter where the food detail prisoners picked them up and plunged them into a tub of boiling water. The prisoners were told to sit in one section of the dining room.

Soon a uniformed man appeared in front of them. He was Captain Rurik, the number two man at the camp. He began to speak. "Prisoners of the Soviet people. I am Captain Rurik and I am in charge of your rehabilitation. When you have served your time here, you will go back to your towns with skills that will make you valuable to society. I will go into that in more detail later. First I want to introduce you to our camp commander Major Gregor Mikoyan." He pointed toward the door.

The Major came forward and waited for absolute silence. He began, "Prisoners of the Soviet. It is my order from the Supreme Soviet to administer this camp in an efficient manner. I call on you to give me your cooperation. You each will have a job to do. How successful you are, depends on how well you do the task assigned to you. There are rewards for hard and efficient work and there is punishment for not doing your assigned work. It is as simple as that.

The food you have just eaten should indicate to you that it may not be caviar, but it is healthy. There is extra food for extra work. I leave you now in the hands of Captain Rurik who will explain some of the rules and what it is we do here." The Major turned and went through the door where two guards snapped to attention.

Captain Rurik came forward again. "Prisoners of the Soviet, what we are doing here is building a road from Krasnoyarsk to Norilsk along the Yenesey River. When I worked in a steel mill my job was to put carbon on steel cable and heat them in a pot for four hours. I had no idea what the heat and carbon did to the steel and to this day I still do not know. So this is why I tell you what we are doing. So you have some idea of the enormous project that lies before us."

Rurik continued, "There is a crew working from the north and we are working from the south. The northern crew refers to this as the tropics. So be appreciative that you are here and not in the north. Last year, we completed ninety miles of road. We have about a thousand miles to go on our section and we hope to complete two hundred miles of road in the coming year. We have five years to link up to the crew coming south. This means we will have to double our efforts." Rurik paused to see if there were any changes in expressions of the prisoners. All were staring blankly at him.

Rurik went on. "Captain Yaroslav will give you a few pointers on what is expected of you." Rurik motioned to the other captain who was seated near the stove.

Captain Yaroslav came forward. "Welcome prisoners. We are always happy to see some new faces around here. The rules are simple. If you try to escape, you will most likely be captured and shot. We have never had an escape from Camp 193. There is no where to go. The road to Krasnoyarsk is heavily guarded. The mud road to the north has some small villages who will turn you in or else face retribution. You cannot go east or west since the forest and swamps will get you. You have food, clothing and shelter here and a noble enterprise. Make the best of it."

Yaroslav continued. "You will rise an hour before daylight, eat breakfast and report to your group leader. Your group will depart to your duty station. You will work to sunset and come back here for supper and then return to your barracks. The barracks leader will check you in, and if you are missing, he will report it to the sergeant in charge who will look for you. You will not be happy when he finds you if you do not have a good reason for your absence. The outhouse toilets are behind every barracks and you should notify the door keeper if you are going to the outhouse."

Rurik rose to add something to the Yaroslav discussion. "We are located about sixty miles north of our road and this summer we should easily pass these premises and move on further toward our destination. We will probably spend next winter building new barracks and facilities about two hundred miles north of here. If you have any carpentry or building skills, let us know, and we will keep you in mind for this duty."

Yaroslav again took the floor. "If you are sick and miss a day of work then two days will be added to your sentence. So it is important to work even if you feel slightly ill. You may be able to relax on your job if you have a sympathetic group leader. However, if your group does not meet its quota assignment, then your illness might be considered as sabotage. After this meeting you will line up at our medical clinic and each of you will receive a purple tattoo on the upper tip of your right ear. This is an identification mark which means you are part of our camp. It is a simple dot and will not pain you."

The meaning was clear, if one escaped, he would be easily recognized as a prisoner and be exposed. Despite the knowledge that some men were sent to prison on trumped up charges, most of the population believed that a prisoner must have done something to warrant his incarceration.

Yaroslav motioned a guard to him. "Private Kharkov will escort you to the medical center for your tattoo."

With that Kharkov told the men to line up and follow him through the door. He led them to a small building with windows on every side. Each man was led to a table where a needle was inserted in a vial of dark fluid and plunged into the upper tip of the right ear. When it was Ivan's turn he noticed several hospital beds in a room off to the left. There were men in underwear on a couple of them.

They were next told to report to their respective barracks and wait for their group leaders to find them and give them some orientation. The sun had just set, so it would be another hour before the old gang was fed and another hour before the group leaders would be free to find them.

True enough! About two hours after sunset, the sixty working residents of Barracks 14 started showing up. They took off their heavy coats and hung them on their bunks. They wearily took off their boots and placed them by the stove, leaving just enough room for someone to get in and feed the fire. Then there was some knee bends and other stretching as the men tried to loosen their overworked muscles.

Ivan lay on his bunk number 74 which was a lower bunk and observed the scene. He remembered Mr. Speaker's advice about staying back and observing and not to jump into things. Apparently Mr. Speaker was in barracks 16, because he was no where to be seen in number 14.

A tall thin man, holding a sheet of paper, approached Ivan. "Number four forty one," he ventured. Ivan rose to sit on the bunk. "I am that number."

The thin man held out his hand to shake Ivan's. "I am a group leader and you have been assigned to my group. My number is 167 as you can see, but when we are alone you may call me Boss."

"O.K. Boss," smirked Ivan.

"It's good that you can still smile. After tomorrow, there will be very little smiles for you, just as there are little smiles for the rest of us. However, we are all prisoners of our minds, rather than prisoners in body."

"What do you mean by that," queried Ivan?

"It's just a philosophy. I think you can put up with anything if you have a strong mind. God will take care of your body but not your mind."

"I'm afraid I do not believe that there is a god that does anything for anyone. My mother prays so why am I here?"

"Then why are you here, you belong with the godless communists. Ah, but I make jokes. Just follow my orders and everything will go well for you. Don't volunteer to be a group leader, it is not worth the trouble. They are always looking for people who want to be leader and then they figure out ways to punish them for their aggression. If they appoint you group leader pretend you don't want to be and they will force you and that will mean you have no ambition. Why am I telling you this? You will find it out for yourself. I must move on and find my other three additions."

Ivan spent a fitful night, but with surprising anticipation of what tomorrow would bring. He tried to look at each man in the barracks before he finally settled down for the night. There was not much room to move around. He saw Sergei Plushna who also saw him but they made no recognition. They both had been warned by Mr. Speaker to avoid giving the impression of alliances."

The next morning, an hour before sunrise, a horn sounded and the prisoners started getting to their feet and dressed. They filed into the outhouse which had eight holes and a urinal trough and relieved themselves. Just in case, Ivan took a piece of newspaper from the stack used for the toilet. A man next to Ivan looked at his new clothes, "Just hope you don't have to shit out there. If you can, hold it until after supper. If you organize your diet, you can shit the first thing every morning."

Ivan remarked, "How can you organize your diet when we eat breakfast and supper."

"Don't worry you will get the hang of it. You probably have twenty years to work on it."

Breakfast was a wheat kasha, bread and hot tea. It was hearty, but nothing to cause ecstasy. Ivan sat next to the boss since he wanted to learn as much as possible as quickly as possible. It appeared that number 863 was also a member of his group, since he sat on the other side of the boss. The boss informed them they were a labor group and he hoped they had some strength; after all, they had a full days rest.

After eating, the boss said, "Let's go and get in formation."

When they reached the outside the groups were already lining up in front of barracks 14. There were eleven men and one leader in each group. Each leader reported to Private Vilnius that his group members were all present. When the eighth leader finished reporting, Vilnius reported to Sergeant Vilko that barracks 14 was ready to go.

The boss led his group to the gate under the watchful eyes of several guards. The large gate was opened and the men filed into an open bed truck which held twenty four men and four guards. Ivan's group was first in line. They filed into the truck followed by two other groups. The end gate was raised and the truck moved out.

Forty miles later the truck came to a halt and emptied its human cargo. Ivan followed the boss off to one side. He looked around to see the faces of the members of his group. He recognized Sergei Plushna and Sergei acknowledged him. Sergei asked, "I never did get your name." Ivan responded, "I am Ivan Ivanov."

The boss snapped at both of them. "Don't ever mention your real name in front of anyone you do not know personally. Pointing to Ivan, "You are 441 and pointing to Sergei "You are 560 and don't you forget it, ever."

The boss crew was one of the crews in charge of laying down stones and gravel. There was a mound of stones in the middle of the road which was the last load dumped there from the night before. Wheelbarrows were removed from their parking space by the road. Six men were given the honor of wheeling stone. Six others took tampers and sledge hammers. The tampers were flat pieces of steel about six inches square with a metal post. The idea was to pour the stone and the tampers would spread it out with the metal square and tamp it into place. There was also a large roller that two men pulled behind them. This was not used until at least twenty feet of road had been put in place.

The boos told Ivan that whoever the engineer was on the project figured that the road level should be about three feet above the floodplain. The land to the west of the Yenesey River was a broad plain and that was the direction of flooding. Since it was flat, it was easier to build the road on that side than on the east bank which was rugged.

Some workers were engaged in building the road to the three foot level. Fill dirt was brought in by trucks and smoothed to that level. Many men were engaged in augmenting the fill dirt with pick, shovel and wheelbarrow. They had a three foot deep trench on the east side. This was a drainage ditch between the road and the river. The fill dirt crew operated about a mile ahead of the paving crew. When the fill dirt crew started lagging, men were brought up from the paving crew to move forward faster.

It was smooth going at this time of year when the ground was frozen. Soon the ground would thaw and the work would be more difficult. The fill dirt trucks came from the north and the stone paving trucks came from the south. A big rolling vehicle pressed the stones of the paving crew further together making it a flat surface since the eyeballs of the paving crew were not always accurate. The human pulled roller merely aligned the stones for the big roller.

The driver of the roller truck was a skilled technician. He had to be able to repair the vehicle as well as drive it. In 1934 only about five percent of the people of the Soviet Union had a driver's license. Most of the vehicles in the country were driven by the military or drivers for the bureaucracy. On this project, skilled truck drivers, steam shovel operators and loaders were at a premium.

Gasoline was stored in very large tanks along the river. The tanks were located near the villages and a villager was responsible for the safety of the gasoline. There were two gasoline tanks near the stockade. A smaller gasoline tank was located near the officer housing area. This was used to produce electricity for powering the lights and appliances in the houses. The barracks had no electric except for searchlights set up at different locations over the stockade. These were seldom used but they could be turned on at any moment.

A string of electric lights was strung over the main avenues of movement in the stockade. These lights were turned on from dusk to dawn. Kerosene lamps were used in the barracks, the outhouses and the infirmary. A prisoner in each barracks was designated to care for the kerosene lamps. No one was to touch these lamps except the designee. The work crew of the lamp tender had to operate with one less member.

The stones came to the project from two sources. There was an alluvial operation which lifted the alluvium to a twenty feet height and let it sift through screens into different sizes. The bigger stones were used for paving and the smaller material was used as bottom fill for road projects to the south.

The other source of stone was a quarry where drilling and dynamiting took place. These workers were not prisoners, but mostly volunteers who wanted to build a better Soviet Union, as well as get away from their present situation. They enjoyed good food and, on their one day of rest, free movement. However, they were virtual prisoners of their occupation. They often went into Krasnoyarsk for the social life that existed there.

When the quarry stone appeared at the paving site it was not welcome since it had to be further reduced with sledge hammers. When a particularly hard rock came in and couldn't be reduced, it was taken up to the dirt fill area and buried. This was time consuming and frowned upon by Sergeant Vilko who was in charge of this area of paving.

There was a small lunch break of bread and tea and then it was work again. Ivan tried to get as much information as possible such as "Where were the other nine hundred prisoners?" He was informed that they were spread around the camp in various capacities of tending to the goat and pig farm, working the alluvial quarry, repairing barracks, cooking meals and cleaning up operations. Several prisoners were engaged in keeping up the major's and captain's houses. One lucky fellow took care of the guard dogs which were stationed everywhere large numbers of prisoners worked.

During the course of the day Ivan was warned to look out for Private Kharkov who was vicious and often beat prisoners for no apparent reason or for a trumped up reason. One of Ivan's compatriots referred to Kharkov as that Ukrainian son-of-a-bitch. Another Ukrainian to avoid was Private Donbas. The other privates were all acceptable, especially Private Vilnius who was from Belorussia.

The day plodded on and soon the clouds darkened and trucks arrived to carry the workers back to the barracks. Ivan noticed the boss handing a blue poker chip to one of his workers. The boss noticed Ivan looking.

"Number 441, you wonder what is going on. When you work here, there are three types of rations. One is your basic food ration, the second is a bare existence ration and the third is a double ration for hard work. I am given a blue chip each day by Private Vilnius and I am to give it to the worker who earned a double ration. The worker presents it to the food line and they throw extra food on his plate. What I try to do, is give it to a different person each day. That way, we all get a double ration every nine days. Your time will be coming."

At supper, on Ivan's first day on the job, there was fish, boiled barley, half a boiled potato, bread and tea. This would be the supper pattern for many days to come. Ivan was informed that some prisoners were engaged in catching and cleaning fish. They operated up and down the Yenesey and into the Angara. Fishing was good at the junction of those two rivers. Fish was also obtained from citizens of the nearest small village who welcomed the soldier guards into their midst and offered them entertainment in the form of music and drink on the night of their day off. They would turn in an escaped prisoner without hesitation.

The days plodded on and one day was like another. Near the end of April Private Kharkov had beaten a prisoner so badly he couldn't walk. This was buzzing around camp. Prisoners were usually encouraged to work when they seemed to be lagging and an occasional kick in the pants was tendered. However, Kharkov took most any opportunity to whack a prisoner. A prisoner who couldn't work was not desirable and Captain Yaroslav called a meeting of the guards who were not on stockade duty. These meetings were usually held in the recreation room of the guard barracks.

There were about 50 guards crowded into the recreation room. It could hold 80 men if need be. Most of them sat on the floor while a few used the available chairs and tables. Yaroslav entered and the men rose to their feet.

Yaroslav commanded, "Be at ease men." They returned to their positions.

The captain made his usual pause for attention. It was a trademark of his. If any man so much as breathed out loud, or made a noise, he was taking a risk.

"Soldiers of the Soviet, guards of Camp 193, I welcome this opportunity to talk to you. Yesterday Private Kharkov beat a prisoner on the legs and now he is in the medical facility recovering. According to Private Kharkov, the prisoner deserved it. We hope so. There is no need to beat prisoners who do not deserve it."

Yaroslav continued, "When questioned about the matter, Private Kharkov referred to the prisoners here as a bunch of shit. I assure you, the prisoners we have are not a bunch of shit. They are probably better educated than most of you. They are all able to read

66

instructions of behavior and did sign their names legibly on their confessions. Most of them are here because of petty and political crimes. None of them are hardened criminals. The hardened criminals are sent deeper into Siberia."

"If a prisoner is not working properly then you are to contact his group leader to keep him working. If you must hit a prisoner, then do it in such a manner that he is not injured to the point where he cannot work. It is better to not hit the prisoner and let him sleep in the ice box overnight. That will get him working the next day."

The ice box was a small room isolated from the barracks. It was made of cemented stones with a wood roof. There was no heat and prisoners were usually put in without their jackets if their disobedience was particularly bad.

"Remember we have an obligation to build this road. If the road is not completed on time it would not be good for the careers of any of us, including privates. Are there any questions?"

A guard rose to his feet. "Private Pesco here Captain. What if a prisoner attacks us physically?"

"You are to defend yourself and if necessary shoot the prisoner. However, if you kill a prisoner, you better have some witnesses willing to testify on your behalf. Are there any other questions?"

There were no other questions. Sergeant Vilko called the men to attention. Captain Yaroslav saluted and left the room. The soldiers broke into small groups to continue the discussion and swap stories about abusing prisoners.

At the end of April, ice on the river began to crack and blocks of ice slowly moved north. Here the ice met the still frozen river and an ice dam was created. Ice dams on the Yenesey are not as great a problem as on the Ob and Lena since much of the Yenesey valley is deep and drains effectively. Waters of the Ob and Lena back up considerably. This has given rise to a proposed engineering project where the Ob will be dammed and the waters backed up to irrigate the arid areas of Kazakhstan.

The road work was pretty much halted in June. By then, the mud road was beyond help. There was still a skeleton crew that worked at paving with stone brought up from the south, but the base on which these stones were placed was lacking because the sorted gravel could not easily come from the north.

July and August were the months when three hundred prisoners were taken approximately two hundred and fifty miles to the north. Here they would cut timber and worked at building a new stockade and barracks. Captain Yaroslav would be the man in charge and one of his duties was to scout out housing for himself, Rurik and Mikoyan. Heaven forbid that they would all have to live in the same house.

Mikoyan insisted on keeping wives and family with them. They all had children. Rurik and Yaroslav's four children were in elementary school in Krasnoyarsk and were brought home at intervals. Mikoyan's seventeen year old daughter was in a private high school in Krasnoyarsk. She would be finished with her studies in a year and her parents had to decide what the next move for her should be. The thought of her living five hundred miles north of Krasnoyarsk in a prison camp was not appealing.

Ivan had a variety of jobs during June. He was not selected for the minimum paving project and was sent to do farm work with the goats and pigs. He didn't mind this at all since his biology interests were augmented by studying the animals and how they were kept alive. He worked the hay fields which were cut to stack up food for the animals in winter. He pondered a statement made by Captain Yaroslav at the first meeting. He wondered what skills he was learning that would help him when he returned to society. Was there a demand for people who used a wheelbarrow and cut hay?

The fields were cut with a scythe and Ivan became adept at it. As his mind wandered during the cutting he thought he might write a book on the use of the scythe. He learned to keep it level as he swung to get more efficiency. He noted that he could get more grass cut if he used a shorter bite into the uncut grass. When he first started cutting, he would take about a ten inch cut and swing around for about four feet. He learned by trial and error and found a four or five inch cut and a three foot swing more effective.

When the hay was dry in the hot rainless beginning of July he and his partners loaded it onto a wagon. The small bits of dry grass went down his shirt and he had severe itching. By turning his collar up he could avoid the hay down the neck, but it was much hotter work.

When the temperature reached 85 degrees on several days Major Mikoyan ordered that every prisoner should sit and rest between the hours of noon and two o'clock. Where there was a small stream the men were encouraged to swim or lie in the water. That way, they could cool off and bathe at the same time. The prisoners usually made up for it by working beyond sunset. These summer daylights were sixteen and seventeen hours long. A lot of work was done and a lot of tired men moved through the food line each evening.

During the middle of that first July, Ivan was put on digging the three foot deep trench that paralleled the road. He would wheelbarrow mud from the ditch to the end of the filled area. There were about thirty prisoners with wheelbarrows doing this task. Private Kharkov was often guarding at this location and the men were very careful not to cross him in any way.

Ivan would fill his wheelbarrow and his mind would wander. He became proficient at shoveling mud and sandy soil. He thought he might write a book about it. He learned not to shovel mud from the back of the wheelbarrow, since a slip of the shovel will get the handles wet and he would have to work with wet muddy gloves. So, he loaded the barrow from the side. He learned to put the heaviest part of the load up front and use the mechanical advantage. He thought about fulcrums and ran formulas for calculating mechanical advantage of the wheelbarrow through his mind. He also concluded that taking a four inch cut of the soil was better than taking a ten or twelve inch cut. He did as many loads as the other wheelers so he was not obvious in this endeavor.

Ivan's ditch would meet a small tributary stream and Ivan would move across it to the other side. Most of the streams were shallow and from four to five feet wide. Some were as much as ten feet wide. There were planks for moving across the stream. Larger streams needed logs and planks on the logs for wheeling. Generally the ditch diggers would place their mud and soil right on the proposed roadbed. By doing this, they avoided the long trip to the end of the road.

About once a day, a load of large cut stone was brought to the tributary streams where a bridge was to be built. To build the road, a gravel base was pounded into place and the cut stone was placed on top of this. Logs were placed across the stream on the stone and these were faced with sawn timber which was coated with oil.

As Ivan worked along these areas he thought he might write a book about building bridges across streams. A thought occurred to him about the bridges. It was burning on his mind for several days and when Sergeant Vologda came to check on progress and talk to his guards, Ivan worked his wheelbarrow, toward him.

Vologda had positioned his guards and was about to return to his motorcycle which was his mode of transportation through the rough terrain and mud. Ivan said, "May I speak with you comrade sergeant."

Vologda anticipated some complaining. "Yes, you can talk to me, what's wrong?" He started to light a cigarette.

"There is nothing wrong comrade sergeant. I just had an idea about these bridges that go across the small streams."

Vologda laughed, "Prisoners aren't supposed to be thinking. Tell me about your idea."
"Well," said Ivan, "The cut stones for the bridges are transported by trucks that get stuck in mud and have to be rescued all the time. There is a lot of gasoline wasted in this operation. The stones come from a quarry just north of the big city. Why not put the stones on flat boats and tow them up river and when you get to the tributary that needs a bridge, the flat boat is loosened and towed up the stream to the bridge site. We could dredge the stream to a three foot depth by using a horse pan."

"What's a horse pan?" asked Vologda.

"It's a scoop made of steel with handles like a plow. A man gets behind it and shoves it downward and it loads itself. Once loaded, the man turns the scoop flat and the horse easily takes it across the land. We could dump this on the road site."

Vologda didn't like the idea of discussion with a prisoner, but he was fascinated by Ivan's proposal. "We are about a mile from the Yenesey. That's a long way to drag a horse pan."

"Not really," said Ivan. "It is deep where tributaries enter a major river and you would have no more than a couple hundred yards of dredging to do. The smaller streams do not get the cut stone

70

so you wouldn't be hung up there."

Vologda smiled. "That's a pretty good proposal four forty one. I'll think about it."

Ivan became bolder. "You could also ship cement up the river. We have the sand and gravel here, so we could make some of the bridge supports out of concrete or at least make their base out of concrete."

"You are full of ideas young man. Let me know when you think of other schemes."

Ivan thanked him for his audience and went back to wheeling mud. Other prisoners and guards noticed the discussion. One prisoner passed Ivan with his wheelbarrow and said, "Were you ass kissing?"

"No I am sick to my stomach and I thought I could go to the infirmary, but he told me to vomit on the next guy who talked to me, so watch it."

A week later, Ivan was still wheeling mud when Sergeant Vologda approached him and told him to follow him to his motorcycle. "Pretend you are looking at the motorcycle, like it needs repair," he said.

Ivan got on one knee and started poking at the wheels. Vologda said, "I talked to Captain Rurik about your bridge cut stone scheme and he liked the idea. He is sending me to Krasnoyarsk, to the shipyard, to see if we can get boats and cranes to handle the big stone. He also likes the idea of shipping cement and making concrete. He said these would be stronger bridges with a concrete base. I thank you four forty one."

"It is my pleasure comrade sergeant. I picked you because you are the most humane of the sergeants around here."

"I don't think that's a compliment four forty one. However, I will accept it as such. Take the taped packet below my saddle bag."

Ivan saw what the sergeant was talking about. "Put it in your pocket. There are five blue chips in there. Keep them until you decide you need an extra ration, then use them. You have given me some prestige with the captain and I appreciate it. Of course I did not tell him it was your idea."

Ivan stood up. "Of course not: I hope it works out for you."

71

Then he moved back to his wheelbarrow. No one mentioned this incident to him or to anybody else. Ivan felt he now had a friend in high places.

It was the third week of August and Ivan was still wheeling mud and putting it on the road. The night before, he had been on his bunk when number 863 came over to him with something in his hand which he held out to Ivan. Number 863 was Gregor Mishkov who was at the head of the line of prisoners attached to the cable. Ivan held out his hand and something was dropped into it. Mishkov had a smile on his face. It was a small chunk of hard sausage. Mishkov said, "Eat up friend Ivan."

Ivan whispered, "Where did you get this?"

"My family sent me a package. Maybe you don't know it, but you can get packages here. The packages are opened and the contents usually taken by the guard that opens them, but sometimes the package gets through. My family sent me some sausage. I know it was bigger, but I am happy to get this and share it with my friends. Do you want a cigarette?"

"I thank you from the bottom of my heart. No I do not smoke."

"You are welcome. I know you would share anything with me. Why don't you let your family know where you are and that you are fine and they can send you things?"

Ivan lied. "There are no family members who would do that for me. My mother is old and she would be confused by all of this. It would be hard for me to contact her because she was moved to a new apartment after I was arrested, and I don't know the address."

Mishkov was also on the wheelbarrow crew this day. Another wheeler purposely ran his wheelbarrow into Mishkov's knocking it over. The aggressive man said, "You clumsy bastard Ukrainian, watch where you are going."

Mishkov said, "You purposely ran into me."

The man punched Mishkov and knocked him to the ground. Private Kharkov was on duty in this section and he liked to see a good fight, so he took his time getting to the scene. A second man came over and kicked Mishkov when he was down. Both men then kicked Mishkov and moved back to their wheelbarrows. Private Kharkov then shouted, "You men stop playing around and get to

72

work."

When Ivan saw the melee, he did not know what to do. Should he help Mishkov? They might all get sent to some ice room. It might be a black mark against him. Who knows what lies Private Kharkov would tell about the incident? Fortunately, it was all over in two minutes and order was restored.

Mishkov slowly got to his feet and fell to his knees. He stood up again and braced himself on the wheelbarrow. He went to the water bucket and took a drink. After getting his composure, he began working again.

Ivan maneuvered his wheelbarrow so that he and Mishkov would meet at the road where the load was to be dumped. Ivan whispered, "What was that all about? Are you okay?"

"I really don't know what that was about. I got the license numbers of the trucks that hit me, 834 and 621. Yes I am okay."

The barracks roof was made of logs and covered with earth to keep in the warmth of winter and protect it from the heat of summer. The logs were braced with smaller logs about four feet in length. These logs were nailed to the larger logs of the roof and to the beam logs within the building.

It was four days after the incident with Mishkov. The lights out signal had been given and everyone should have been asleep. It was about four in the morning when a loud thud was heard, accompanied by a shout as if someone was in pain. Then there was a groan and silence.

The man in charge of the kerosene lamps lit one and asked what happened. A man said something occurred over there in the corner. When the lamp was brought over there was an unconscious man on an upper bunk. Apparently one of the four foot brace logs had come loose and hit the man across the face and head as it fell.

The man in charge of the lamps said, "Stay in your bunks, I will get the guard."

The lamp man went to the door and called the guard outside to come forward. "There has been an accident tonight, come in."

The guards of the stockade felt no threat from prisoners. They knew that if there was a revolt in the barracks, the entire barracks might be annihilated.

The guard shined his flashlight on the injured man then said, "You two, carry him and follow me to the infirmary. We better check all of those support beams tomorrow."

The two designated prisoners removed the injured man from his upper bunk. His head was bleeding and he was unconscious. As they passed Ivan's bunk he noticed the number on the man's jacket which was thrown over him. It was number 834, one of Mishkov's tormentors.

The next day Ivan did not say anything to Mishkov nor Mishkov to Ivan. They wheeled their barrows and sweated in the warm sun. Number 834 would not be wheeling mud for a long time and his sentence would be increased two days for every day of work he missed. Ivan noticed Mishkov deliberately cut his wheelbarrow in front of Number 621, his other antagonizer.

For the next week, number 621 slept with one eye open. Every day he appeared more haggard. Was this over the sausage that Mishkov had shared? Perhaps number 834 and 621 did not like their share, or perhaps they didn't get a share. Mishkov would often stop his barrow and rub his chest and take deep breaths. The kicks in the chest still bothered him.

It was early September and barracks 14 began to light a fire in the stove to heat water and make tea. A new rule had been passed. Prisoners could take cups with them and keep them in the barracks and they could use them to drink tea. The tea was rough cut leaves imported from Georgia. The leaves were simply thrown into a pot. Tea leaves were often dispensed with the tea. The night temperatures began to drop below freezing and the extra warmth was welcome in the barracks.

Since each night was like every other in the barracks and each day was like any other at work there was no need to keep track of the day of the week. Every once in a while someone would say something like it was Thursday September 5 or 6th. Then there would be a discussion as to the exact day of the week and day of the month. The prisoners liked speculation better than asking a guard for the exact date.

The stove fire was also a source of dim light and prisoners could move about in it without stumbling. One night, about four in the morning, there was a scream and everyone sat upright in the

74

bunks. There was a lower bunk on fire near the stove. Its occupant was being burned. He managed to wiggle out of the bunk and throw himself on the floor. The man in the upper bunk threw his blanket over the burning mess and others rolled the mess until the fire was out.

The guard was summoned and the burned man, who was grimacing and gasping, was carried out of the barracks. Two guards returned with flashlights gleaming and wanted to know what had happened. The man in the top bunk said he found a cigarette half smoked at the foot of the bunk. Apparently the prisoner was smoking in bed when it caught fire. The guard said it was unusual for the wool blankets to burst into flame like that. Maybe the man had spilled kerosene on his blanket at one time when he was in charge of the lamps and it ignited. Several prisoners nodded their approval at this explanation.

The guard accepted this explanation and said, "This matter is finished, you can go back to sleep, you have a lot of work to do in the morning."

Ivan noticed that the locker under the bunk had a number 621 painted on it. This was the other attacker of Gregor Mishkov, the mild mannered man. Ivan did not think it prudent to point this out to Mishkov.

The First Full Winter

By the end of September the ground was frozen in the mornings. The crews sent to build the new barracks had returned and something like a normal work schedule was resumed. Ivan was again wheeling rocks or pounding them on the road. He also spent a lot of time getting vehicles out of mud ruts. They all looked forward to October when the ground would be frozen hard enough for trucks to move on it.

The autumnal equinox had passed and daylight was slightly less than twelve hours. The road was progressing nicely and everyone was doing his duty. Then came a break in the routine.

One of the new prisoners had escaped. Since they worked in the open air, he simply waited for his opportunity, then disappeared. Speculation was that he had stowed away on one of the last trucks heading south for the stone quarry, then jumped off in the darkness.

The Boss relayed this to Ivan. The crew with the missing man was late and had to report the status of one man missing to their private guard. They would be the last group to eat supper that night.

Ivan asked, "What will happen now Boss?"

The boss paused, "Well, the camp employs a Nentsy tracker who is related to the devil. This man will find the missing man and bring him back dead or alive. If he is dead and the body is too far to carry he will bring back the right ear, the tattooed ear of the man, after burying the body. If the major wants to see the body then the tracker will take him to it. This missing man is obviously new or he would know about the tracker and that the tracker always gets his man. Once it took four months, but the tracker came back with the man."

About a week later the assembly whistle blew and the big search lights were turned on. Everyone assembled in the usual place. Major Mikoyan was at the center position with Captain Rurik on his right and Sergeant Vologda on this left. The compound door opened and the tracker rode in on his horse with another horse in tow. On the other horse, a body hung loosely over it. The tracker halted beside the major.

The major spoke in a loud voice. "Prisoners of the Soviet, this is what happens when a man tries to escape from our establishment. If he did not resist, he would still be alive. Let this be a lesson to you, especially to you people who are new to our establishment. Be thankful you are in our facility and not in some other. Now go back to your bunks and think about what you have seen here. Get a good night's sleep for you have work to do tomorrow."

Sergeant Vologda stepped forward. "Group leaders, take a count of your men and report to your private guard. Once your group has signed in, return to your quarters."

The tracker was a short oriental Eskimo dressed in a hooded parka. The hood was down and his eyes reflected the search light. He cut the cadaver loose from the horse and dragged it to center stage. As each man looked forward, they witnessed the proceedings.

76

In the morning the corpse was still there. Boss came over to Ivan. "Number four forty one, I am assigning you to the burial detail. You and a prisoner from another barracks will accompany a guard to the site. Take a shovel from the shack with you and stand by the corpse. You will receive orders there. It's a day off for you."

Ivan went to the lean-to shed and retrieved a shovel. Another prisoner showed up with a shovel. Soon a guard appeared with a horse drawn cart. He looked to Ivan's partner and said, "You know what to do."

The prisoner got in the drivers seat with the guard beside him. Ivan was put in the cart next to the dead man and they drove off. After about a three mile drive they came to a cemetery. The guard turned to Ivan. "This is where we bury the dead. We really don't get too many dead here. Prisoners here have short sentences and this is a new camp so not too many people have died."

Ivan and his partner went about digging a grave. When they were down about four feet the guard said that was deep enough. The corpse was wrapped in a canvas blanket and laid in the grave and the two prisoners went about covering him up. When this was completed, the guard took a hand sledge hammer from a tool box and drove a stake in the ground. The stake had the number 727 carved on it.

Ivan asked, "Are there any guards buried here?

The guard answered. "No, none have died here. Most guards are young and we don't expect them to die. This camp has only been open four years. We spent the first two years getting things organized. One guard was killed in a power shovel accident. He sat in the wrong place to observe prisoners. His body was sent home to his family and buried in their family plot."

The other prisoner asked, "Shall we head back now?"

The guard answered. "No, let's just rest for a long while. I'm going to smoke a cigarette. Do either of you want a cigarette?" The other prisoner took one, but Ivan protested again that he did not smoke.

The guard was Private Penza who was also on the good guy list of the prisoners. "You men walk around if you want. We should be here another two hours before we head back. That way, the sun will be almost down, and it will be too late for you to go to your work station." He looked at Ivan. "Don't think about escaping unless you want to be wrapped in canvas and have your number on a stake."

After walking around and checking about thirty graves, both prisoners went to a small clump of trees and took a nap. Private Penza worked on his fifth cigarette and drank from a flask. Two hours had elapsed when he called to the prisoners to return with him to the stockade.

7 The Salt Run

Sergeant Vologda had worked out a new assignment for Ivan. He was transferred from the work brigade to the service brigade. Ivan received a bunk assignment in Barracks Number Ten which was reserved for the service personnel. He was glad to get out of working in the open air, since summer was a time for mosquitoes, horse flies, black flies, blow flies and grasshoppers that made working outdoors miserable. Unfortunately for the prisoners, this area was one of the worst places in the world for mosquitoes and horse flies.

Service personnel worked at various tasks around the compound. They were mostly cooks and cook helpers who prepared meals for the prisoners. Others took care of the dog's housing and welfare, burial details, processing new arrivals, wash house duties, latrine clean up, service to the three households and whatever else could be assigned to them. There were a large number of horses in the stable. Other than the cooks and helpers, these prisoners were trustees and many of them were well known and could pass in and out of the guarded front gate without suspicion.

The service barracks had an outhouse with sinks and a large vat of water which was kept warm in winter. The warm water was used for washing and shaving. Since these men dealt with officers, they had to be more presentable than the work crews. Many kept small moustaches and beards. Ivan chose to be clean shaven. While others exchanged hair cuts, Ivan chose to cut his own hair.

In this new capacity, Ivan's first task was to take wasted food to some barrels outside. There was not much waste food on the prisoner's plates, but there was waste food such as carrot tops, beet stems, potato peels and the like. He passed through the gates unchallenged as he carried waste food products in two large five gallon pails. He deposited these in two large thirty gallon drums. It was a stinking job, but it was better than digging ditches in the hot sun and when winter finally arrived, in the cold. His new barracks was comfortable, but just as crowded as the former..

Sergei Plushna and Gregor Mishkov were also assigned to the service barracks. Ivan didn't know what their duties were, but he would see them in the barracks at night. Mishkov must have had some connections, since he received regular food packets which he freely shared. All Ivan knew about Plushna was that he had large ears and seemed to be very alert. Michkov told Ivan that when he was assigned to the service corps, Sergeant Vologda remarked, "Maybe this will keep you alive a little longer."

There was a mysterious man in Barracks Ten. He would hover in the dark corners and do incantations over candles. Ivan was told that this man's nickname was Rasputin and his prisoner number was 666 at his own request.

Rasputin was a tall man with a long oriental face. A black moustache and goatee beard added to his mystery. Ivan's new work boss told him that Rasputin can go into a trance and predict the future. He had correctly predicted that a certain prisoner would die on a certain day. When the man died on that day, Rasputin's reputation soared. No one suggested that Rasputin might have aided in the outcome of the prediction.

Rasputin did the same chores as the rest of the service group. He seldom talked to other prisoners, except to give them warnings and advice from time to time. He gathered weeds when he was outside in summer and dried them. Throughout the winter, he rolled cigarettes out of newspapers from the toilet and used these with his dried weeds. The aroma of the burning weeds kept others away from him. Rasputin's main job seemed to be cleaning dog shit out of the dog pens and dumping this into a small ravine at the end of the campgrounds.

In early October, the frosts were getting thick, but the river was still flowing. Ice was forming on the river at the northern end near the Arctic Ocean. Sergeant Vologda told Ivan and Rasputin to get a good night's sleep for they would be on a hard trip for a couple of days. They were told to get their identification cards from the infirmary since they would be leaving the compound area. Rasputin grinned at Ivan, "You lucky son-of-a-bitch."

In the morning, Sergeant Vologda, Private Penza, Rasputin and Ivan walked toward the small dock on the river which served the camp. It was about two miles from the stockade and the distance was covered in less than a half hour. The two soldiers were armed with pistols, but there was no need to brandish them. Adventure was high in the air.

The men sat on the pier and Vologda said that they were waiting for a boat going north with a truck on it. It would be the last boat heading to Dudinka to pick up ore and the truck would be theirs for the task at hand. The task was to pick up a truck load of salt from a small Evenki village, about a hundred miles to the north. The boat would take them to the village and unload the truck. Ivan and Rasputin would shovel ten tons of salt onto the truck and the four of them would bring the truck back to camp over the hundred plus miles of road. When Ivan questioned, Vologda explained that the salt shipment to the camp was always inadequate and Major Mikoyan had given Volodga money to buy the salt from the Evenki.

Vologda looked at Ivan and pointed to Rasputin. "We would have shot this useless bastard long ago, but he is the only one around who can speak Evenki. So we feed him and put up with his behavior."

Rasputin smiled. "I not only speak Evenki, but I know all the dialects of the Siber, Nentsy, Samoyeds and Komi. I even speak Russian." They all laughed at the way he said that. "The sergeant will not shoot me because he knows I would give my life to protect him. I will get us all a good deal with this group, since I have been there before. I know the village well."

Vologda turned to Ivan. "Have you ever been on a big river before?"

"I lived in Voronezh on a tributary of the Don River. We students at the university would go downstream and study aquatic water life."

Penza joined in the conversation. "Like mermaids and bathing beauties."

"No, we were serious students." Ivan didn't understand that

Penza was joking. Penza shrugged his shoulders.

With that said, the boat rounded the bend. It was an ore barge with a platform built over one of the open hatches. On the platform was a large dump truck. The boat was drifting more than it was running, but it moved along nicely. A small boat was sent out from the barge to pick up the four men.

As they climbed up to the platform, Ivan noticed that there was room for lying down if he wanted to. They could also sit in the truck or ride in the back of it.

The captain of the barge hollered to Vologda. "Hey, sergeant, we will get you there this time for sure." Vologda waived at him. He told Ivan that the last time he made this trip, the barge was stuck along one of the banks and they had to unload the truck prematurely. Rasputin had also been on that trip and made an additional comment.

The men settled down to looking at the river. Ivan identified some bird life along the river. There were cranes, egrets, ducks and blackbirds. A sailor fishing up front pulled in a small sturgeon and yelled, "We might be eating caviar this evening."

The barge was making about twenty miles an hour. After about fifty miles, the river narrowed and the surface current was swifter and carried them along at a faster rate of speed. Vologda checked the chains holding the truck in position and declared that they were sound.

The ship passed a large raft of logs which was heading toward the Arctic Ocean. Vologda said that the logs were necessary, since the cities of Dudinka, Norilsk and Igarka had no forests. They were cities on the tundra.

It was late in the day when the barge docked at the pier in the small village of Evenki. The village had no recognizable name and the Russians simply called it after the ethnic group living there.

The village consisted of fifteen houses made of logs, all lined up along a corduroy street facing the river. A corduroy street was made of logs laid down and covered with earth. Eventually the logs began to poke through the dirt. There were outbuildings behind each house for housing animals and an outhouse. At the southern end of the row of houses was a large gasoline tank belonging to the Soviet Military and at the other end was a larger building which held the salt. Where the Evenki got the salt was a secret and no one questioned them. Salt was a valuable commodity in every area and a source of revenue for the Evenki.

What appeared to be the head man came hurriedly to the dock and shook hands with Vologda and hugged Rasputin, kissing him on both cheeks. Rasputin turned to Ivan. "I am loved in this village."

There were still a couple of hours of daylight left and the head man of the village invited the four to dinner at his house. Through Rasputin, he explained that there were few people in the village at this time. Most of the men and women were out setting traps or fishing or going to the secret salt gathering grounds.

The head man was a short muscular man dressed in skins. He had graying hair. Ivan guessed his age to be about sixty years old. His wife served a brisk tea made from local leaves of some sort. There was fried reindeer meat, even though the herds were fifteen hundred miles to the north. There were also roots of some wild crop which Ivan could not identify.

Rasputin and Ivan were brought along to shovel the salt onto the truck, but Vologda had made a deal for two local men to do the job while the four of them slept. He asked Rasputin to ask the man about getting women for the four of them. Ivan wanted to interrupt, but he thought the better of it. He didn't want to show any evidence of lack of support for the sergeant.

After talking to the man in deliberate tones, Rasputin turned to Vologda. He said, "He can get four women, but the donation to the town would be three rubles each for the night." Vologda said that he had calculated six rubles and this was a sign of hard times for the village. It helped to explain why most of the village people were out on foraging, trapping, fishing and hunting assignments. Vologda told Rasputin to tell the head man that he would give him five rubles for each of them.

The extra income prompted the head man to produce a bottle of liquid and pour each of them a drink. They all sipped it slowly. It was almost pure alcohol and Ivan wondered if it was wood alcohol and they would all be dead by morning.

When the head man poured Ivan's drink, he paused and looked deep into Ivan's eyes. Ivan felt embarrassed. The man looked at Rasputin and said something in Evenki. Rasputin looked at Ivan and nodded. It was a nod of approval.

The head man disappeared for about a half hour while the men enjoyed another drink. Rasputin looked at Ivan and said, "The head man is a wizard and he said he detected greatness in you. He thinks you might be his son from another life." Ivan made no response.

When the head man came back, he said something to Rasputin who said, "It's all finished. We have women to sleep with tonight."

Rasputin turned to Ivan. "These are not professional prostitutes. The Evenki and other native groups have found that inbreeding causes deformities at birth. They have a high infant mortality. It took them centuries to discover this. They welcome new blood into their society, since it cuts down or eliminates many birth defects. He is probably hoping that one of these women will be pregnant from this night."

Rasputin told the others to follow the head man as he went out the door and down the street. The man stopped at a house and a woman came to the door. She was assigned to Private Penza. He nervously followed her into the dimly lit log house.

At the next stop, it was Vologda's turn. As he stepped over the flimsy stair to the house he turned and said, "You boys better be here in the morning, sober and ready to go."

It was Ivan's turn and a young girl came to meet the men. The head man said a few sentences to Rasputin who in turn said to Ivan, "This is the man's youngest daughter. She is fourteen years old and a virgin. He would not offer her, but the village has an obligation to guests. Anyway, it was time she learned the facts of life and participated in them."

The girl came and took Ivan by the hand as Rasputin and the head man moved down the street. The small hand was strong and held a firm grip on Ivan who wanted to pull his hand away.

She led Ivan thorough the door which opened on a kitchen with a small stove burning and a tea kettle heating on it. She pointed to the tea kettle and a cup and Ivan shook his head from side to side.

The next stop was a small bedroom with two single beds.

Ivan sat on one of them. The girl sat on the other bed and they stared at each other. After about ten minutes of staring, the girl rose to her feet and started undressing. Her immature breasts were exposed and her pants and leggings made of fur slid down over her hips as she was about to step out of them. Ivan went to her and said, "No, no. I don't want to do this. I will only do this with the woman I love."

The girl couldn't understand the language, but she got the idea as Ivan pulled her pants back up. Ivan picked her up and laid her on the bed where she had been sitting. Ivan kissed her on the forehead and put her top over her. "Let us go to sleep my little one and you can, like me, save yourself for the one you love." The girl stared at the ceiling. Perhaps, she didn't like the rejection.

They both went to sleep and early in the morning the door to the bedroom opened slightly and the looker closed it again. Ivan was awake and thought it must be the head man checking up on them.

The girl was also wakened by the door and she opened her eyes. Light from a lantern in the kitchen filtered into the room and everything was dim, but visible. The girl still with her small breasts exposed came over to where Ivan was lying. She lay down beside him, put her hand on his chest and they both went back to sleep.

Morning seemed to come fast for Ivan. It was a very good night's sleep and the alcoholic drinks probably contributed to it.

There was a breakfast of boiled rice and milk waiting for Ivan. There was also a cut-up apple, something Ivan had not seen in a long while. The head man was there at breakfast which was being tended by a lady, presumably his wife.

The young girl talked hurriedly and the lady and the head man looked at Ivan curiously. Obviously, she had told them of the inactivity of the evening.

Ivan finished eating and went out to the log street. He sat at the end of a log closest to the river and watched as an ore boat lumbered by. Soon, he was greeted by Penza, then Vologda and Rasputin.

Rasputin spoke to Ivan. "How was your stint with the virgin?"

"I didn't do anything. How could a man have sex with a child ten years younger than himself?"

Rasputin answered. "My good man, they do it all the time in

84

Russia. My mother was married at age fourteen."

Vologda laughed. "You are a bastard, your mother was never married."

"My good sergeant, watch what you say about my mother.. Maybe, I will withdraw my pledge to give my life for you."

Vologda slapped him on the back. "I apologize for the joke I tried to make about your mother. Let's go and see if the truck is loaded." They all rose and ambled down the street to the north and where the truck should be waiting.

The truck was there and loaded with salt. Vologda instructed the men to put the canvas, which came with the truck, over the salt and tie it down. Penza checked the gas gauge and said it was full and that should easily get them the hundred plus miles back to camp. Ivan wondered how they would get to the other side of the river. He never noticed any bridges on the way upstream Vologda said he will soon see how that is done.

The head man had packed a satchel of food for the four and delivered it to them as they stood by the truck. He motioned for Rasputin and Ivan to follow him and he led them away from the truck. He spoke to Rasputin in serious tones.

Rasputin turned to Ivan. "He says you are an honorable man and he would be proud if you decided to marry his daughter."

"Tell him that she is one of the most beautiful women I have ever seen and I hope she saves herself for her husband. He should not offer his daughter to strangers."

"That's their custom Ivan. You have a mysterious quality of getting people to like you. You have endeared yourself to this family and if you should decide to escape they will protect and hide you. All you have to do is figure out how to cross the river and head upstream. The river will be frozen soon and you would have no trouble crossing it. Ah, but, you would think it dishonorable to escape."

"Don't bet on it, my mysterious friend. My only obligation is to myself."

"I am your friend Ivan, and you can count on me. I have no doubt that you feel an obligation to friends and would honor that obligation."

Before they went back to the soldiers, the head man handed Rasputin a small package. Ivan asked, "What's in that?"

"These are weeds that put one's anxieties to rest."

The head man turned to Ivan. He took a leather thong necklace from his jacket and put it around Ivan's neck. It had a small ivory carving attached to it.

Ivan looked ill at ease and asked Rasputin, "What's this?"

Rasputin looked wide eyed for a few seconds. "If you ever wander through Siber lands wearing that necklace, people will do just about anything for you, even risk their lives. It is a religious carving, only bestowed on people of high honor among the Siber."

"Will I be able to keep it or will it be confiscated?"

"Vologda saw him give it to you. Remove it and put it in your pocket once we get underway. I don't think he will take it from you. He likes you or you would not be on this excursion."

Rasputin said that there was little room in the cab of the truck and he would ride on top of the salt. Ivan agreed to try that also. Vologda got in the cab and Penza got behind the wheel. The truck started easily. Just as it was pulling away, a woman came out of the shadows to the passenger side and gave Vologda a small bunch of flowers which he accepted. He kissed her on the forehead and off they went.

The ride across the log street was bumpy. Rasputin decided to put his legs under the set of ropes that was holding the canvas over the salt. Ivan thought he didn't need to be tied down even though he was bumping up and down. Soon they were on the frozen mud road heading south on the east side of the Yenesey River.

The truck stopped after an hour's driving. Vologda got out and said, "Time for a rest. We will spend an hour here."

Both top men climbed down from their covered salt seats and stretched out. Rasputin went to a large evergreen tree, rested against its trunk, took out a piece of newspaper and tore it into a four inch square. He took out the packet given to him by the head man and poured some of the dried weed onto the paper and rolled it. When he got to the end of the paper he wet the flap with his tongue and put the roll in his mouth. He produced a match from somewhere in his garments and lit the crude cigarette. He puffed contentedly.

Vologda and Penza were soon asleep. They had probably been up all night with their women. The sergeant seemed to be in no hurry to get back to camp and no one objected to that attitude.

Ivan went walking along the road they had just come over. He had a lot of energy, since he had had a good nights sleep. He noticed a small green object on an area between the mud ruts. He picked it up, thinking it was a piece of green glass. When he examined it, he thought differently.

It was a green stone that had been worked into a triangle. Its thickness was little more than that of a fingernail and its size was the size of a thumbnail. On one of the sides was a spur or else the stone would have formed a perfect triangle. He put it in his pocket.

Ivan noticed the woods for the first time this season. There were many evergreens and protruding among these were yellow leaves of poplars. It looked like a wall set against the plain of the river bank.

When Ivan got to Rasputin he asked, "Can you really tell fortunes?"

"I have told fortunes and they have always been accurate, as far as I know."

"How do you do this?"

"My mother was gypsy and my father was a Samoyed and I believe I have inherited supernatural powers from them."

"You are kidding me, of course."

"Of course. But I do dip into the mystical and supernatural and there are a lot of things that are unexplainable. I talk to spirits and spirits talk to me."

"Would you tell my fortune?"

"That is a broad request. Give me a specific question and I will answer it."

"Will I ever take a wife and have children?"

"That is two questions. However, they are related and I will give you an answer based on my mystical research."

Rasputin handed Ivan his cigarette that was half smoked. "Here, take a puff of this and breathe it deep into your lungs."

Ivan did so, with much coughing, and handed the cigarette back to the mystic. "Wow! That was awful, like smoking dried dog shit."

"Have you ever smoked dried dog shit?"

"No, that is just an expression. Now can you tell my fortune?"

"I have smoked dried dog shit. Maybe I can't tell your fortune. Wait a while until I can evaluate your situation."

Both men sat looking at the trees and the truck parked on the frozen mud road. After a few minutes, Ivan's body jolted and he yelled out. It was as if lightning had struck him in the head. He turned to Rasputin who was smiling his evil smile. Ivan asked, "What was that?"

"Describe what happened."

Ivan spoke slowly. "There was a pain in my head and flashes of lights."

"What color were the lights and how many flashes?"

"They were bright yellow and there were three of them."

"Well, my good friend Ivan, that indicates you will marry a fair haired woman and have three children."

"Really! Are you ever wrong?".

"I am never wrong in these matters."

When the soldiers awoke, Ivan produced his stone. Vologda thought it was serpentine. Rasputin thought it was a stone worked by some craftsman. Penza said he was certain that it was jade and was traded for furs. It looked like there was a place for a string, but it broke and the owner probably lost it.

Everyone agreed then that it must be some form of jade. Ivan said, "Too bad the spur is on it, otherwise it would be a perfect triangle." Penza asked to see the stone. Ivan handed it to him. Penza put it in his mouth and bit off the spur and handed it back. "Now you have a perfect triangle of jade. Remember this Ivan. If you give a piece of jade to someone, you give them a piece of your soul."

Soon it was time to get rolling. Vologda decided they would drive until the road started to get muddy again. They would stop for the night and continue in the morning. He was in no hurry to get back to camp. If they didn't return on the third day, Mikoyan would get concerned and send someone to investigate on the fourth day, probably the tracker.

They came to a wide place in the road where it was

obviously more muddy than usual. The road ahead was a mass of ruts. Vehicles using this stretch went around it and there was about sixty yards of diminishing turns off to the left. Each subsequent driver made the curve yet ever wider.

Rasputin who was now in some form of Nirvana had lashed himself on top of the salt. Ivan rode the side running board and hung onto the window for several miles just to get a break and add to his adventure.

The truck stopped after about a mile beyond the ruts. There was a road leading down to the river. Vologda called to Rasputin. "We are at the swing ferry and will cross here." Rasputin never answered.

The swing ferry consisted of a huge raft which was able to carry large vehicles. It was attached to a long steel cable which was fastened upstream. As the current moved the raft, the steering mechanism was activated. This consisted of a large rudder which when placed at an angle to the flowing water would move the raft across the river. It was a cheap, but effective system.

However, getting the truck onto the raft was another problem. One edge of the raft had an extension and this pulled up to the road. Many planks were laid down and anchored on the road side. The truck was slowly moved onto the planks and then onto the raft. Despite the shifting and plunging of the raft, the truck was on and secured with chains.

Getting the truck off the raft was the same problem in reverse. All planks were moved to the other side of the raft and the truck unloaded. The three men loaded into the cab and the truck got underway. Rasputin, lashed to the top of the salt, was not disturbed by the entire procedure.

When the group was about thirty miles from camp, Vologda decided they would spend the night and wait for the road to freeze by morning. He said they probably could make it back to camp on this day, but they would have to constantly be getting the truck out of mud ruts and the hassle wasn't worth it.

There was a campfire in the evening and Vologda shared the food that the head man had packed for them. Ivan remarked that he had not expected to be treated so even handed by Vologda and Penza. Both soldiers shrugged their shoulders.

Vologda looked at Ivan. "Number four forty one, don't you realize that we are all prisoners here. This place, which has been forsaken by God, is lost to the world and we are lost in it. I don't know when I will see my family again. If war breaks out, most of us will be killed. We are better off staying here if there is a war. However, I would like to see my children grow up."

Ivan asked. "Don't you get a leave or holiday break and then you can go home?"

"Not very often."

With that said they decided to sleep. Penza and Vologda went to the cab of the truck. Ivan and Rasputin went back to the salt bed. They would have slept on the ground, but were afraid of unknown animals which might lurk in this edge of the forest.

The next day, they made it back to camp by noon. Unloading the truck was easy, since it merely dumped the load onto an elevated platform. There was a little straightening up to do and the salt was covered with the canvas. Rasputin and Ivan were given the rest of the day off, except to help the cooks of Barracks Ten during their evening meal.

8. Dog Days

Out of the many jobs Ivan had under the service barracks he liked taking the slop out to the hogs. He had to hitch a horse to a cart and load three barrels of food scraps and move over to the officer's areas where they and their prisoner servants added another barrel.

Between the stockade and the officer's houses he passed the dog kennel where the guard dogs were kept. He would often see Privates Donbas and Pavlov working with the dogs, teaching them to attack and possibly kill. Other guards could be seen walking the dogs on leashes and teaching them leash behavior.

Ivan would often stop at the dog cages and look at the dogs in the exercise yard. Generally the dogs were kept in individual cages that could be opened and closed to the exercise yard. Usually the dogs did not fight, but when they got together there were some skirmishes in establishing a pecking order.

When Ivan first stopped with the horse, there was a tumult of growling and a few barks. The guard dogs did not bark often. They usually growled. When they growled at each other they showed their teeth and once the teeth were bared they would grab at another dog.

It was an interesting stop which usually lasted about ten minutes. When Ivan first stopped by the exercise yard, the dogs came to the chain link fence and growled viciously at him. All the dogs came to the fence except a medium sized whitish shepherd .that had gray spots on its back and black ears. It stood back and stared at Ivan who was fascinated by the dog's eyes. Could a dog be a kindred spirit? Dogs consider eye contact as a threat to them, but this dog seemed to welcome the eye contact. Ivan said to the dog, "I will call you Latko since you look like a big pan of milk." As a child, Ivan used the term Latko for milk. The dog did not respond.

This pattern of stopping at the kennel continued over a period of weeks. It was November and winter was already in full swing. Siberians have a saying, "Winter does not start until after the third snow." This is understandable, since the first two good snows usually melt and the third one sticks.

The dogs were fed a mixture of different grains as well as grain cakes embedded in frozen lard. The refuse of bones with some meat and gristle on them from the goat and pig farm was fed to the dogs. The bones were put in individual pens, while the grain was often dumped into a feeding trough in the exercise yard.

Ivan's interest in the dogs did not go unnoticed by Privates Donbas and Pavlov. Once when Ivan was there, Private Donbas came to the dog pound to put his working dog away. Ivan tried to mount up and get out of there when he saw Donbas coming toward him. Donbas was one of the guards Ivan had heard was to be avoided.

"Hey, four forty one," said Donbas, "Do you like my dogs?" "I think they are interesting to study. You must have fun working with them."

"It is not fun, it is work. It is my job to train these dogs to kill scum like you." Then he laughed.

Ivan made for the horse and wagon. Donbas followed him as he mounted the seat. "I am supposed to find a prisoner to clean out the dog pens. I'll see if I can get you. Then you can see the dogs from inside the cage."

Ivan grimaced, "You already have someone, I see him in here every day."

Donbas laughed, "Oh, that weasel, the dogs killed him."

Ivan shook his head and snapped the reins. The horse moved forward.

True to his word, Ivan was assigned to clean the dog cages in the morning. His new boss told him of the assignment. This relieved him from some of the kitchen duties, but not all of them. He still had to take the run to the animal farm every afternoon. The evening meals were too late for him to be out with the horse and cart. Gregor Mishkov had been assigned to work with the horses and he was always punctual with a horse and cart for Ivan.

Mishkov and Ivan had an understanding, even though it was never stated. They would protect each other as much as possible under the circumstances. Mishkov asked Ivan why he seemed to always be cheerful,

Ivan responded, "I look upon this experience as if I were an insect. You know, entomology is my profession. During my childhood and university days, I was in the larva stage. Now, in this prison, I am in the pupa or cocoon stage. When I get out of here, I will emerge as a butterfly and soar into the sky. It will be a metamorphosis for me." He made a soaring gesture. Mishkov laughed so hard he began choking.

When Ivan first went to the dog pound Private Pavlov was there to greet him. He took off the lock and informed Ivan that he only had to clean the dog shit from the exercise area, since the dogs did not shit in their individual cages. Most of them waited for their leash run, but there were those who could not wait and did their business in the exercise yard.

Ivan entered the exercise area. Pavlov closed the gate behind him. There was a scoop shovel in the yard and a five gallon bucket. Pavlov said, "You know what to do. When you come out, make sure no dogs get loose and close the gate behind you." He then walked away from the enclosure.

Ivan picked up the scoop and the bucket and moved forward. The dogs in the yard came to life and started to form a half circle around Ivan. Everything seemed calm until one dog started growling. This set up the dogs to staring at Ivan, baring their teeth and growling. Ivan thought he should bolt for the gate and get out of there. When he made a move toward the gate, a large black dog moved to stop him.

Ivan lifted the scoop and was about to start swinging at the large black dog when Latko appeared and got between Ivan and the black dog. Latko bared his teeth and the black dog backed away, its tail slinking. Latko eventually got all the dogs to back down and return to their cages. Ivan began scooping up dog shit and putting it in the bucket.

Ivan knelt down and called Latko to him. The dog did not make any effort to come forward.

"I thank you Latko from the bottom of my heart. If there is anything I can do for you please let me know." Latko didn't answer, but Ivan thought he saw Latko smile.

So it was that Ivan had made a friend of a guard dog. It was a pleasure to see Latko and get some response from him on a daily basis. On some occasions, Latko was locked in his cage. This meant he was about to get some training or just leash exercise.

When Ivan returned from the pig farm with bones for the dogs he usually gave Latko the choice piece. Other dogs did not fight over this because there was often enough bones to go around.

December had arrived. The air was cold with temperatures ten to twenty degrees below freezing. Ivan was informed that the January and February temperatures were often thirty to forty degrees below zero which was considerably below freezing. He was told to walk slowly under these conditions, since the wind created by walking would freeze his face.

The service crew had access to razors and most of them were clean shaven as was Ivan. Most of the other barracks relied on scissors to trim beards and cut hair. Since many of the service crew had contact with the authorities they were expected to present a better appearance than the work crews. Their laundry was more active and their washing facilities and toilets were more convenient. Ivan was careful to not have the smell of dog shit on him.

The latest camp rumor was that a new load of prisoners

would come to the camp. The camp prison population had been reduced to eight hundred and twenty from nine hundred and one when Ivan arrived. Prisoners did not keep track of this but relied on rumors of camp numbers. When Mikoyan sent in his reports to the office of General Frunze he would always request more prisoners to make the higher authorities think he ran a stern efficient operation and needed expansion. His requests were not always honored.

Many of the new prisoners would go all the way to Norilsk and Dudinka in this dead of winter. Most often the northern batch arrived in winter and was taken there in trucks which used the frozen river for a road. The old boss told Ivan that once a truck full of prisoners on their way to Igarka broke through the ice which was usually three feet thick. All the prisoners and the driver and two guards were killed. Those that did not drown were killed by freezing once they made it to shore.

Ivan was assigned to take photographs of the prisoners as they were processed. He thought this was a good assignment since the prisoners would be washed, beards and hair cut and deloused. He did not relish working with the men before they were deloused. He expected many of the men to go into shock when they moved through the cold shower.

The big day arrived. Forty new prisoners entered the stockade around noon. They went through the same routine that Ivan had gone through less than a year before. Ivan considered himself lucky that he had arrived when the worst of winter was over. Many of this new batch had frozen fingers and toes.

Ivan and his assistant went about the job of putting the men against the white background, getting their identification correct and snapping the picture which would be developed later and made into an identification card.

The process went rather quickly. After about twenty men had passed through Ivan's sector, a prisoner stepped forward that Ivan thought he recognized. He pondered the recognition when he finally realized who it was.

"Lev Lefkovich, you lawyer bastard. Welcome to the tropics. You must have friends in high places."

Lev looked at Ivan and recognized him immediately. "You

are Ivan Ivanov aren't you?"

"I used to be Ivan Ivanov but now I am number four forty one." Ivan motioned to Lev's crotch. "I see you made it without any frozen parts."

Lev said, "I noticed we were being dragged over a good hard road. Why didn't they move us here in trucks? I see a couple of trucks parked outside."

Ivan's assistant gave an opinion. "If someone is weak and about to die, our commander would like to see him die on the road, rather than in his jurisdiction. That is why our camp has few natural deaths."

Lev was processed and as he left for the infirmary Ivan said, "Maybe I'll see you around and clue you in on the situation."

Ivan's partner in the film studio said, "It is not good to make alliances. If the guards find out you have a friend, they will think you are conspiring, getting your heads together for some anarchist purpose." Ivan agreed with him.

Sergeant Vologda heard this conversation and gave it affirmation. "Don't be too obvious about the friends you make. When one prisoner commits a crime here, his friends usually go to the ice house with him."

Ivan thanked him for the advice and said, "Comrade Sergeant, step up to the wall and I will take your picture. You can send it to your family back home. I won't even charge you my usual fee for it."

Vologda thought for a moment and responded. "Why not?"

He moved over to the wall and took a serious military pose. Ivan took the photo. Once the photos were developed, he would see that Sergeant Vologda got his picture and Ivan would destroy the negative, just in case there was some problem. Often problems arose in situations where there was no obvious problem.

9. The General's Visit

The leadership of Camp 193 was in an uproar. General Mikhail Frunze was coming for a visit. It was going to be a surprise; but after thinking about it, Frunze decided to make his visit known in advance. The last time he tried a surprise inspection and visit, it was at the camp outside of Igarka where a prisoner crew of road builders were heading south along the Yenesey. For sure, the camp commander was taken by surprise. He did not have time enough to procure champagne and hard drinks in advance. Russians were reputed to love vodka, but they preferred the more expensive stuff, wines from Armenia and whiskey from Ulanovsk, the city where Lenin was born and the city renamed after him.

It was March and the Vernal Equinox had just passed. The Yenesey was still frozen. Frunze would come by a plane equipped with skis. He liked these dramatic entrances and always wore his military finery in case there were photographers around. He really did not need the publicity, since he was truly a national hero.

Major Mikoyan was a specialist in organization and even if Frunze did appear out of nowhere, he would find ample food, drink and everything in good order. General Frunze did not lean heavily on the major, since it was widely known that the major had an uncle in the politburo and if something untoward happened to the major, there would be heads rolling in the streets.

Frunze had a reputation as a womanizer, even though he was getting up in years. When he led his troops through the Central Asian Republics, he let them rape at will. The question that Mikoyan posed to Rurik was whether or not to have some willing women ready in case the general did want some sexual gratification.

The two captains and the major had women prisoners working at their households. They were, of course, slave labor, arrested for some questionable crime. Stalin did not like uppity women and this filtered down through the system. Stalin had his two sisters-in-law sent to prisons in Siberia, as well as the wife of his foreign minister Molotov. The latter's wife was sent to prison just after the signing of the Molotov-Ribbontrov Treaty with Germany. For good measure, he sentenced one of his daughter's suitors to prison in Siberia.

The women in the camps were supposed to have the same duties as men, but Major Mikoyan isolated them into the household and maintenance staffs. Their wives liked the idea of having cooks and servants, even though these were young women, mostly in their twenties, whom their husbands might find attractive. Most of them had been raped by guards on their way to their prison assignments, so, they had already been exposed to that indignity.

Mikoyan told the woman boss about the predicament and she said she would have women ready for sex just in case there was an emergency.

She said, "If things don't work out I'll have sex with the old guy myself and he will be in for the ride of his life."

She often made ribald jokes to Mikoyan and his wife Lorraine. Mikoyan permitted her to have a sexual liaison with one of the men working at the Yaroslav household. He warned her not to get pregnant because he would have to send her to another camp.

The day before the arrival of General Frunze, Sergeant Vilko had Ivan and Mishkov checking the walkway from the river to the camp and scraping off snow or ice if necessary. For good measure, the two prisoners spread sand on the walkway. Vilko personally checked the mooring and lashing site to make certain it would hold the plane in case of wind. Generally there were no winds or storms at this time of year; but, the temperatures could be bitter cold.

Major Mikoyan and Captain Yaroslav were there to greet the general's plane. They had two armed guards with them. One of the guards had a leashed dog in tow.

General Frunze's plane landed with much noise. The pilot had been here before and knew exactly where to land. The side door opened and a landing flight of stairs came forward. Two armed soldiers stepped out and surveyed the situation. This was followed by a woman whom Mikoyan recognized as the general's wife. There would be no womanizing on this trip.

The general and his wife were both in their late sixties with graying hair. The general had his hair dyed from time to time, especially when he made public appearances. His wife was distinguished looking with her silver gray hair which she fashioned daily into many different styles.

After various hellos and embraces, Yaroslav offered his arm to the wife and the major walked with the general. The camp guards walked ahead of the procession and the two guards from the plane brought up the rear.

Mikoyan could have had a vehicle pick them up, but he thought that walking past the camp would be part of the general's inspection. The prisoners within the camp were hidden from view and only soldiers could be seen inside the enclosure.

Once the royal couple was settled in Mikoyan's best room, the general was anxious to take the tour of the camp and get that out of the way. An open air vehicle was at hand even though the temperature was slightly below freezing. They were all used to cold weather, so no one was inconvenienced.

The tour included the compound where the general insisted on seeing one of the barracks. Mikoyan asked which of the ten barracks the general wished to see and luckily he pointed to barracks 15 which was the best constructed of the lot. Barracks 10 had the reliable prisoners, but most of them were around the barracks while barracks 15 was all but empty, except for the barracks master who tended the fire, filled the kerosene lamps, checked and cleaned the outhouse, stacked firewood, kept water in the bucket used for tea and made certain every prisoner kept his bunk area neat and everything put in place.

When they came out of the barracks, Frunze turned to Mikoyan, "It's like the Garden of Eden compared to what we had to endure. This is probably why you never had a prisoner escape."

Mikoyan retorted, "We have had several attempts at escape, but we have an excellent tracker who brings them back in a few days. After a couple of nights in the ice house, they never want to escape again." Frunze laughed.

The tour included the stables, the dog pound, the infirmary, the soldier's quarters, quartermaster building and mess hall. The general was very pleased with what he saw.

That evening, a semi-formal dinner was served in the Mikoyan dining room. Only adults were there. This included the captains, Mikoyan's wife Lorraine, the captain's wives and the major.

Goat meat was one of the general's favorites, since he lived on goat meat during the campaign. He liked it roasted over an open fire.

During the meal he said, "I like the way your cook did the meat. I don't like beef and that seems to be all we can get at the Headquarters. I guess you're able to get it from the natives."

No one answered or offered a comment. Mikoyan wasn't sure he wanted the general to know about the goat and pig farm. It could be mistaken for a native farm from the air.

Frunze said that he thought war with Germany was inevitable. Russia had made a pact with Germany to split Poland and give the Baltic States to the Soviets. This was hush-hush, but Frunze liked to leak these bits of information to show that he considered his hosts honorable and trustworthy. Also, it indicated he was on the main line to Moscow.

The general passed on information that was common knowledge to the military officers, but they would not admit to knowing it. He said he thought he was in danger since half of the generals in the Red Army were shot for suspicion of plotting to overthrow Stalin. This included the Chief of the Red Army, General Tukhachevshy. Even Admiral Orlov, Commander-in-Chief of the Red Navy was shot. About seventeen thousand officers with field battle experience were purged and executed.

What Frunze didn't know was that the German General Heinrich had faked documents which he let fall into the hands of the Soviet secret police, the NKVD. The documents made it seem like the doomed men were communicating with the West. Stalin, who was suspicious of everyone, took no chances, he had everyone whose name appeared in these documents executed. It was a counter-intelligence coup for Germany.

There were spies everywhere and everyone in authority was suspect. It did not pay to discuss the purges and executions of the Soviets under Stalin. High ranking officials confessed to crimes in order to spare their families, who were often exiled to Central Asia anyway. The Old Bolsheviks that led the revolution were all tried and executed. They were heroes and yet they were executed. The list included Bukharin, Kamenov and Zinoviev. The number two man Trotsky had taken flight to Mexico. It was only a matter of time before he and his politically active son met the fate of his former comrades. Of the 140 members of the Central Committee in 1934 only 15 were still free in 1937, the rest had been liquidated or sent to prisons.

During the purges before 1939 more than ten million people had been arrested and three million of those where executed. Ivan and his prison mates were among the fortunate seven million, if one was considered fortunate to be in Siberia..

After a pudding desert, Frunze lit a cigar and asked about the children of the officers. The wives of Yaroslav and Rurik gave a brief statement about their children who were in boarding schools in Krasnoyarsk, and how the boys enjoyed the roughness of soccer. They wanted to assure Frunze they had tough genes to pass along.

Frunze asked Lorraine about their daughter. "How old was Ludmilla now?"

Lorraine's face lit up. "She will be eighteen on April 20. She has just finished her studies at the technical school and will be eligible for the university this fall. She was at the top of her class and her teachers said she should try to get into the university at Tomsk which was just given the government contract for aeronautics and rocket programs."

Frunze said he was familiar with the aeronautics program at Tomsk. He could assure her entrance to the university, but not into that aeronautics program since admission was by examination. Frunze said there might be as many as two thousand applicants, but only thirty or forty students would be accepted.

The Mikoyans pretended that Frunze was saying something new to them, but they had researched the program completely. There was a foreign language exam, as well as a rough technical and science exam, and having relatives in high places didn't help here.

Frunze's wife asked if Milla, as she was called, was home, since she was finished with her studies. When informed that Milla was indeed home, she insisted on seeing her.

Mrs. Mikoyan left the room and returned with Ludmilla. The daughter was a beautiful young lady with a full figure, large eyes, full lips and long brown hair. Frunze looked as if he was going to start foaming at the mouth when he saw her.

"Ludmilla, you were just a little girl when I last saw you. Now you are grown up and a mature young lady. And not only are you as beautiful as your mother, but you are as intelligent. Come over here, where your uncle Mikhail can give you a kiss."

An embarrassed Milla went over. Frunze pulled her onto his lap and kissed her on the cheek twice. His left hand roamed down and rested against one buttock. Most everyone felt uneasy. Frunze relaxed his grip. Milla stood up and went to stand by the chair of her

100

mother.

Frunze spoke, "I hope you study hard so you can get a good place at the university. I would come here and tutor you myself, but my duties deny me this privilege."

Milla was smiling, "Maybe you can take the test for me. I am sure you could pass it without difficulty. We studied your treaty with the Muslims in school. Everyone was impressed when I told them I had met you five years ago."

Frunze smiled at this buttering up. "Let us see if I am still in t   he textbooks five years from now."

Milla said, "We might change textbooks, but we cannot change history."

Frunze was very pleased with that statement. Milla excused herself and left the room. The wives moved to one end of the large table and the men to the other.

Major Mikoyan lifted his glass to General Frunze who responded by lifting his glass. Mikoyan spoke in a serious tone. "General, the troops here have had little combat training. The only experience most of them have had is guarding prisoners. Would it be possible for you to give them at least an hour talk on military strategy and perhaps what it is like to be in a serious combat situation?"

"Major, that is a good idea. Get set up for two o'clock tomorrow and I will talk to your men who are not on duty. But I have to leave immediately and fly to Dudinka."

The general and the major finished their drinks. The captains did not speak but were mere drinkers and observers of the situation. Mikoyan thought he might be considered as buttering-up Frunze, but he was serious, his men had no combat training and it looked like he might have to go to battle in the future, and most of these men would be there with him.

A skeleton guard corps was sent out to tend to prisoners. There was no expectation of trouble. Benches were put on what passed for a parade ground. It was the field where the troops played soccer when they needed to let off steam. Sometimes, but not often, the field was used for practice in marching.

Sergeant Surgut usually handled parade and organizational chores around the camp. He had a slight platform installed, since he wanted the general to be higher than the men. The Soviet flag was off to one side. There were no weapons at this meeting.

All the sergeants were there, as well as the two captains, and, of course, the major. The privates were the most trusted of the camp. Surgut made certain that Privates Donbas, Pavlov and Kharkov were out with the prisoners. He didn't want them embarrassing the camp with their trademark boorish behavior..

Precisely at two o'clock General Frunze appeared with his two body guards. Major Mikoyan called the troops to attention. The two body guards moved to a position behind the platform while Frunze was motioned to a seat next to Major Mikoyan. When Frunze was seated, Mikoyan said "At ease, return to your seats."

Still on his feet, Major Mikoyan said," It is my pleasure to know and introduce to you, one of the greatest heroes of our military history. Here is a man whose troops were outnumbered eight to one and yet he was able to annihilate the enemy and bring him to his knees. In one battle, the battle of Ashgabat, only one man in three had a weapon while the enemy was heavily armed. He not only destroyed the White Army in this area, but he also secured it against the Mongol descendents of Genghis Khan and Tamarlane. Let me give you General Mikhail Frunze, hero of the Soviet Union."

The men rose spontaneously and applauded vigorously as Frunze rose to his feet. They had genuine admiration for him and he knew it. He stretched his arms out and motioned for the men to sit down. They would not, but continued to applaud. Mikoyan rose to his feet and shouted, "Be seated men." They sat down.
"I apologize for their behavior general." Frunze smiled, turned slightly and shook Mikoyan's hand.

Frunze began, "It is a pleasure to be here in such a well organized camp. Your officers and sergeants are to be congratulated. You men are to be congratulated for running a camp with so little dissent and great production. I salute you all."

He continued. "Major Mikoyan has asked me to talk about my military strategy and to give you some tips in case you ever get into battle in a leadership capacity. My first tip is for the officers at all levels to know the men under their command. Know them inside and out. You will know whom you can trust and who is to be watched for weakness. Let the weak get killed first and save the

102

meat of the battle for your best soldiers."

He paused and looked at the faces of the sergeants sitting in the first row. "You men who are sitting up front are the key to victory or defeat."

There was a continuation of the trustworthy theme and then a shift to another topic. "Major Mikoyan pointed out that in one battle only one man in three had a weapon. What we did then was to let the men with weapons advance and the men without weapons follow them. When the man with the weapon was killed, or wounded, the second man would pick up the weapon. In that battle, we were shy on ammunition and each man was given ten rounds to carry. If the man with the weapon was not killed, but used up his ten rounds, he would pass the weapon to man number two and number two would pass it to man number three. Fortunately we killed so many of the enemy with our first blast that within a half hour all of our men were armed, most with enemy rifles."

"My philosophy is simple. If you have the numbers and superior force you attack straight on, right down the middle. If you do not have superiority, you attack the flank. In many of the battles I would send a nuisance force of volunteers ahead of us, at least three days in advance. They would enter the enemy camp and cause havoc and demoralize the enemy. The enemy would get no sleep for the next three days and by the time we attacked, we were well rested and the enemy was harried. That strategy has worked many times."

The speech continued in this manner and finally the hour was almost up. The general knew he had won the audience and asked, "Do any of you have any questions?"

Everyone sat stunned, not knowing what to do. They were too uneducated in warfare to even think of a question. Finally, Private Penza rose to his feet. General Frunze acknowledged him and asked, "What is your question?"

"I am Private Penza general and I read a description of the Battle of Ashgabat. Later when I read about a battle near Irkutsk, the author said the major in charge had made the classic Frunze Movement. Later on, I read about the Frunze Movement again, but I don't understand what it is. Unless it is a secret, would you explain that?"

"Very good private. It is good to see a soldier reading military journals instead of romantic stories about soldiers and their love escapades. The Frunze Movement was simple, but difficult to carry out. It is my knight's advance. If you play chess, you know that the knight advances by two blocks and then turns one or vice versa. What I did was to move my troops into the front of the enemy and then when we got sufficiently in his face we made a quick move to the right. The enemy had shifted all of his troops to the front and had depth there. When we shifted to the right, we had fewer of their troops to fight, and once we got rid of them, we had the rest of their army trapped in a flanking action. This has worked for me with shifts to the left as well as to the right. I would recommend that all of you learn to play chess. It helps to organize your mind and see how the enemy can be made to move in chaos."

"Something else happened at Ashgabat. We took a large number of prisoners and my lesser officers wanted to shoot the entire batch rather than hold them. However, killing those who surrender is not always a good option. It is true, you don't have to worry about them when they are dead, and you don't have to feed them, or tie up troops holding them, or moving them to another location. But, prisoners are often a valuable resource. They can do menial work for you, like digging trenches and transporting heavy loads of materials. Many of our prisoners turned out to be our most dependable people, and many of them became our friends."

When Frunze made that remark, the image of Ivan ran through the minds of Sergeants Vologda and Vilko. Who would not be friends with such an honest person?

The meeting was concluded to thunderous applause. Sergeant Vilko shouted to Major Mikoyan who quieted the applause. Vilko said, "Would it be possible for us to shake the general's hand so that we can tell our children about this great occasion."

Mikoyan looked to Frunze who was pleased to shake his head yes. Frunze moved off to one side and his guards moved behind him, but to his sides. The men lined up and moved forward, giving their rank and name and shaking the hand of the general. When Private Penza appeared, the general remembered him and said, "I am certain that I will hear great things about you in the future." This was not wasted on Mikoyan or the captains.

When the men returned to their seats, they remained standing. Major Mikoyan said, "Be seated." They all sat.

Mikoyan said, "There is one story about General Frunze that I must tell you."

Frunze looked puzzled. The major went on." Our small army was heading toward the high mountains of Kyrgyzstan and were moving at a fast pace. I was in General Frunze's command group and we had moved ahead faster than our support group and major fighting force. The general was not one to waste time and he kept us moving. We had run out of food and had not eaten for three days."

Frunze smiled because he knew where this was heading. Mikoyan went on. "We were a group of about three hundred. There was a halt in our movement and the general wanted scouts to go on ahead and report back. I volunteered to lead this scouting group of eight."

"We rode about five miles over a hill and found ourselves surrounded by warriors that we could not identify. I told a private next to me to head back to the general. He turned around and went back. The seven of us were soon surrounded and I told the men to hold their fire, since we would be cut down immediately."

"We were taken to a large tent. One of our men could speak their language and they wanted to know who we were and what we were doing there. Nobody gave any information. They told us to sit in one corner of the tent with our tied hands on our heads. They had already removed our weapons."

"We sat there for about a half hour when we heard the sound of hoof beats. Our men came into the tent with guns blazing and the captors that were left alive surrendered. Guess who was among our small group of rescuers. General Frunze. He personally cut the bonds from my hands."

"We began an immediate interrogation, and like us, the men refused to give any information. There were about thirty of them. The general had selected three men whom he thought to be their leaders and told them if they did not tell us everything, their eyes would be cut out. Needless to say, they began talking so fast our interpreter couldn't keep up with them."

"They told us that their commander had trained huge dogs to attack and when we reached a certain point on the route, he would send about two hundred dogs at us. The idea was to soften us up with the dogs and then their warriors would finish us off."

"General Frunze turned to me and said this was great. I asked him what was so great about the situation. He said that we hadn't eaten in three days and the enemy was sending us lunch."

At this, the soldiers broke into laughter and General Frunze turned to Captain Rurik and shook his head yes as he was laughing.

Mikoyan went on. "When the dogs came at us, we killed about half of them with the first volley and the other half went running. The enemy saw this, and like their dogs, they turned tail and ran. We piled the dead dogs on stretchers and carried them back to our cooks, who had large kettles of hot water boiling.

One of the prisoners said that he was forced into this band. His family had a ranch nearby and he could make a deal with his father to exchange food for the hides. We let him go and he came back about an hour later with his father and a wagon load of milk and beets. Our cooks made a milk base and we had a great meal of dog meat. One of the finest meals I think I ever had."

With that, the men started applauding. The major turned to the general who was standing and beaming. The general waved to the troops as he left the platform and they continued to applaud. When he disappeared, Rurik gave orders to Sergeant Surgut to dismiss the troops.

10. A New Assignment For Ivan

It was a cold first day of April and Ivan was sent to scrub the floors of the infirmary. He obtained the proper tools, a hard bar of soap and a bucket of hot water from the kitchen and went to his designated workplace.

When Ivan arrived, he looked around before deciding which of the floors to do first, the outer office or the ward.. There were three prisoners on cots in the ward. They were in their underwear and lying on their backs, all looking at the ceiling.
Ivan said to them, "This will cost you two extra days, maybe it's worth it if you can relax and get your strength back."

106

One of the prisoners sat up. "Ivan, is that you?" It was Lev Lefkovich the one-time lawyer.

"Lev," glowed Ivan. "Looks like you are already pulling your influence."

"No, Ivan, I am sicker than a dog. Watch so I don't vomit on you."

Ivan smiled, "Maybe you can tell me how you came to be in this unfortunate situation."

Lev shook his head yes. "Let's go out into the office where we can talk freely."

The other two prisoners did not seem to mind. Lev wrapped a blanket around himself.

Lev sat in the doctor's chair with a writing pad holder while Ivan sat in the patient's chair. Ivan stared at Lev's face. It was gaunt, not like the robust lawyer Ivan once knew. Soon though, with hard work and nutritious food, Lev would be back to normal.

Lev began his story. "You know my occupation and my duties, which were to help determine the punishment for the crime. The punishment never fit the crime, since in most cases, there was no crime, merely some neighbor getting back at another for some argument. Or often, the informer wanted the neighbor's better apartment."

"One afternoon, I was summoned to defend a young woman who was about to be brought into the interrogation room where you and I met. Her file said that she had cursed an officer representing the Soviet people. That's all it said, no more details, except, she was nineteen years old, five feet four inches tall, black hair, brown eyes, the usual stuff"

"When she came into my office, it was obvious that she had been having a rough time. She was beautiful. My mother would have been proud if I married her. She was slumped in the chair and could barely talk. I tried to discuss the situation with her, but she refused to say anything except 'you are just like the rest of them.' I wondered what she meant. I got her a cup of hot tea which she accepted."

"A while later, she said she had been raped repeatedly the previous night. There was so much semen in her that it was still oozing while we were talking. She collapsed several times with her head on the desk."

"After our meeting, she was taken back to a cell. I thought I better speak to the prosecutor and tell him abut the situation because, under Soviet law, rape is a serious offense. When I met with the prosecutor, he said that often women in prison would offer their bodies to guards and others in hopes of getting special favors. My client was probably one of these types of women. There was no changing his mind."

"When I met with Anna, that was her name, again I mentioned that I met with the prosecutor whose name was Brezla. She perked up and said he was the first one who raped her and told the guard he could be second when he was finished. Other guards came later and continued into the night. Last night, the raping continued, but not at the feverish pace of the night before."

"It was hopeless for her and this would probably continue, since the prosecutor moved her trial back two weeks. I guess that would give him time to get some more action. She wanted to know how persons went about committing suicide. I didn't want to get involved in this, since I always suspected the room had listening and recording devices attached to it."

"I motioned to the walls to tell her that the room was bugged. She understood, but still wanted to know how to commit suicide. I told her I did not know how to do it, but it was in her best interest to go to trial and be sent to some prison somewhere and serve out her sentence. I said she would probably get ten years and she would still be less than thirty years old when she got out. That was the same advice I gave to you."

"She persisted and I put my finger up to my lips and passed her my cyanide pill. Anyone living in our hellish society should carry a suicide pill. I hated to give mine up. It was in a small pocket in the lining of my coat. I wished I had two of them. She put it between her cheek and teeth before she left the room. I said I would meet with her tomorrow and see if I could get her trial date moved up and get this show on the road. I never should have used the term 'show' since that was the term the western newspapers used to refer to the trials of a couple of years ago. Show trial is what they called them. They were right."

"When Anna got back to her cell she swallowed the pill and

died a quick but painful death, but it was preferable to what she was experiencing. The prosecutor confronted me with the use of the term 'show' and said I was in contact with enemies of the Soviet people. I knew it was futile to deny it, but I did, and received a pistol whack on the side of my face. I asked Brezla what I should confess to and he already produced a document for me to sign which I did."

"So here I am in the tropics with you and I didn't even have friends in high places. I think Vishinsky would have helped me, but I didn't know how to contact him on such short notice. I don't think Brezla wanted a trial, because he knew, I knew about his escapade with a female prisoner. Even though nothing would come of my mentioning it, there would be a faint smear on him, which might lead to bigger things. Probably if I hadn't signed the confession I would be dead now."

Ivan sat in wonder and finally said, "Look at it this way, the air here is cold, but it is fresh and clear and healthy if you are not worked too hard. The food is lousy, but it is not scarce, unless you get on the deprived basic ration list."

Lev went back to his bunk and Ivan finished scrubbing the floor. It was comforting to both of them to know that they had a friend in the group even though they would never acknowledge the friendship. Perhaps it was Lev who sent Ivan the package of clothing while he was in prison. Ivan never mentioned it.

In the middle of April Sergeant Vologda told Ivan that he had a new assignment for him. Major Mikoyan had a large garden next to his house which had not been planted for some time. He was looking for a prisoner who knew horticulture and could work the garden and get it to produce flowers as well as fruit. Vologda figured Ivan knew plants and animals and could handle the task. Ivan said he had no choice, but to do it. Vologda assured him that he had a choice, and if Ivan did not want to do it, then he would get someone else. He assured Ivan that people would kill for this opportunity.

Ivan said that he was enthusiastic about the assignment and he learned to show a lack of enthusiasm in such things, because, as a prisoner, the people with whom he dealt were not pleased to see a prisoner smiling. Ivan thanked Vologda and asked when he would start. Vologda said he talked with the service barrack boss and they agreed Ivan would clean the dog compound in the morning, do the pig slop run in the afternoon and start working on the garden in the afternoon and evening. Vologda said the boss would get someone else to do the pig slop run as soon as possible;

The major's house was about a half mile from the stockade. It was a large house with ten rooms. There were four bed rooms on the second floor, each with a large triple glazed window. The outer two windows could be removed in summer. The house had been confiscated from a successful fur trapper, who operated in this area before the prison was moved here. For some reason, he put the upper windows almost at floor level which was the reverse of most buildings that had the tops of windows at ceiling level. This was only on the second floor. Windows on the first floor were normal. Ivan reasoned that the trapper used the second floor for his business and it was easier to remove the windows at floor level and push things out, instead of taking them down, what he assumed were narrow stairs, or lifting them up to normal window level.

   The house was made of sawn lumber which was unique. The houses of the captains were all log with cement between the logs. The trapper must have been wealthy, considering the size of the house and the two floors. Ivan's garden was on the south side of the house. A single window on the second floor looked out at the garden.

   Since the ground was still frozen in mid April, Ivan constructed hot beds near the garden area. He figured he would spade about a third acre of ground for the garden and he would surround this with flowering shrubs. He knew plants and could dig the shrubs out of the forest. He noticed many blackberry plants along the river and would set aside a section for blackberries. In the hot beds, he would start tomatoes and cucumbers, the mainstay of the Russian summer diet. He would make a small dark shelter, cover it with earth, include horse manure and raise mushrooms, another Russian favorite.

   Soon he was taken off the pig slop run and now had the entire afternoon and evening to work on the garden. Often he would notice Major Mikoyan observing him from a lower window, which was his office when he was not at the stockade. He noticed the

110

beautiful daughter Milla studying in the second floor window of her bedroom. She would sometimes rest her eyes by looking out the window and watching Ivan at his work. Ivan had already started bringing shrubs in from the woodlands and planting them in the half frozen earth. He had a couple of nice hedge rows growing.

Major Mikoyan came out to talk to Ivan who dropped his shovel and stood at attention. The major said, "You don't have to stand at attention when I come to talk to you. Just continue working and I will stop you if I want to ask you something."

Ivan relaxed, "You will have to forgive me comrade commander, but I do not know the proper etiquette when talking to or addressing someone of your importance."

"Commander will be fine number four forty one. What is your name, in order that I may address you by your given name?"

"It is Ivan Ivanov."

"How old are you? How long are you in for Ivan?"

"I was given a ten year sentence and I have served over one year already. I am twenty three years old."

"Good Ivan, you will only be thirty two years old when you get out. There is a lot of life left after thirty two. I didn't get married until I was thirty five. You must be very reliable to have this job, since Sergeant Vologda would not assign just any one to this task. How do you know gardening?"

"I studied biology at the university at Voronezh. My professor's specialty was insects, but we studied the entire spectrum of science. It's all related, biology, chemistry, earth science, soil science. Russians are the world experts at soil. Our soil terminology is used all over the world. This soil is classified as podzol, or ash like earth, and I know what it can do and what it can't do. Don't expect any bananas or oranges."

"Just give me tomatoes, cabbages, potatoes and cucumbers that I can share with my friends and I will be satisfied. Maybe some beets and carrots would be nice. Good day Ivan, I will be out to check my garden often. Just ignore me unless I speak to you."

"Goodbye commander and thank you for taking time to talk to me." Mikoyan gave a half wave and moved to the house.

It was the last week of April when Mishkov told Ivan that Plushna had escaped. He had taken a horse from the stable and rode down the road in the darkness. No one missed him until daybreak. He had abandoned the horse after about twenty miles. The tracker was already on his trail.

Six days passed before the lights were turned on inside the stockade and the prisoners were called to assemble. The tracker rode his horse through the gates. He had an empty horse behind him. Ivan thought perhaps Plushna had eluded the tracker and was the first to escape. This was wishful thinking.

Captain Rurik was in the center of the assembled group and the tracker dismounted his horse and walked up to Rurik. He presented Rurik with an ear, a large ear with a purple dot on it.

Rurik took the ear and walked down the first row of prisoners in each of the ten groups and displayed the ear. Then he went back to center stage.

"Prisoners of the Soviet people, no one escapes from Camp 193. If you have some personal problem, go to your boss who will direct you to one of the sergeants, who might be able to help you. But, do not try to escape. Prisoner number 560 thought he could solve his personal problem by leaving the camp. He hopped on a railroad coal car at Krasnoyarsk and was shot from the car. His body fell beneath the train and was cut into several pieces. It was too messy to bring back, but this is his ear."

When the ear had passed before Ivan and Mishkov they both knew it was Plushna's ear. No one else they knew had such large ears, at least no one they knew with a purple tattoo on the tip of the ear.

The end of winter was always a trying time for people of Siberia. They suffered from being confined to the indoors most of the time. Cabin fever was the humorous name for this condition. Plushna was said to suffer from cabin fever and that is why he attempted to escape.

Near the end of winter everyone's nerves were frayed. The guards were particularly testy. After all, they were prisoners in their own system. They did get time off and could go to visit the new bustling town of Lesosibirsk which was just north of the junction of the Angara and Yenesey Rivers. When the new road reached the town last winter, the town had only three hundred residents. Once the road reached there, the population soared to almost three thousand, with hunters and trappers coming from the interior to barter their wares for knives, pots and other necessities. A small band of women supplemented their incomes by part-time prostitution.

The road was now nearing a native village called Yeniseisk and its population was beginning to increase. There were twenty seven log houses at Yeniseisk and three more were under construction.

These were the recreation outlets for the soldiers of the guard. In their recreation room they had chess and checkers, dart board, sometimes beer, cards, a small library and some after-hour foods such a jerked reindeer meat.

It was in this setting that the frayed nerves of Private Kharkov unfurled. He beat the driver of the roller machine so badly, the man died. The machine had stopped running and the driver said there was something wrong with the fuel line. Kharkov hit him with his rifle butt and kicked him in the stomach and said the man was looking for any excuse to stop work. The man did not get up from the ground and after a few more kicks Kharkov decided the man was not pretending and had him removed to the infirmary where he died.

The investigation was carried on by Sergeant Vilko under the direction of Captain Yaroslav. They informed Major Mikoyan of the circumstances and the major decided on a formal hearing. Witnesses would be Privates Penza and Vilnius, as well as Sergeant Vologda and Sergeant Surgut who would record the proceedings.

The hearing took place in the camp office of Major Mikoyan which was just outside the stockade. The major was behind his desk and Private Kharkov was in front. Kharkov gave his rendition of the story and often inserted the phrase "these shit prisoners." After about fifteen minutes, nobody in the room liked his attitude.

Mikoyan said, "How did you know that the fuel line was not blocked?"

"I worked with these machines many times. If it was an air lock, all he had to do was wait for twenty minutes and the air lock would disappear and the machine would start. These gasoline rollers are much easier to fix than the steam rollers they use up north."

Mikoyan looked coldly at him. "What would have been your reaction if the man was sitting idle for twenty minutes waiting for the air lock to break? Would you have permitted twenty minutes of idleness? There are not many people who can run these machines. You know that hardly anyone can do that. Was it necessary to hit the prisoner repeatedly?"

"I found hitting a prisoner to be an effective method for getting more work done."

"I sent down a directive a few months ago about beating prisoners until they could no longer work. Did you get that message?"

"I do remember a talk by Captain Yaroslav concerning this. He said that it was permissible to beat a prisoner if he attacked you."

"Did prisoner number 234 attack you?"

"It was a verbal attack. He argued in a threatening manner. He called me a Ukrainian son-of-a-bitch."

"We have the testimony of two prisoners who said that was not the case."

"You can't take the word of a prisoner over mine. I am a soldier of the Soviet Union, sworn to duty and to uphold the constitution."

"We are not taking the word of those prisoners. The fact is, a valuable prisoner who can drive heavy equipment is dead."

Before he could finish the sentence, Kharkov broke in. "Anyone can learn to drive that equipment."

"Let me finish Private. Do not talk unless I give you permission." Kharkov stood up straighter.

Mikoyan looked Kharkov in the face. "Private Kharkov, take your uniform off."

Kharkov was bewildered, but complied with the request except for his socks and underwear.

"Take off everything private." Kharkov removed the rest of his clothes.

Mikoyan looked at Privates Vilnius and Penza. "Take this man to barracks number 16 and dress him in the clothes with number 234 on them. The dead man will no longer need these clothes, but this prisoner will."

114

Kharkov protested, "I was doing my duty."

"Your new duty will be driving the roller machine and caring for it." To Sergeant Vologda, "See that this man's ear is tattooed and a new identification card is made out for him."

Kharkov again protested. "The prisoners will kill me."

Mikoyan said, "That is your problem. However, we have a rule here. No one is to hit prisoners without good cause. You should not be killed, because we have a rule here that does not permit killing anyone except prisoners trying to escape. Move out now."

May Day was celebrated in the stockade with roasted goat meat. At the beginning of winter, many of the goats and hogs were slaughtered and hung up to freeze. As the sun edged further north, the meat began to thaw and Mikoyan thought this was a good way to give the cooperative prisoners a treat and remind them of this important holiday.

A few days after the celebration, Ivan was in the garden working and looking at his hot beds. These were glass covered frames that let the sunlight in and held the heat at night. He had placed a lot of horse manure in the pits and covered this with earth. The bacterial action with the horse manure also added heat to the structure. He was now ready to start tomato seedlings.

Major Mikoyan came around the house and approached him. Ivan nodded his head in recognition. Mikoyan came all the way over to the hot beds.

"Ivan, how is it going?"

This took Ivan by surprise, since he expected to hear his number rather than his name. "Everything is going fine. I am ready to start the tomato seeds. I might try a few different types of squash. Captain Yaroslav said he was going to Krasnoyarsk and he would pick up some seeds for me, if I give him an order. We have plenty of time, since the actual growing season doesn't start until the middle of June. Even then, we can have some killing frosts."

Mikoyan was only making small talk. He had something else in mind. "Do you know I have a daughter?"

"Yes, I see her from time to time." Ivan wanted to say that she was very beautiful, but he thought it best not to offer that analysis.

"She is studying for exams to get into a special science study program at a university. She must take a test in English and in technical sciences. She is having difficulty studying for the exams, since there is a lot of material to cover and she doesn't organize very well."

Ivan offered, "Wouldn't it be better if she tried to learn German which is the international language of science?"
"We thought about that, but every student is trying to learn German in order to translate scientific literature, but there are few who are learning English. We think she would have a better chance if she learned English. However, let me make a proposal to you."
Ivan didn't know what to say. Here he was, talking boldly to one of the most powerful men in Siberia. He was trying to be subservient, but he was talking as an equal, which was always dangerous.

Mikoyan went on. "I have been looking at your impressive university record. You have almost five years of science in your background, plus your secondary school science work. I sent to your university for your records when I found you were a university scholar."

Ivan said, "You are very kind in your remarks."

"I want you to tutor my daughter Milla in science. We have all the books that cover the topics, mostly physics with some chemistry. You can use my library to study the books and tutor Milla. We can set aside time each day for the lessons. You will have to clean yourself up, shave and wear a clean uniform. Your clothes will be washed and cleaned with the clothes of our household staff. You will move to a room in that shed over there." Ivan looked around as the major pointed.

Ivan thought his fortunes had been made. "I think I can handle the task, if the idea is just to pass a beginning test to get into some special program, but I can't handle English since most of my translations have been from German."

"That is good to hear you say that. There is another prisoner here with a university education and an excellent reputation in English language. He will be the other tutor. He will meet with Milla in the morning while you are studying for the tutorial lesson. You will meet with my daughter in the afternoon and eat supper with our staff. In the evening, you can do your gardening. We have electric lights in the library and reading conditions are excellent. As you are relaxing, remember you have an important job to do."

"I won't forget the importance of my job and I thank you for the confidence you have in me."

"Good, you can come to the side door of the house at one o'clock every day and go to the library. You will tutor Milla in the guest sitting room. Tomorrow you can meet Milla. We will go over the tasks, the books, and the schedule. If I am busy at that time, my wife will help you. Be certain you are clean and neat. My staff will have two extra shirts and pants for you. Leave most of your clothing issue in Barracks Ten. Only bring what is necessary with you to your new quarters, which you will be sharing with the other tutor."

Ivan went back to his hot beds. The May sun was warm, but the nights were still freezing. He took off his light jacket and was absorbing the sun through his shirt. He looked up at the middle window of the second floor of the house. A young beautiful girl was looking back at him and his muscular body.

The next day, he did the last dog shit job which seemed to be some sort of irony. Latko always came up to him and Ivan had been able to touch Latko now. He slipped Latko a wad of goat meat he had saved from the May Day supper. "Latko, my true friend, after lunch I will be on easy street." Latko wagged his tail in happiness. It was the first time he had done that with a friendly motion. He had often moved his tail slowly when he was in the attack mode. Ivan made a promise to visit Latko every day.

11. The Tutors

When Ivan went to his new sleeping quarters, he found two new shell tops and two new pairs of pants on one of the two bunks. Each shell had the number 441 neatly placed on the back of the sleeve and the number 441 down at the cuff of the pants. He thought his prisoner status would not be so obvious now. Under the bunk was a pair of black leather shoes, almost dress shoes.

The room was simple. A small window let in inadequate light. There were two tables, one for eating, perhaps, or writing, and the other held a kerosene lamp. A wind up clock set to the correct time was beside the kerosene lamp. No electricity was in evidence. There were clothes hooks near each bunk, a small wooden locker at the foot of each bunk and a sink, but no running water. A five gallon bucket beneath the sink was full of water. A small dipper hung on the side of the bucket. A sink drain led to the outside.

The building had four small apartments such as this. The other three were occupied by four women and four men who worked at the main household. A double seat outhouse was at the end of the apartment. The captain's properties also had this same outbuilding construction which was inhabited by their household staffs.

Ivan dressed in his new clothes, which fit well. There must be a tailor who created his outfit from the dimensions of his identity card. The clothes were basic olive drab and dark green. They were soft, not like his other prison clothes. He lay back to think of his new position of trust. He felt he was back at the university. Ivan would meet with his student in thirty minutes.

In a very short time, there was noise outside the room and the door was pushed open. In walked a big man who went immediately to the other bunk and sat on it.
Ivan looked at him and smiled, "Mr. Speaker, so you are the other professor. I knew you were educated, but I didn't know the extent."

"Hello Ivan, I figured you would work yourself into some kind of deal, and here you are. If you can only keep this tutoring job going for ten years you will have it made."

"I have less than nine years to do now. Did you meet the daughter yet?"

"No, you and I are going over to meet her and whoever else will be involved. I was here earlier as you can tell by my great looking outfit. We are to go together."

Ivan was happy to see his new room mate. "What is your name? I can't call you Mister Speaker in front of anyone. There might be an inquiry as to how you got that title?"

"You can call me Alexander, my last name is unimportant in this situation. So is yours by the way. When you introduce yourself to someone do not give your last name unless it is requested of you."

"Mr. Speaker," he paused, "Alexander, ever since I first saw you, I said to myself, if I ever need advice, you are the man I would approach."

118

"Good Ivan," Alexander held out his hand in friendship, "Now let us go to meet our future."

The two men tried to ignore the two armed guards near the house. They made their way to the side door, wiped their shoes on the outside mat, and entered. They removed their hats and stood in the doorway.

Major Mikoyan came to the hall. "Come this way teachers." He waved them toward him and directed them into the guest waiting room. Seated at a small table was the beautiful Milla and her attractive mother Lorraine.

Mikoyan introduced the men to his family. "This is Ivan who studied at the University of Voronezh and this is Alexander who studied at the University of Rostov. This is my wife Lorraine, and this is my daughter Ludmilla." Both women nodded. Milla smiled and a sunbeam moved about the room.

The major went on. "Mr. Alexander will tutor in English in the morning, starting at nine o'clock, while Mr. Ivan is in the library. Mr. Ivan will tutor in science in the afternoon, starting at one o'clock, while Mr. Alexander is in the library. They will have supper with our household staff and report to other duties after supper. The sun is getting higher in the sky, so they should have a lot of time to tend to their other duties."

Milla spoke as her mother chastised her with her eyes. "Mr. Ivan I see you working in the garden. Are you going to guarantee us a good crop?"

Ivan hesitated. "It depends on the weather. I guarantee, however, that you will work hard in science and pass your test at the end of summer."

Milla just wanted to hear their voices. "And Mr. Alexander, I understand you were a writer before coming to our town. Did you work for a newspaper?"

"No, I wrote some essays for our university lecture series which led to my trip to Krasnoyarsk."

Mikoyan looked at the men. "My wife, Lorraine, will be here during the tutoring. So in effect, you will also be tutoring her. Then she can discuss the lessons with Milla who will be studying in the evening. It is important that she pass the science and the English exam. If she passes, she will be entered into the prestigious program

119

and her future will be assured. Now that we are close to war with Germany, this is especially important."

A war with Germany! Each of the men acted as if this was common knowledge. There were rumors to that effect, but these were never confirmed until now.

Mikoyan made farewells to his wife and daughter and bade the men to accompany him to the library. It was a small room with well stocked bookshelves. Two easy chairs were placed around a small table. The major turned on the electric light. "See, gentlemen, you have a good light for reading, a table for working and unless I am mistaken, a pot of tea is forthcoming."

The tea and service were brought to the room by a middle aged lady with the number 804 painted on her sleeve and hem of her dress. She looked healthy and well fed.

"This is Pauline," said Mikoyan with a hand gesture toward the woman. "You better get to know her, because she controls the food in this household. Pauline, this is Ivan and this is Alexander. They are new members of our household staff."

Pauline looked the men over. "I know about you from your ID cards that Sonya used to adjust your clothes. I welcome you to our staff. If you need something within reason, don't hesitate to contact me."

Both Alexander and Ivan picked up their cups of tea and started browsing the bookshelves. The books were divided according to topic and Ivan found the science shelf. They both were surprised at the quality of the tea. Pauline explained it was imported from India rather than the tea of the Caucasus that most Soviets drank.

Ivan blurted. "Wow, look at this. Just what I need." He held up a book.

The major grinned, "What is it.?"

"It is a classic work. It is Tomato by Dr. Jon Mulhauser, the famous German horticulturist. It is in German, but I shouldn't have any trouble reading it. My German will come back to me."

Mikoyan got serious. "Don't let too many people know you can speak and read German. You will find yourself out of here and on the front lines. The enemy would also like to get a hold on you. It would make interrogation easier if you spoke their language. Don't let anyone, but the two of us in here, know you can do German."

Ivan hesitated, "I understand, and I thank you for the advice."

Mikoyan then added, "Don't let your gardening duties interfere with your main job right now, which is to tutor my daughter."

"Believe me sir, nothing will interfere with my duties toward your daughter. I will forget that she is the most beautiful woman I have every seen and remember that she is a student and I am a teacher."

Alexander stifled a smile in order to keep it from breaking out into a laugh. Mikoyan grinned. "Take whatever materials you need back to your quarters and begin your lessons tomorrow. How will you begin Ivan?"

"First I will have summary questions about the various sciences involved in this test. Once I find her level of expertise, then I will proceed to the more difficult."

Mikoyan turned to Alexander. "And you?"

Alexander spoke with definite authority. "I will give her a reading to do and I will discuss the meaning of the reading. I will also establish her level of expertise and take it from there. I will keep in mind the importance of our assignment and I am certain you will find our work will meet your satisfaction."

"Thank you gentlemen, let us not forget that you are prisoners of the Soviet people. However, even as prisoners, you have a duty to those people. I will leave you now. Be out of here within an hour. Then change clothes if you must and go to your work stations."

The prisoner tutors looked over the library and each took a couple of books. Then they headed back to their bunkhouse. They paused in the open area out of earshot of anyone.

Ivan turned to Alexander. "Just what is your other duty here?"

"I work at processing camp documents, who died, who is still here, what are their duties. I make lists for Sergeant Vilko. I am Vilko's boy and you are Vologda's."

"I guess that's true. What do you know about the war?"

"There is no war yet, but everyone except Stalin knows it is coming; German troops are massing along their eastern border."

They went back to the bunkhouse and each settled onto his bunk. Alexander rose and lit the kerosene lamp. The light was adequate and each poured over the books he had just borrowed.

Ivan kept going back to the book on tomatoes. It was fascinating and had a section on building a greenhouse. He thought that he could use the second and third windows of the house since they were not used in summer. He could build a small greenhouse using the windows and return the windows in October to be used back on the houses.

The First Lesson

Ivan walked into the sitting room for the first lesson. Lorraine and Milla were at the table with looks of anticipation on their faces. Each had a sheaf of blank paper and a pencil at their disposal.

Ivan said, "Dobra dien, good day" and the women responded in kind. He sat down opposite them and said that they better get started. His first questions to Milla pertained to the behavior of gases.

He began, "When you increase the pressure on a gas, what happens?"

Milla took on her best serious voice. "The pressure of a gas is inversely proportional to its volume."

"What does that mean?"

"It means that as the pressure increases, the volume decreases?"

"What's the relationship between temperature and gases?"

"The temperature is proportional to the volume. If you increase the temperature, the volume will increase."

So it went. There were mathematical problems involved and Milla got everything correct. She knew gases at the college entrance level fairly well, but there had to be some touching up. Ivan made notes to that effect.

As the lesson continued, Ivan noticed Lorraine rubbing her left arm. She was wearing a blouse with sleeves that came down to her wrists while Milla wore a blouse with sleeves coming down to her elbows. Ivan didn't want to be rude, but he was distracted by this arm rubbing.

After an hour of questions, answers and explanations, Pauline came in with tea for Ivan. He took a quick break while Pauline waited for the cup and saucer. Pauline spoke to Lorraine in French and Lorraine responded.

Lorraine explained that she is French on her mother's side and she learned French there. Pauline was French. She had married a Russian who had been to France on a diplomatic visit. Later her husband was declared an enemy of the state and executed. She was sent to Krasnoyarsk and ended up working for the Mikoyans. It was not clear to Ivan whether Pauline was a prisoner or just working here until he remembered the numbers on her clothing of yesterday. She had no numbers on her clothing today.

Pauline asked Lorraine something in French. There was concern in her voice. Lorraine answered in disgust and rolled up her sleeve and exposed a red sore looking rash. Ivan wondered what it was. Lorraine said the army doctor in Krasnoyarsk had been treating it for two weeks now with no results. In fact, it was spreading and getting more painful. They have tried salves, potions and powders with no luck.

Ivan finished the tea and Pauline took the cup and saucer out with her. Lorraine rolled down her sleeve and the lesson continued for another hour and a half.

Ivan complimented Milla and said she was much more advanced than he was at that age, especially in mathematics. He said, he was satisfied with Milla' s abilities and tomorrow they would discuss, the behavior of liquids. She was to also brush up on weights and measures.

The arm rubbing of Lorraine was getting to the point of distraction. Her face expressed continuous pain. Ivan considered this situation a challenge and he figured he would contact the one person he knew who had knowledge of such things, Rasputin.
First, Ivan had to come up with a reason for going to Barracks Ten. The guards of the compound knew Ivan well and that he had some special connection with the major so they never challenged him. They made him sign a sheet stating his purpose which he said was to pick up some of his clothing. He could use another set of underwear. Most prisoners were down to two sets and Ivan was in luxury, he had four.

In the barracks, he went straight to the corner where Rasputin conducted his séances. The air was heavy with candle wax and some foreign smell, maybe cinnamon. Rasputin was behind a candle and his face glowered in its light.

Ivan approached cautiously, not wanting to break the spell. Rasputin stared ahead and ignored him. Finally, he broke the spell and said, "Ivan, my good friend, it is good to see you. My heart soars like an eagle when you come into my life."

Ivan went right to the problem and told about the rash. Rasputin asked questions about its color and location and whether it was spread in spider-web fashion or was a continuous sheet of sores. When he had all the basic information he nodded and smiled.

Rasputin hummed and in a hushed voice said, "It's a fungus. The army doctor is treating her for bacterial infection when it is a fungus. Sulfa drugs only agitate that kind of condition."

Ivan was pleased. "Do you have anything to treat it with that I can take with me? If I can cure her rash I will be like a prince at a royal ball."

"Yes I do. I have this powder that I use when I get a rash between my toes or up around my balls. Those are usually areas where fungus grows if those areas are not kept dry. Before I got this stuff from my Evenki friends I used ground up powdered birch bark which worked fine but this stuff will cure it in one day."

"I have nothing to pay you with, but when my garden comes in, I will reward you with fresh vegetables."

Rasputin patted Ivan's hand. "I consider you one of my best friends here and if they shoot me they will probably shoot you as a collaborator with me. Let me get the stuff for you."

He went to his bunk and lifted up the mattress. Under it were several leather bags and some that appeared to be made out of dried intestines sewn together. He took up one of the intestine bags and poured a little of its contents into a square of paper which he folded into a neat packet and handed to Ivan.

"It doesn't take much. Put it on lightly."

"I will repay you somehow. What is your real name anyway?"

"I have accepted the name of Rasputin and I can see into the future. I have predicted many events which came true."
"You did predict I would get married and have three golden haired children."

"Yes I did Ivan, but I have had a disturbing vision three nights ago. I saw you and Plushna drinking wine and clinking glasses over a grave marker. When the grave marker emerged into my view it had the number four forty one on it, your number."

"How can I get married and have children and be dead at the same time."

"I don't know Ivan. My visions are never wrong. Maybe you will meet Plushna in the afterlife, after you have been married and have the three children. I could be wrong about the three children, since you were in no condition to give me an accurate description of the lightning bursts in your head."

"That was one of the best days of my life, being on that trip with you and the two soldiers."

"By the way, do you still have the amulet the head man gave you at the Evenki village?

"Yes I do and I also have the triangle stone I found."

"If you ever leave the compound make certain you are wearing that amulet."

The men parted and Ivan went back to his plush quarters in the back yard of the residential property. He felt content that night and slept soundly.

On the next day's lesson, he asked Lorraine about her arm. He explained that he was a biology student at the university and had studied some diseases. He brought this powder with him and wanted her to try it. She responded that anything was worth a try.

Ivan asked her to go to her bathroom and wash the rash area and dry it thoroughly. She rose and told Milla to go with her to help in this matter. Actually she did not want to leave Milla alone with Ivan. If something untoward happened, there is no telling what reaction the major would have.

When the women returned, Ivan looked at the arm. He took the muscle of her left arm which was the arm with the rash and twisted the arm slowly. He finally got it into the position he wanted and reached in his shirt pocket and extracted the packet. He slowly sprinkled it on the rash and rubbed it softly.

As Ivan did this, a strange thing happened to Lorraine. She felt a twinge in her pubic region and warmth spread into her legs. What was happening? She couldn't understand it. Did she have a sexual attraction to this young man who was young enough to be her child, or was it just a coincidental reaction to the gentle massaging of her arm. Whatever it was, she liked the touch of Ivan.

The lesson continued in its usual vein and Ivan had supper with the household staff and worked on his greenhouse now that he had Pauline's permission to use the windows. He had obtained some lumber, blocks of stone, nails and a hammer from a prisoner who worked for Captain Rurik.

The next day, Lorraine's rash was gone, just as Rasputin had predicted. Ivan's fortune was made and Lorraine was happy and said she would call him Dr. Ivan.

When Ivan went to Rurik's property to borrow what he could from the man in charge, he was introduced to Magda, a pretty young woman about twenty years old. She was with Rurik's household. She had brown wild hair which reached to her shoulders. Around her waist she had a red sash, and on her feet were the typical red boots of a Russian peasant folk dancer.

Magda took a special interest in Ivan. They were nearly the same age and they hit it off immediately. There could be fireworks here, but Ivan did not want to get involved and risk his present situation. He had to control himself.

The greenhouse progressed nicely and soon it was finished. The final result was a low building, five feet high, ten feet long with a canvas door on one end. Ivan put sod around the base and had yet to figure out an easy watering system for the plants once they were transferred from the hotbeds. He had already set up used metal oil barrels at the apartment to catch rain water. He figured eventually the oil residue would be washed out. He even considered that he could take a bath in the water if necessary. However, the wash room was adequate and he was able to maintain good hygiene there. .

It was near the middle of June when Ivan decided to put out the tomato, cucumber, and squash plants that he had raised from seed. He had already dug up a sizable portion of the garden and had planted lettuce, radish, cabbage, beets, onions and potatoes. First he planted tomatoes and two squash in the greenhouse. The excess plants were put out in the garden once Ivan felt the danger of frost was gone..

It was after supper and Ivan was working in the garden. The day was June 20, close to the summer solstice and the sun was high and daylight lasted almost seventeen hours so there was a lot of time for work and little time for sleeping.

As Ivan compacted the earth around the cabbage plants, he heard the sound of a balalaika. Soon he could hear it loudly playing Alle Aleuska, or Meadowlands, as some called it. This was followed by a lively tune, one of Brahms Hungarian Dances. Ivan, who was somewhat of a music buff, thought it was the fifth dance. He pretended to work but listened to the music which was coming from the half opened window of the sitting room. Ivan could not wait to find out about the musician.

When he approached Milla and Lorraine the next day, he couldn't contain himself to find out who was playing the balalaika. Lorraine admitted to being the musician and said that now that her rash is cured, she feels better and happier, and this spurs her on to playing happy songs. She was instructing Milla in the balalaika, but academic studies had absolute priority now.

Milla and Lorraine were both growing closer to the warm personality of Ivan. Alexander was an excellent teacher, but he was stern and his personality was absolutely administrative.

A cold air mass had pushed down from Siberia. The camp was not freezing, but the temperature had dropped to fifty five degrees. Not having scientific equipment at his disposal, Ivan assumed there would be a frost. Sergeant Vologda said the last frosts of spring occurred around June 10, but sometimes, they occurred at the end of June. Ivan thought he might have put out his tomato plants too early.

There was panic. The plants in the greenhouse would be fine, as would the cabbage, onions, and radish. The potato plants might be damaged, but they would recover. There was only one thing to do and that was to cover the plants before sunset. Ivan went to Pauline for help. She said she would recruit help from Rurik's household. In about a half hour, a skinny young man and Magda showed up to help.

Pauline provided a pack of old Pravda newspapers to use as covers. She showed Ivan how to make them into hats which she had made as a child. The hats could be put over the plants. She made a sample hat and put it on Ivan's head.

"You look like a sea captain now Ivan." She laughed.

Pauline and Magda made the hats while Ivan and the Thin Man put them on the plants and covered the edges with a handful of dirt. There was progress and when they were almost finished the strings of the balalaika could be heard. This gave a festive atmosphere to an activity that was already festive and communal in nature.

There was a pause in the music. Then it started slowly and picked up speed. Magda danced her red boots toward Ivan. "Chardash Ivan, dance with me." Ivan complied and they did a traditional folk dance that every Russian school child learned. Madga put her face in Ivan's and they smiled and the dance moved on. Finally the music stopped and both dancers caught their breath.

Milla was in her bedroom and had observed the entire scene. She felt possessive of Ivan and pangs of jealousy set in. The young Magda, with her flying hair and firm body, was competition to the princess for the attention of her tutor, whom she considered her property.

Lorraine started another tune. Milla dashed from her bedroom to the sitting room.

"Mama, would you stop playing tonight."

Lorraine stopped. "I thought my playing helped you to study."

"It does, but not tonight. I am having trouble with my concentration."

Lorraine put the balalaika aside. Milla went back to her observation post. The music stopped and the work was quickly finished.

Magda punched Ivan in the arm. "You are a pretty good dancer Ivan. How is your sex life?"

"I am in prison and have no life other than that of a prisoner."

"Oh, there are ways to get around our confinement. Give it some consideration."

At the next tutoring session, Milla asked Ivan if he enjoyed the dance with Magda. Ivan said it was a good break from the routine and it was like being out on the town. He complimented Lorraine on her playing.

Lorraine finally realized why she had been asked to stop playing. She was unaware of the dance and questioned Ivan about it. Ivan said that when she played the chardash it enlivened them to dance, since they were almost finished with their tasks.

Milla started to pout. She questioned, "Magda is very pretty, isn't she?"

"I really didn't notice that. She is a nice person and she will make someone a fine wife someday. Being a prisoner is good training for marriage."

Lorraine didn't know how to stop this conversation. She tried to interject some humor, but it didn't work.

Ivan went on. " I am saving myself for the woman I love."

Milla said, "And who might that be?"

"I don't know, but I feel a new presence entering my life. A fortune teller said I would be married and have three children. But, you can't believe in fortune tellers."

The lesson began to a sober class and went well. Milla was very positive in her answers and Lorraine took copious notes.

On June 22, 1941, the Germans put Operation Barbarossa into effect. It was the invasion of the Soviet Union. They made huge gains in the weeks after that. The news of Barbarossa was kept from the prisoners and almost everyone else, except the officers and the sergeants.

However, Alexander had his sources and informed Ivan that the war had begun. "The Germans invaded the Soviet Union despite the Molotov-Ribbontrov Treaty. In the first couple of months, they caught us by surprise. Stalin went into hiding and finally emerged to make a radio speech. Rather than ask the people to fight for communism, he was very clever, he asked them to drive out the invaders and fight for the Motherland."

"What else can you tell me?"

"In those first couple of battles, we had more than a half million men taken prisoner by the Germans. Stalin put out an order that if any man is taken prisoner, his wife or mother, will be sent to Siberia. We already have a few of those wives working for the officer's households here. Everyone is warned not to discuss the war in any manner, so these wives are afraid and comply. Stalin's son was taken prisoner and when the Germans wanted to make an exchange for one of their general's, General Secretary Stalin said he had no son."

"How do you know so much about this Alexander? I didn't even know a war had started. I thought it would be with the English."

"The English are our allies at this time. I have my sources, which I will not divulge to you. That way, you could never compromise me, or them."

"I understand and I thank you for your indulgence."

"Ivan, you are too polite, always thanking people. It might be good if you got a little insufferable."

"It is my nature. I can be tough if I have to. As a student at the university I was very active in gymnastics and I have kept my body fit, except for those early days in prison."

"I am glad to hear this, my little friend. Keep fit. Concentrate on running. Concentrate on speed and distance. Be able to outrun anyone who is after you."

12. A Night At The Opera

It was the last day of June and knowledge of the war had spread throughout the compound. It was business as usual at the camp as Alexander and Ivan continued their tutoring sessions.

At the end of the session on this last day of June Major Mikoyan was in the house. Usually he went to his office at the compound and didn't return to the house until supper. Often, he missed supper, but Ivan was unaware of this, since Ivan ate with the household staff.

The major had the tea service brought into the sitting room at precisely four thirty when the session was to be ended. He brought a chair for himself.

Mikoyan addressed Ivan. "Ivan, how are things going with you?"

This was strange behavior and Ivan thought something was up, other than the usual routine. The major referred to the German invasion and said that all of their lives would be changed by these events. Probably, the road project would be abandoned.

The major questioned, "Do you like music Ivan?"

"Yes, I do. Your wife's balalaika playing is like angels dancing around in my head."

"Do you know anything about opera?"

"Some. I have been to several opera productions?"

The major sniffed. "Lorraine and I have been invited by General Frunze to attend the opera Boris Goudunow with him and his wife in Krasnoyarsk. Milla will go with us, so there will be no lesson for three days. She can study at Krasnoyarsk and look up old friends, while I attend to business, and we go to the opera. Anyway, what is this opera about? "

Ivan took a deep breath. "It was based on a work by Pushkin and composed by Modeste Moussorgsky, whose most famous work is A Night on Bald Mountain."

Lorraine broke in, "That's your opinion."

Mikoyan stared at his wife for a second. It was a signal to shut up. He then turned to Ivan. "Could you give me the details of the story?"

Ivan began. "It follows history pretty accurately. Boris is feeling guilty for his role in the murder of Ivan the Terrible's son. He has confined himself to a monastery. In Act One, the people are at the monastery chanting for Boris to declare himself Czar. A monk in an adjoining cell leaves the monastery and goes to Lithuania where he declares himself to be Dimitri, the slain son of Ivan the Terrible. In Act Two, Boris is established as czar and there is a lot of squabble between him and the children of his accomplices. In Act Three, the false Dimitri is still active in overthrowing Boris. There is an excellent love duet in this scene. The scene now changes to cries of 'Death to Boris'. The stage is emptied and the village idiot sits alone contemplating the misery of Russia. In the last scene, Boris is dying and gives instructions to his successors."

131

Mikoyan paused in contemplation. "Could you go over that again?"

Ivan complies, but adds an event where a blind man prays at Dimitri's tomb and has his vision restored. He added that it is a great opera and only wished that he could attend.

Mikoyan, Lorraine and Milla traveled down the new highway in one of the two cars of Camp 193. Private Penza had been recruited as driver and body guard. The Hotel Krasnoyarsk had been taken over by the military and General Frunze had his headquarters there. The three travelers were assigned rooms on the second floor. Private Penza was billeted with the guards.

When Mikoyan went to meet the general, he was pleasantly surprised to find Major Timko there. Timko was the commander of Post 195 which was the road group working from the north. His base was just south of Igarka on the Yenesey River. They embraced in front of General Frunze.

Frunze grumbled, "You two embrace each other, but neither of you embraced me."

Timko smiled. "You are our superior, but Gregor and I are equals."

Frunze grumbled again. "It's the price of being at the top. You can't have true friends."

Timko assured Frunze that he and Mikoyan were the best friends Frunze could ever have and he could rely on either one of them to give their lives on his orders.

It was July 3 and the opera was scheduled for seven o'clock. The group of six headed for their seats. The sixth person was the wife of Timko.

There was a free bar for the officers and wives and some hard cakes to go with it. The men drank lustily. The women drank the watered down punch, which still had a kick to it.

They were seated in the front row of a balcony with a good view of the stage. The general and his wife sat in the middle. Mikoyans were to the right and Timkos to the left. The men put their hats under the chair and settled back.

As the house began packing, Lorraine innocently asked her husband. "Could you tell me something about this opera? I am not very familiar with it. I know who Boris Goudonow is, but that's about as far as it goes."

Mikoyan went into the details he had garnered from Ivan. The others were silent, leaning toward him and listening intently. Mikoyan passed himself off as an intellectual and the others approved, since they were all friends caught up in an opera of their own.

Moscow was several hours behind Krasnoyarsk in time and when the group had left the opera they were told about a speech that Stalin had given. It was Stalin's first appearance since the invasion of June 22. He avoided any reference to the Bolsheviks and the communist philosophy, but concentrated on the invasion of foreigners and how we must all fight for our homeland. It was well thought-out since Stalin had killed off most of the military leaders, as well as twenty million of his own citizens. There were few families that had been untouched by the cruel regime. About five million prisoners were now in the camps of Siberia. There were two million more prisoners in the west.

In his speech, Stalin called for a scorched earth policy of leaving nothing for the invading army to use. He called for an intensive guerilla effort behind enemy lines. He defended his 1939 non-aggression pact saying that he only wanted peace for his country.

There would be no easy sleep for anyone. The women went to bed. Frunze, Mikoyan and Timko sat up until after midnight talking about the future of their commands. Frunze had something else to tell the majors.

The general began, "There was a message that came down from the top regarding prisoners and their treatment. It was okay to starve political prisoners and even torture them, but it was not okay to starve and torture prisoners assigned to work camps. You both run work camps. I also have three political camps under my jurisdiction."

He went on. "The government goes to great expense to ship prisoners to us and they expect decent work out of them. When they have served their time and been rehabilitated, they should be sent home in good condition. That does not mean you shouldn't take measures to encourage slacking workers to do better. If you must execute them, I will understand that, but, at least give me a good reason for doing so."

The general paused to finish the bottle from which he had been drinking. "Encourage the prisoners to make chess sets and let them play. If you can get decks of cards or books in Krasnoyarsk, take them back to camp with you. Even encourage the men to hold talent shows of singing and dancing. I know that Major Mikoyan lets the prisoners have tea in their barracks."

He looked at Mikoyan who was about to say something. "You may think I don't know what goes on in your camps, I have informers. I am pleased with both of you and you are my two top commanders. If I should go into battle again, you two would be my first choices to accompany me."

"I might add, if you are ever in command in a situation such as I am, have at least two informers that do not know each other. That way, you can cross check on the information they give you."

Timko interjected. "I'm sure that I speak for Gregor in thanking you for your confidence in us." Mikoyan uttered a low, "That's correct."

Abut two o'clock Frunze went to bed, but Mikoyan and Timko sat drinking. Mikoyan raised his glass, "I hope the general is not called into battle soon."

Timko asked, "Wouldn't you like to give up this project we have and go into battle somewhere? I don't like rusting here in the middle of the earth."

Mikoyan retorted, "To tell you the truth, I would rather survive the war which we should win, considering that the English have superior air power right now and are keeping half the German army busy on their western front."

"Not me. We could probably become generals with our own commands if we got into the war."

There was more talk of their duties and the war. There was more vodka and champagne which was almost free to the majors. Mikoyan and Timko exchanged the status of their family activities. Mikoyan told Timko how Milla would take a test and if she passed, it would qualify her for intense training in an important government scientific program. He did not mention the prisoners acting as tutors. Timko assured him that Milla was a bright girl and should do very well.

Mikoyan leaned forward. "What is it like in Igarka?"

"Do you want a travel inducement? I would gladly change places with you tomorrow. As I have said, I am willing to go into battle to get out of there."

"Give me a rundown on what it is like up there in the frozen north."

Timko started in with a sigh. "At our location, the Yenesey is four miles wide and it takes a while to cross it. Here the water is too rough for small river boats. If you go further north on the river it widens to over fifty miles so ocean vessels can come all the way to Igarka and dock. We are about four hundred miles from the ocean. At Igarka, ships are loaded with ore from Dudinka and Norilsk, as well as lumber from your region. These are shipped out to other ports in the six months of ice free river. Actually in some of these months, we have to use ice breakers."

Mikoyan inserted. "So you get your heavy equipment for the roads from your ocean port advantage."

"Yes that's right, but we still have steam shovels and steam rollers while you enjoy the luxury of gasoline."

"What's the city like."

"We are about a hundred miles south of the city which sits on a terrace about a hundred feet above the river level. Even when the spring floods occur, it does not reach the city, because the water expands to the west, where the land is lower. When the spring ice causes a jam, the water might rise ten feet in an hour. These jams are short lived."

Timko continued. "To travel from your city to mine takes about a day by plane. That's how we got here. To go by boat takes a week and if you want to travel the mud road, it takes a month and a half and you must cross the river. The boats coming into Igarka come from many countries. Last year we had one from Africa."

Mikoyan had questions about industry and the population. At this time, there were about fifteen thousand people in Igarka. The city was built by forced labor, first sent there by the Czar, and now by the communists. Many of the people who have served their time on the prison crews have elected to stay in the city. Timko thought that most of his prisoners would do likewise, because he referred to himself as a humane, but stern, commander.

Great rafts of logs are floated downstream to Igarka from the Angara River area. Some of the logs are two feet in diameter. At Igarka these logs are cut into sawn timber and shipped out through the port to ports in Western Europe. Local timber is too small in diameter to be of much use in big construction.

Most buildings in Igarka were of log construction. One of them was three stories tall. A water system was established and the water pipes were in the same ditch as steam pipes used to heat most of the main buildings. The ditch was also filled with sawdust which was plentiful. The ground is permanently frozen at a depth of two feet. When spring thaws arrive, the area is a sea of impassable mud. People prefer the frozen surface, since it is easy traveling, even walking.

The streets are surfaced with planks. To make a road, scraps of wood from the sawmill are laid in place and on them other scraps are laid at a right angle. As the scraps sink into the ground other scraps are put on top of them. Most of the transportation is by horse drawn carts. There are few automobiles.

One of the attractions to keeping former prisoners here is high wages. Also an inducement is the variety of consumer goods brought to this remote region. General stores have such things as perfume and other cosmetics as well as fashionable dresses which could rarely be found east of the Urals.

Snow begins in mid-September and stays until the middle of May. Frosts occur as late as June, and begins again in August.

There are excellent schools for elementary children, as well as a hospital. Most people stay indoors and semi-hibernate in winter.

Buildings do not have basements and are constructed by driving poles into the permafrost. Under each house, there is a foot of sawdust. The houses are banked all around with moss, soil and sawdust. The roof is usually planks covered with earth.

There are many areas of greenhouses along the river, but most of the fresh vegetables are brought down river from Krasnoyarsk. Experiments with crops have proven unsuccessful. Potatoes can be grown, but they never get much bigger than a golf ball. Berries are large, but have little taste. Cabbages are in the same category, large, but with little taste or texture.

At Igarka, there are a few stunted trees, but further north at

Dudinka there are none. It is in the tundra and the Eskimo population tends to their herds of reindeer. The Eskimo lives in nomadic units, while the Russians live in the log houses. Both make a fairly good living from furs and fish. There is also a trade in ivory collected from frozen ice-age mammoths. Migrating waterfowl adds to the diversity of a menu."

The sun was coming up in the long daylight at this time and the two majors decided to call it a night. When Mikoyan got back to his room, he found Milla and Lorraine huddled in bed. He took off his shoes, pushed Lorraine over and fell asleep on the side of the bed.

The trip back to Camp 193 was mostly a silent trip. Milla asked Private Penza how he spent his time. The reply was that he was up most of the night telling lies with the other soldiers and drinking vodka, lots of vodka. Many of the soldiers were women who drank as much vodka as he did. He said in a devilish manner that he wished his commander would provide vodka in the same volumes as General Frunze. Vodka was at least germ free, while their camp water supply was always suspect.

Milla and Lorraine came back to the classroom. Alexander and Ivan had taken to hiding on their time off. It was the duty of the sergeants to keep prisoners active and they didn't want any action. Ivan had taken extra rations of goat and pig meat to Latko and had many pleasant conversations with him. Of course, the dog did not engage in conversation, except to show approval with his body.

In one month, the Germans had advanced to the Don River. They had gained control of the Caucasus and the Baltic area and were on the outskirts of Minsk. Camp 193 went about its business of building the road, but everyone was holding their breaths, waiting for some word to come down about their fate. For the time being, no word had been forthcoming.

By the end of July, Ivan had started harvesting his vegetables and everyone complimented him on the great success of his mission. The Thin Man from Rurik's household came over and pilfered whatever he wanted. Ivan chastised him for it, but it was not serious.

It was the first Thursday in August and Ivan's lesson was on airplanes and how they flew. There was numbness in the air as Milla answered questions and gave explanations and Lorraine took notes. Ivan wanted Milla to explain how the rudder controlled some of the plane's movement.

Milla rose to her feet. "Rudder, budder, smudder." She did a little dance and started laughing. "Rudder, budder, smudder"

Ivan got to his feet and stopped her in the dance. He was facing her and held her muscles above the elbow. "You silly goose, stop this right now. We have work to do."

Milla got serious "Work, work, work. What's it to you what we do. You will be a prisoner and I will be gone. It doesn't matter. What do you care what happens?"

Ivan grew stern, "It matters that you will be successful. I care because, because-" He caught himself. He almost said something he would have maybe regretted. He still held on to her as she looked into his face and he into hers. Then he let her go and sat down.

"I care because your success is important to your future. Without an education you will be nothing, but an unimportant player in the scheme of things."

Milla sat down and looked at Ivan. It was a look of admiration and more than that, it was a look of genuine affection.

Lorraine had been startled by all of this and she wanted to interfere, but could not. She knew well the look on the face of Milla. She too had been grabbed by a strong gentle man who held her for a moment in time. When their eyes met, it was all over, formalities were gone. Yes, Lorraine knew this look well, but, what could she do. She could see the love slowly building between Milla and Ivan, but there was no way to prevent it.

Lorraine finally broke in. "In less than a month Milla will take her test and if she passes it will be off to the University of Tomsk. If she doesn't pass it, she will be off to the University of Krasnoyarsk. So, all of our problems will be solved."

Milla offered, "Perhaps we should take time off from our studies and discuss the war and what it has in store for us."

Ivan was still stunned. "No, we must put all of our efforts into your study. We only have three more weeks to go.'

For the next several lessons there was an atmosphere of business in the air. Everyone did his duty of teaching, studying, learning and transcribing.

About a week after "the incident" Milla stopped the beginning of the lesson by commenting to Ivan and Lorraine that she had read a poem in English that she thought was beautiful. It was about this man, who was dejected and depressed with his station in life, but when he thought about his loved one his life became like a lark at daybreak singing at heaven's gate. When he thought about his loved one, he would not change his status with kings. She said that she was like that, when things got tough, all she had to do was think about her love and then she became like a lark singing at heaven's gate.

Ivan asked her about her loved one. She replied that he was still in her imagination, but he was real, and they would be together.

She then asked, "What about you Ivan, how old will you be when you get out of here?

"I have a little less than eight years, I will be thirty two at that time."

Milla looked at the table. "I will be twenty six."

No one asked her why she had asked that question or what significance it had. Ivan and Lorraine were both afraid to hear an honest answer.

Two lessons later, Milla had another English reading to tell them. It was about how this young man Romeo stood beneath the balcony of Juliet and poured out his love to her. She said she wished she had a balcony and a young man would look up to me and pour out his love. Ivan thought of himself working in the garden and constantly looking up at Milla's window, hoping to see her there looking back at him. He was often rewarded.

That night in the bunkhouse Ivan challenged Alexander. "What are you teaching our girl in English? There is nothing but nonsense about love. Shouldn't you be teaching her scientific English?"

Alexander gave a weak laugh. "I teach her scientific English. She is reading all of this love baloney on her own. She is in love my young friend and we better accept it."

After supper one evening in the second week of August Milla was at her window, as she usually was, looking at Ivan, who was picking tomatoes from the field. They paused to stare at each other.

In that moment of viewing pleasure Milla took off her blouse and exposed her beautiful breasts. She stood motionless and breathed heavily, trying to breathe in the same air that Ivan was breathing. Ivan clutched a tomato in his hand. The tomato was red and ripe. Its soft skin felt nice to the touch and as Ivan watched Milla he slid his palm over and over on the tomato.

This trance had to be broken. Ivan hoped no one was watching him as he kissed the tomato as he looked up at Milla. She put her right hand under her left breast and held it up as if it was the tomato that Ivan was kissing. Ivan stopped and went back to gathering his harvest.

That night, he took the tomato into the bunkhouse. Alexander remarked about the lovely tomato and could he have it to eat. Ivan said no, it was a sacred tomato, and that this was the culmination fruit of his labors and he wished to preserve it as long as possible.

August was midway through. Soviets begin to counter attack the Germans and have some success around Riga, the main port of Latvia. This is temporary however, and the Germans get control. Their front extends from Latvia south to the Caucasus.

Ivan had eaten his tomato and had enjoyed it immensely. He felt like some sort of pervert because he equated the tomato with the breast of Milla. Their lessons became a friendly, but serious matter. Lorraine just accepted the situation and reasoned that Milla would soon be off to some university and Ivan would still be a prisoner. If he should try to escape, it was her husband's duty to get him back or have him killed.

The air temperature during the day was in the eighties in mid-August, but went down to the forties at night. Winter was on its way and the lessons would soon reach their climax.

At one lesson, Pauline brought in some punkushki, along with the tea. When Ivan commented that these were the best treats he had ever eaten, he was informed that they had been made by Milla who was beaming. Lorraine explained that even a woman scientist had to know how to cook and bake.

That evening, Ivan was still harvesting and looking to the

window of Milla. She arrived on schedule and bared her breasts again as she had done several times. As Ivan looked to the window, Milla slid off her skirt and stood there in her brief underpants. Ivan felt a lunge growing in his balls. Milla stood awhile and took off the underpants. Ivan could see her from her knees to the top of her head. She stood with a look of longing. He stood with a look of longing.

He thought 'Surely there was no one more beautiful.'

As if on key, Lorraine began playing the balalaika. It was Meadowlands again but in slow tempo. Ivan and Milla looked into each others eyes from a distance. Milla turned slowly in the window exposing her buttocks and beautiful shape. She again faced him and again turned slowly. She wanted him to see her in her entirety. And he did.

As Milla stood there nude, Lorraine in the other room started playing a sad slow song on her instrument. Tears formed in Ivan's eyes. Tears formed in Milla's eyes. After the music ended, Milla began putting on her clothes in full view of the window. When fully clothed, she blew Ivan a kiss and disappeared into the bedroom.

At the next lesson, Ivan complimented Lorraine on her beautiful music. He said the last number she played, brought tears to his eyes. "What was it?"

Lorraine looked serious. "It is something I wrote myself."

Ivan said that it was remarkable that it brought tears to his eyes. Milla said that it also brought tears to her eyes. Lorraine said that it also brings tears to her eyes.

Lorraine said, "It is my musical expression of love. A song of true love is a sad song. I imagined these young lovers in a hopeless situation and this is the music that came out."

Ivan said, "It is a sad song and an obvious song of love."

August was passing quickly, and in the last lesson before the test, Ivan said he wished to give Milla a good luck charm for the test. He produced the green gemstone triangle that he had found near Evenki. He asked Lorraine if it was permissible to give it to Milla and Lorraine said it was. Milla said she had nothing to give Ivan and Ivan said that the memory of knowing her would always be good luck to him.

When Ivan presented the gemstone Milla gave him a kiss on the cheek. She looked at Lorraine who was smiling. She wanted to do more than that, but Ivan was a prisoner and she was the daughter of the commandant and she had obligations of decorum.

The lessons with Milla were finished. She went to Krasnoyarsk to take the exams.

Ivan went back to the dogs and still tended the garden. He was permitted to live in the household barracks until the garden was harvested. Once the harvest was complete, he had to dismantle the greenhouse and go back to Barracks Ten. Alexander was already at Barracks Ten.

It was two weeks after the last lesson when Major Mikoyan came to the garden and stuck out his hand to shake Ivan's. This was unheard of. Mikoyan said that Milla had finished among the top ten of over two thousand entrants. She had finished third in English language. Mikoyan purposely taunted Ivan by withholding how she finished in science and made small talk.

Ivan grew serious. "If you don't tell me how she finished in science I might kill myself tonight."

"Don't do that my valuable prisoner. She finished second."

Ivan could not believe his ears. He dropped to the ground on his knees and held his hands over his face. The tears flowed freely along with audible sobbing. Mikoyan stood there for a while and finally said, "Thank you Ivan, I have to go now."

He left Ivan still on his knees sobbing uncontrollably. When Ivan rose and made his way back to the bunkhouse, he kept mumbling, "Oh, my love, oh my love."

13. Lev and Mishkov

August had ended and the September sun was heading toward the equinox. The gardening was done and Ivan went back to tending the dogs, slopping the hogs and helping Gregor Mishkov with the horses. He had a lot of time to talk to Mishkov and they exchanged stories.

Gregor Mishkov was born on a little farm in the Ukraine. Joseph Dzhugashvili, otherwise known as Stalin, came to power and established the massive collectivization of agriculture and intensified industrialization of the country. The collectivization program was begun in 1928. In order to get the peasantry to go along with the plan, the more successful farmers had to be eliminated. The successful farmers were called kulaks and it was easy to get their employees set against them. The government promised that all people would be equal and share in the profits of the collectivized farm. What was not stated, was that the products would be shipped to the cities and the peasants would be left with little food for themselves.

The first estimate of the farm population was 7 million poor peasants, 16 million intermediate peasants and 2 million kulaks for a total of 25 million peasants. By the end of 1929, Stalin had called for the liquidation of the kulaks as a class. Many of the peasants, as well as the kulaks, fought collectivization. The scheme called for the transfer of all property, livestock and equipment to the state. About three million peasants were immediately wiped out financially. All those wiped out were called kulaks whether they fit the definition or not. Eventually, the program called for implementation by the police. Peasants had always considered the state as their enemy, whether it was the Czar or the communists.

Most peasants hid vast quantities of food and slaughtered their livestock rather than turn them over to the collectives. Some villages refused to comply. These were surrounded by units with machine guns and forced to surrender. Those kulaks and imaginary kulaks were rounded up by the thousands and deported to cold Arctic regions or hot dry desert regions of Central Asia.

The First Five Year Plan was instituted in 1928 and by the end of the period more than 60 percent of the independent units were converted to collectivization. Stalin, in an uncharacteristic disclosure, admitted that there were 34 million horses in 1929 and less than half that number existed in 1934. More than a hundred million sheep and goats had been slaughtered.

The grain and animals confiscated from the peasants was sent to the cities or to foreign countries in exchange for machinery. Millions of people in the food raising areas of the Ukraine died of starvation. Stalin told Winston Churchill that more than ten million people had been eliminated by starvation. Hundreds of thousands were machine gunned by special political police units.

Cattle and horses were used as draft animals, and once they were killed off, there was no way to get the land back under cultivation. Large areas of the steppes were set aside for tractor cultivation. The tractor drivers worked night and day to try to increase food production.

The industrialization program was increased in order to provide more tractors and other implements for agriculture. With the deportation of the more prosperous peasants, there was no leadership in agriculture.

Even the government elite in the Soviet Union were affected by the shortages of food and consumer goods which ensued. The sacrifices of the people created an immense concentration of heavy industry. A new elite class of technicians had been created. Stalin was counting on industrialization to effect economic changes. The police force, secret and obvious, was increased tremendously.

Gregor Mishkov said he worked his way into the stable job because he loved animals. Besides, he didn't like the hard work of road building.

Gregor's family consisted of himself, two parents and a sister. They were successful in that their family had worked the same land for over a hundred years. When the order for collectivization came, they and their neighbors rebelled. Police agents were sent into the town to gather evidence against trouble makers and resistors.

Gregor explained. "My family worked hard on the land. As a boy of ten, I put in fourteen and fifteen hour days. We had farm implements that could be pulled by our horse. We had some chickens, one horse and two cows. We had our own milk supply and a surplus of grain that we sold. Then came the order for collectivization."

He paused to catch his breath. He was becoming more emotional. "When the first police agents came, they called my parents kulaks. My mother asked them to define kulaks and they said it was anyone they wanted to call a kulak. So we were put on a list of kulaks that was posted on a bulletin board outside of town. Everyone in the village, including our friends, started to avoid us. Our only friends were those also called kulaks."

Gregor started rubbing his nose and chin. "The police had

authority to shoot anyone they wanted. They took all of our grain. They even dug up the yard around the house looking for more grain. They found some grain hidden in our root cellar that we thought we had disguised very well. We were wrong.'

"Two men from the village were shot for resisting the confiscation of their grain. This was a signal to all of us. We were told that we were to leave our house and take whatever we could carry with us, but we were not to take any food. Our house and sheds were to be used in the collectivization scheme. They had already ripped down one of our small barns."

"We had one day to get out of the house. When the police came to evacuate us, my mother got on her knees and prayed for the safety of the house." Gregor began to cry. "My mother went to the horse and kissed it. Then she went to the two cows and kissed them and blessed them with the sign of the cross."

Gregor paused and wiped his eyes with his sleeve. "We were put on a horse drawn wagon along with another family of four and taken to the Volga River. We were ferried across the Volga and told we were exiled in Kazakhstan. We were not to leave Kazakhstan under penalty of death. We could roam anywhere in the province we wanted to, but not leave it."

"My father, who was a good trader started fishing and trading his fish for cloth. He sold the cloth and became a kulak in Kazakhstan. He avoided farming, since the farms were the former range lands of the nomadic people. It was a disaster in Ukraine and it was a disaster in Kazakhstan. Not only were the Kazaks subjected to the same treatment as the Ukrainians, but now they had us to contend with."

Ivan was fascinated by the discussion. He asked, "How did you end up here?"

Gregor answered. "My mother told me she had buried a gold crucifix, some coins and gold and silver jewelry near one corner of the house. She said she had put them down about two feet. I made my way back to our home. It took me about a year. When I got to the village I thought I could count on former friends of our family to hide and take care of me until I completed my mission. The first woman I talked to turned me in."

"When I went before the court the judge said that I was too young to have been a kulak, but I was forbidden to return to Ukraine.

He sentenced me to ten years and, like you, I wound up here."

"As you know, I receive a parcel of food about once a month. Sometimes I get them, sometimes I don't. I think they just want to know that I am alive."

Ivan reflected for a moment. "I wish there was some way I could contact my sister and tell her that I am well and will probably survive this adventure."

Gregor grimaced. "That would not be a good idea because then she would be identified with a criminal and be under surveillance forever. My family members are known criminals and so it doesn't make any difference to them. Actually we are the innocents and those who sent us here are the criminals."

Ivan agreed with his stable mate. As Gregor had testified, working in the stables was better than pushing a wheelbarrow in hot and freezing cold weather. At least with the horses, there was some warmth on the job in winter. Gregor stated, "The horses are not used in road work because they are considered more valuable than the prisoners."

Gregor said that he was accused of helping Plushna steal the horse but Sergeant Vologda testified that Gregor was on an assignment for him when the horse was taken.

Near the end of September, Private Penza informed Ivan that he was to report to the office of Major Mikoyan at nine the next morning. Ivan thought he had an in with the major and was not apprehensive about this order.

The next morning he was dressed in a clean outfit and clean shaven. As he made his way to the major's office, he came across Sergeant Vologda going the other way. He said "Hello Sergeant Vologda, I am going to the major's office."

Vologda assumed a military pose. "Prisoner number four forty one, you are to address me as Comrade Sergeant and not speak unless I speak to you."

Ivan was taken aback. He made a feeble attempt to apologize. Vologda had him straighten up.

Vologda went on. "Ivan, it is not good policy for us to be on friendly terms. There are spies in this compound and they might think I am building up a complement of loyal prisoners and privates. If there was some difficulty, it will be all of our asses in the gutter. We think the secret police have planted some agents in our midst. You stand at attention until I walk by you. Okay, keep faith my friend."

Vologda took big strides beyond Ivan who waited a few seconds and then continued to the major's office. He announced himself to the guards stating that he was expected by the major. After the guard announced him, the major asked him to come in.

Mikoyan got to the point immediately. "Ivan, how are you on reading the law?"

"I can read it, but I can't interpret it very well. Sometimes words have different meaning when they are used as legal terms."

The major looked grim. "I have a problem that needs a devious legal mind and there is no one I can turn to."

Ivan said, "What about Lev Lefkovich?"
"Who?"

"Lev Lefkovich is a prisoner here at the camp. He graduated from Moscow University with a law degree. He was a student of Vishinsky's. He was my interrogator before I was sent here."

"I read over all the files on the thousand prisoners here, but I never saw that in the Lefkovich file."

"He is a lawyer," assured Ivan, "and a man that can be trusted."

"I will see about this prisoner Lev Lefkovich and thank you for the tip. You may go back to your dogs and horses now."

Ivan hesitated. "May I ask you a question sir?"

"Yes, but I may not answer it. I will not answer any question pertaining to my daughter."

"No, I have a question about Alexander. I don't see him around anymore. Has something happened to him?

"Yes, he is no longer with us. General Timoshenko was a lecturer of military science at Rostov. Alexander was one of his students. The general had a shortage of second command officers and had all of his university military students tracked. His men found Alexander here and secured his release. Alexander is now an officer in field artillery somewhere on the front lines."

Ivan hesitated. "He was a real intellectual."

"Yes, he was, and like all intellectuals he wrote too much. People who write books will always get themselves into trouble. Never write anything down. Is there anything else?"

"No sir."

Mikoyan looked down at papers on his desk and shooed Ivan away with his left hand. Ivan had second thoughts about mentioning Lev, but his instincts told him that Lev would welcome the opportunity."

Ivan had hoped to get word to Lev that he had mentioned his name to the major. There was no way to do that now, since Lev was on hard labor and Ivan was living in Barracks Ten. It was not good protocol to leave Barracks Ten and visit other barracks.

In a day, Lev was told by Sergeant Vilko to get himself presentable within the hour. He took an icy shower, shaved and put on his best clothes that were not stained with sweat.

He reported to Sergeant Vilko who escorted him to the office of Major Mikoyan. Vilko personally stood guard while Lev entered the office.

Lev entered and stood in front of the major's desk. After a pause of looking at papers, the major raised his head.

"Sit down Lev Lefkowich. Please relax."

Lev looked for the firing squad to enter from a side door. He sat straight in the chair provided for him.

The major began. "I understand you are a lawyer, but this did not show up in your files. How do you account for that? Please speak freely, no harm will come to you.'

"I believe it is not in my files because I worked for the prosecutor and the court that sent me here. They do not want me bad-mouthing them and identifying the bodies."

"That is a funny expression. A great friend of yours recommended you to me because I have a problem. Ordinarily, I would not trust a prisoner, but this man has won my respect and if he recommended you, I can trust you as I trust him."

"I thank you for the compliment and I do consider myself worthy of trust."

"Well then mister lawyer, let me put it to you straight. I have been ordered to report to the front lines at Minsk in three months. I don't want to go. I am also ordered to come with one of my top

148

sergeants and I am dedicated to these men, and I don't want any of them to go. So I want you to look over these orders and see if you can find any flaw in them, so that I do not have to spend this winter in Minsk."

"I would be glad to look over the document you described and give you my opinion on it."

Mikoyan was serious. "Sergeant Vilko will take you to a room near my house. You will be shown to my library where I will give you the document. The library has an electric light. You can spend the night there reading and thinking about solving my problem."

There was no doubt in Lev's mind. If he did not solve the problem, he would be eliminated. At least, that was standard practice with the Bolsheviks.

Sergeant Vilko led Lev out of the compound and to the bunkhouse once occupied by Alexander and Ivan. There were fresh clothes waiting for him and a pair of dress shoes. The wind up clock was running and Lev was to report to the servants table at six o'clock, to eat and then go directly to the major's house.

Pauline met him at the door of the house and escorted him to the library where Major Mikoyan was waiting. He told Lev that the orders came from the headquarters of General Frunze, but were signed by some lackey major on his staff. The letter stated that Major Mikoyan had been approved to form a battalion at Minsk. Once the details were ironed out, the order would be forwarded to General Timoshenko, commander of that region. It was a letter and not a direct order.

The major handed Lev a packet of five sheets of paper. These were the letter that would be turned into an order. Only five sheets, and Lev had all night to pour over them. The major said he would check with Lev at seven in the morning. Lev could nap in the easy chair if he felt a need to sleep.

The next morning, Lev was awake at seven and the major came in precisely on the hour. Lev stood up as straight as he could.

"Sit down," commanded the major. "What do you have for me?"

"Sir, I can't find any way to get you out of this problem."

The major clenched a fist and waved it at his feet. "There must be a way, have you thought about it?"

Lev said in a straightforward manner, "Yes I have. Could you get me a copy of the orders that sent you to this place? Maybe there is something in them that we could use." He put in the word "we" instead of "you" or "I." He wanted the major to know they were in this together.

Mikoyan told Lev to relax and breakfast would be brought to him and he would get a copy of his original orders for him to look over. He would be back at the end of the day, probably around six o'clock, to see if Lev could come up with something. .

Before departing for the compound, the major entered the library and handed Lev a large brown packet with flaps tied by a ribbon. The packet was constructed of fine cardboard and had been waterproofed. Mikoyan wished Lev good luck in his search.

Lev read the orders which assigned the major to the desolate place and position of authority. He read over them again and again and could not determine anything which could get the major out of the combat assignment.

The lawyer had overlooked one important detail. Just after lunch was served, he saw it. The order to start the road construction came, not from General Frunze, but directly from Stalin. It was signed by Stalin. Lev's mind raced with a plan.

When Mikoyan appeared at precisely six o'clock, he was upset and grim. He immediately asked "How did it go?"

Lev smiled, an oily confident smile. "I think I have found a solution to your problem."

Mikoyan lightened up. His face muscles relaxed. "Don't keep me in suspense: tell me what you have found."

Lev held up the two sheets of orders which he considered important. "These were signed by Stalin himself. It is not a stamp signature."

"Yes, my uncle works in the Kremlin and got this deal for me. I don't dare ask him to get me out of this. He would think it unpatriotic. He is a fanatic, devoted to the cause."

"We won't have to contact him. You can intimidate General Frunze. I don't mean by force, I mean by the power of suggestion, hinting and innuendo."

"What do you mean? Explain yourself."

"You can either write to General Frunze, or see him in person. I suggest you see him in person. Written statements have a way of working against people. Tell him your order to run this camp was directly from Stalin and only Stalin can rescind this order. It would make you very uncomfortable to countermand an order from Stalin himself. If General Frunze would like to contact Stalin, then it would be okay with you. You and I know, nobody wants to contact Stalin, under any circumstances."

"I think you have it, but I would have to be extra careful on how I word it."

Lev brightened. "If you could recommend someone in your place, someone that had a reputation among officers, then that person would do it. Not many people have a direct order actually signed by Stalin."

Mikoyan thought. "I was just in touch with Major Timko who runs the camp coming south from Igarka. He is a zealous military man. I will recommend him for the job, and he will think I am doing him a favor."

"That is a great idea. Please let me know how you make out. If something occurs that we hadn't anticipated, then we can work on it."

Mikoyan thanked Lev and said he would travel to Krasnoyarsk in person. He would get working on this immediately and leave Captain Rurik in charge. He would make an appointment and tell General Frunze that, what he had to say, could not be said over the phone or radio.

Lev was told to move his possessions from his work barracks to Barracks Ten and Sergeant Vilko would assign him to permanent infirmary duty. The major said he would contact Lev as soon as he got back from Krasnoyarsk.

At Krasnoyarsk, General Frunze welcomed Mikoyan with open arms. The two men sat alone in the general's office. Frunze poured a drink for each of them and they raised their glasses in salute.

When Mikoyan told Frunze of the reason he could not take the proposed assignment Frunze looked disgusted. The general knew he couldn't even suggest transferring the major, if

the major wanted to use his trump card. He understood the
major's refusal, since the Germans were slaughtering the
Soviets in every battle.

Frunze also appreciated the fact that Mikoyan had friends in
high places, and perhaps, these friends could help him some time.
What Mikoyan never let on was that his uncle ignored him and didn't
want to expand his circle. When things went wrong under the
present government, the entire circle was eliminated.

Mikoyan told Frunze that he had a solution for him. Why not
appoint Major Timko to the job of forming a new battalion. When he
talked to Major Timko at the opera, Major Timko said he was eager
to get a command and go into battle.

Frunze looked surprised. "Major Timko said that?"

"Yes, I am sure he would consider it an honor, if you
called him directly and asked him. I assure you, he is eager to
leave Igarka and get a fighting command."

"That's great. I didn't know that about Major Timko, he is
always so formal around me. I'll contact him immediately, since we
have to get the battalion officers from our district. Most of the
soldiers will be conscripts."

Mikoyan was relieved. He had won a victory for himself, but
he didn't like the idea of recruiting officers from his command. He
suggested that Frunze let Timko choose his officers. Frunze said that
he expected the major to supply one of his excellent sergeants to
handle the training of prisoner soldiers.

What did he mean by prisoner soldiers? Frunze explained
that some prisoners would have their sentences negated if they
volunteered to fight in the army. He expected the major to come up
with a good sergeant and at least a hundred prisoner volunteers who
were there for petty crimes.

The major said he would work on that problem immediately.
He volunteered to look after Timko' s compound when he left, and
until a suitable replacement could be found for that position. Frunze
shook Mikoyan 's hand vigorously. Not only did Mikoyan get
himself off the hook, but he also got Frunze off the hook. He had
two months to get a hundred volunteers and a good sergeant. But, he
did not want to give up any of the sergeants who were loyal to him.
If he wanted an armed support group for himself, the sergeants

would get it for him.

Lev had demonstrated a keen mind for problem solving and Mikoyan thought he would get Lev's opinion when he explained what had transpired between him and Frunze. He wondered why Lev was not able to protect himself.

At a command breakfast in the library, the details were laid out to Lev. Mikoyan didn't mind the reduction in his labor force by ten percent, but he didn't want to expose his loyal sergeants to the front lines.

Lev thought to himself. Mikoyan drank tea and munched on a piece of bread swathed with jam Lorraine had made from the blackberries of Ivan. . Then Lev said he had it.

"Why don't you promote one of your privates to sergeant and have him start drilling the volunteer prisoners. Then you can tell General Frunze that you are carrying out his wishes and that you would have a sergeant and a hundred soldiers by the middle of November. That will give you two months before the snow really flies and you will help General Frunze meet his deadline."

"Brilliant Lev, have some more jelly and bread."

They sat eating and pleased with the idea. Mikoyan actually smiled at the lawyer in his rumpled prisoner outfit with number 448 painted on it.

Mikoyan tried to think of his private guards. There were about sixty of them. Which one would he promote, and which one would like to be promoted? He thought Sergeants Vilko and Vologda could advise him. On a hunch, he asked Lev what he thought..

Lev got serious. "If you want the best man, in my opinion, it is Private Penza. He is unassuming, does his job, and knows the military. He actually likes the military."

"I like the military too Mr. Lawyer, but I don't want to get shot. I want to be around when the war ends and live a normal life."

Lev looked up from his bread and jelly. "How do you think the war will end?"

"The Soviets are on the eastern front of Germany and the English are on the western front. If America and the South Americans get into it, there is no way the Germans can win. We will be victorious. But after the war, there will be hell to pay and executions will be a daily occurrence. Executions will be administered for such things as not taking some obscure town, executions for being a prisoner of war, executions for loose talk. That's why I want to stay here. You never know who will decide that you didn't fulfill your duties."

Lev looked at the major intently. "We are all trying to survive. Sometimes we need help."

The scheme worked well and Timko thanked Mikoyan for recommending him. When Mikoyan approached the sergeants with the name of Private Penza they agreed that of all the privates, he was the best and did understand military regulations.

When Mikoyan contacted General Frunze and told him that he had the right sergeant and had already had a good response of volunteers, the General was delighted. He was not familiar with Sergeant Penza.

Mikoyan reminded Frunze that it was then Private Penza who had asked Frunze about the Frunze Movement at the lecture to the guards at Camp 193. General Frunze could expect more questions from Sergeant Penza, if ever the two should meet again. Frunze said that he would come to the camp at least once in the next two months before the unit shipped out and formed near Minsk.

The sergeants went about recruiting prisoners for a new role of soldier. Vologda made it a point to discourage Ivan and his other loyalists from this group. He didn't need to warn Rasputin. He said that the new recruits would be the first to lead the charge into battle. Most of them would be killed with the first volley.

In a week, the new group took over Barracks Nine. There was a shifting of bunks and equipment. The new unit was ordered to get better food by Captain Yaroslav, who looked forward to having one hundred less people to deal with. Penza was happy in his new role and took to it with enthusiasm.

Other guards were jealous of the promotion of Penza. One guard in particular, Private Donbas said he would like to meet Penza in the tavern at Lesosibirsk some night, and he would see what the new sergeant was made of.

There was no chance of the two meeting at some town, since

Penza was engrossed in his work. He spent evenings planning the next training sessions. He had wooden sticks made up the size of a gun and used those in marching and drilling exercises. He showed the men how to crawl on their stomachs while keeping the gun from getting contaminated.

The new military unit was a welcome diversion at the camp. Even the remaining prisoners were interested in their welfare. The hard labor prisoners did not see any increase in their work, after all, they were already worked to capacity.

14. The Bear Hunt

The brown bear is a gigantic animal. In eastern Siberia it reaches heights of ten feet and may weigh 1500 pounds. In western Siberia, north of Krasnoyarsk, the bear has dimensions slightly less. It remains inactive in winter, but contrary to folklore, does not hibernate. It will make its home in a cave or dig a deep den in the ground, or just settle against a natural depression near a large tree. The female may have up to three cubs in the spring, so she is careful in her selection of a den site.

In order to support the great bulk through a sleeping winter, the bear must eat heavily in late summer and autumn. It consumes a wide variety of food including berries, fungi, fish, earthworms, insects, deer and elk.

When temperatures rise to only ten degrees below freezing, the bear may leave its den and walk around looking for food, or just to get up and stretch its body. If there are year-old cubs, they will join the mother in her walks.

The den is often covered with a thin layer of snow. Unless drifting, the Siberian snow is scant. Hunters looking for the bear can often identify the sleeping dens by a small vapor trail emitted by the breath of the bear.

It was mid-October when a mother bear and two cubs were seen at the goat and pig farm. This was a great event and everyone was talking about it. A couple of weeks earlier, a goat was missing and the event was blamed on desperate poachers from the small village of Yeniseisk across the river and south of the camp. Now it was blamed on the bear and her cubs.

The farm was basically the domain of Sergeant Surgut. Two extra guards were put on the farm with orders to shoot the bears if they should appear. The sergeant thought that everyone would enjoy a meal of bear meat.

True to nature, the bears came back and one of the guards took aim and shot at the mother. He hit her somewhere in the front shoulder which did not stop the bear. Before he could get another shot, the three bears disappeared into a thicket. The bears were cautiously followed and were seen emerging on the other side of the Yenesey. Shots were fired at them, but there was no evidence of a hit.

Three days after this incident, two men from the village of Yeniseisk approached the compound early in the morning and asked to see the commander. They were not permitted to see Major Mikoyan, but were given a hearing by Captain Yaroslav and Sergeant Surgut. Rasputin was summoned in case they needed an interpreter. Their Russian was so bad, they did need to speak in their native tongue and Rasputin translated.

The men related how the bears came into the village of eight houses and terrorized them. The village consisted of thirty four full time residents with transient hunters, trappers and fishermen staying over for months at a time. One of the transient hunters had challenged the mother bear who was indeed wounded. His small caliber rifle was no match for the bear and he was mauled and was now near death. The men asked for military help. Could some soldiers come to the village and kill the bears or at least get the mother bear, since the cubs seemed easily frightened.

Captain Yaroslav told the men to wait outside while he discussed the situation with Sergeant Surgut. Rasputin was asked to wait outside with the men.

After several solutions to the problem were discussed, the one best suited to Captain Yaroslav was to deny any help and let the village shift for itself. Sergeant Surgut said that if they could kill all three bears then they could have bear meat for the entire compound and it was a money and resource saving opportunity. The villagers could skin out the animals and keep the hides and gallbladders which were an important item in their rituals.

Yaroslav relented and asked Surgut if he knew who was the

best marksman among the guards. Surgut did not hesitate to name Private Donbas. He was the only one Surgut could think of, who would not hesitate to shoot anything with a reflex action. Donbas had accompanied the Tracker on one of his man hunts and had done very well. It was Donbas who had shot the escaping prisoner when the Tracker simply wanted to run the tired man down.

Yaroslav told Surgut to get Donbas and maybe two prisoners to help bring whatever kill they had back to camp. The villagers were not to accompany Donbas and the prisoners on the hunt. They would be notified if a bear was killed.

Surgut relayed the orders to Private Donbas and told him to find two prisoners, who didn't seem to be doing anything worthwhile, and take them on the hunt. They could cross the river in the boat of the villagers. Donbas loved the idea.

Donbas walked around the outskirts of the compound and passed the stable where Ivan and Mishkov were grooming horses. He spoke in authority. "You two come with me. You will have the best experience of your life. Get your warm jackets, we might have to stay overnight." Donbas did not tell them to get their identification cards even though they were leaving the comound.

"Where are we going?" asked Mishkov.

"I would not tell you, but make it a surprise; however, we are going on a bear hunt on the other side of the river."

Both men had heard of the bear and how it was wounded. They had not yet heard the villager's story. Both were intrigued with the idea.

Donbas turned to Ivan. "Get one of your dogs, put him on a leash and control him. We can use him to track the bears. "

Ivan was not really in charge of the dogs. He had never had one on a leash or directed a dog in any way. His main job was to clean the pens, feed the dogs once in a while and report any sickly animal. Private Pavlov was in charge of assigning dogs to guard duty, as well as walking them for exercise, and training them when necessary.

After donning his warm clothing Ivan went to the dog pound and called Latko to come forward. The dog approached Ivan wagging his tail. He had become too friendly with a caretaker. Dogs were supposed to be intimidated by the caretakers and trainers.

Ivan looked at Latko. "I don't know if you have it in you to go on a bear hunt my friend, but we will manage."

Donbas had gone to the soldier's kitchen and obtained food which he put in his back pack. When Mishkov arrived, Donbas gave the back pack to Mishkov to wear. The private was armed with a slightly larger than usual rifle and carried a side pistol. He had a cartridge belt around his waist with twelve bullets in it.

The three men, along with the two villagers and the dog, went to the mooring and crowded into the small boat. The villagers barely had enough room to row but they made the two hundred yard distance in quick time. According to the sun, it was noon.

The villagers quickly showed the trio where the bears were last seen and where the dying man had been attacked. Their limited Russian became a handicap when Donbas wanted more information. The main village speaker had noticed the amulet which the head man of the Evenki village had given Ivan, since Ivan had put it around his neck. He spoke to Ivan in his native language and Ivan said he did not understand by pointing to his ear and shaking his head from side to side.

Donbas picked up the trail of the bears quickly. Like humans they liked the easy way and were heading down a trappers trail. Donbas said, "Let's go," and started along the trail at a brisk pace. They kept this pace for about two hours when Donbas said, "Let's eat."

The trio sat on exposed rocks. Donbas looked at a pocket watch and estimated they had come six miles. The private extracted a piece of cheese from the back pack. With the hunting knife he wore on his cartridge belt, he cut off a slice of cheese for the two prisoners. It was the first piece of cheese either of them had had in a long time and it was much appreciated. He then gave each of them a chunk of bread.

Ivan gave half of his bread to Latko. Donbas growled, "What are you doing?"

"I'm giving the dog a piece of bread. We are eating, I thought the dog should be eating."

"Don't feed the dog, we need him to be hungry. We will be releasing him from the leash soon and he will drive the bears to us. I will shoot the mother bear and maybe one of the young ones before it has a chance to escape. Just like you two, I would not hesitate to shoot you, if you try to escape."

Mishkov retorted. "Where in hell would we go? We would be dead in less than a week in this forest. Last night's temperature was ten degrees below freezing and it's only October seventeenth. Besides, the villagers get a reward for turning us in."

Donbas was stern. "Just so we understand each other." Both prisoners said that they understood the situation.

It was time to get moving again and Mishkov donned the pack. Ivan said he carried the pack well for a man who was good with a shovel and wheelbarrow.

Mishkov smiled, "Not bad for a kulak, right"
Donbas startled. "You're a kulak."

Mishkov realized that Donbas was a Ukrainian. He replied, "No, I'm not a kulak, I just use that term to make jokes."

"I thought you might be rich since you get a packet once a month. Nobody but rich people send their relatives a packet. Let's get moving." With that he slapped Mishkov along the shoulder.

The men marched in silence for about ten minutes with Donbas leading the parade. Then he kept turning around and making insults to Mishkov about being a kulak. He seemed possessed by some demon. Mishkov knew it was useless to protest, but he didn't say anything. Ivan tended to the dog.

Apparently they were near the bears since Donbas slowed down. He said he noticed some bear shit off the trail. It was still steaming in the low temperature.

They came to a small clearing along the trail. It was an obvious place where trappers and hunters made camp. There was no vegetation in the clearing, but the ground was covered with fine gravel and sand. There were some logs near the perimeter which were used as seats. A small fire circle was in the center

Donbas gasped, "Let's sit here a while and collect our thoughts. The bears are just up ahead. Is that okay with the lazy kulak?"

Ivan tried to intervene. "Let's just get one bear and bring it back to the river."

Donbas retorted. "You keep out of this dog man. This is

159

between me and the kulak. We will get the bear. Release your dog."

Mishkov and Ivan sat on the logs which were at right angles to each other. Instead of following a trail Latko sat near Ivan waiting for orders of some sort. Donbas stood in front of Mishkov in a threatening manner.

In a calm voice Mishkov said, "Our job is to get the bears and kill them."

Donbas' voice grew shaky and louder "I'll tell you what our job is." With that he slapped Mishkov across the head. Mishkov rose to his feet. Donbas took the safety off on the rifle and held it pointing downward.

Mishkov stood directly in front of Donbas. Ivan begged, "Please, let's get on with the task before us." Donbas took one step toward Ivan and hit him with the butt of the gun. He then raised the gun to either intimidate Mishkov or actually shoot him. As the gun came up to Mishkov's knee it discharged sending a bullet through the side of his knee cap. Mishkov fell to the ground screaming. "You bastard."

Donbas sneered. "You attacked me and I have a right to kill you."

Ivan, though stunned, leaped to his feet and snatched the rifle from the hands of Donbas knocking him to the ground. Donbas reached for the pistol on his waist. "I guess I will have to kill both of you bastards."

During this entire event Latko had become extremely agitated and made growling and whimpering noises. When he saw Donbas reach for the pistol he sprang at the neck of Donbas, grabbing him by the Adam's apple, ripping it. Instinctively Donbas rolled over and put his hands on his head. Latko grabbed him by the back of the neck and bit down hard dragging Donbas onto his side. Latko continued to bite at the neck while Mishkov and Ivan stood in stunned amazement.

Finally Ivan said, "Pot sem Latko, come here, sit." Ivan had taught Latko to sit on command. Latko stopped his savage attack and went to Ivan's side. The two survivors assessed the situation. Ivan still had the rifle.

The head of Donbas was almost severed. It hung to the body by a thin shred of muscle and spine. Blood was still slowly oozing from the body as the heart had not quite stopped beating.

Ivan turned to Mishkov. "Can you walk?"

"No, I can't. What are we to do?"

Ivan patted Latko on the side. "Let us be calm and think this through. With your wound they would catch us immediately. Especially, if we stay on this trail." Ivan took the hunting knife and cut away the pants around the wound.

Mishkov offered, "My wound has stopped bleeding but I can't walk, probably not even on one leg. My leg will have to be amputated. You have to go on Ivan and I will sit here and wait for rescue and possibly execution. You have to take your chances and escape."

"I won't leave you my friend."

"You and I both know you have to leave. Even though we have friends in the compound they can't ignore the fact that a soldier has been killed in the presence of prisoners. They can't afford to falsify reports or it will be their ass."

Ivan reflected. "How far is it back to the river?"

"Maybe five, maybe six miles. I can't walk it Ivan. The pain is just starting."

"I will dress in the uniform and carry you back to the village. They will think we had a hunting accident and take you over to the camp. How much do you weigh?"

"That might work, but six miles is a long way to carry me."

"I'll leave the guns and ruck sack here and pick them up on my way back here. If you could delay crossing for an hour, it would give me a good head start."

Mishkov moaned. "Ooh let's try it."

Ivan removed his clothes and that of Donbas. There was surprisingly little blood on the uniform which fit slightly large but still fit. Ivan took out the identity card of Donbas and held it before Mishkov. "Do I look like that?"

"I think you could pull it off for a while. Where will you go? That's stupid, of course, I don't want to know your plans."

Ivan dressed in the uniform. He put the rifle, cartridge belt, knife and pistol about ten feet into the underbrush. "I don't think anyone will be here, but maybe the guns will stay hidden until I get back. I might need them for food or I hope not, protection. Come on dear friend, time for our journey."

Ivan put Mishkov over his shoulder and started back on the trail. Latko walked beside him. If soldiers could walk forty miles with a hundred pound pack, then Ivan thought he should be able to carry the thin Mishkov six miles.

There was much struggle to get there but Ivan approached the village with Mishkov on his back. It took about three and a half hours of sitting down, trying to joke, picking up and struggling. But the village was in sight.

A village woman spotted the approaching spectacle and ran back into the village. Ivan put Mishkov down, since someone would obviously come, but he waited to make certain. The two men who had made the plea for aid arrived with the woman..

The men noticed Ivan was now in uniform and they both noticed the amulet around his neck. The woman started tending to Mishkov. She removed her babuska and placed it around the knee. One of the men ran back to the village.

Ivan said, along with appropriate gestures, that he had to return to the forest and tend to the other man. The village man and woman seemed to understand and nodded.

Ivan bent over and kissed Mishkov who hugged him, took Ivan's hand and kissed it. The village man was moved by this and put his hand on Ivan's back. The other man had returned from the village with a blanket and two poles, obviously to make some sort of carrier.

It looked like the villagers were going to treat Mishkov for a while and bid Ivan farewell and waved him toward the trail. Ivan was tired and started walking down the wide trail which would soon narrow to a wide path.

Ivan walked about a half mile then he ran a half mile. He walked and ran. Latko followed him every step of the way.

When he got to the clearing, Ivan discovered that the bears had found the dead man and were eating his flesh. They had dragged the body down the trail about a hundred feet and were working on it. Ivan didn't know what to do. The bears were blocking his escape route, if he was going to escape at all. It was impossible to travel through the taiga without following a trail.

Ivan was able to get to the guns, belt and knife he had stashed. He sat on a log with rifle ready. He wasn't sure he even knew how to fire the rifle. It had a clip and so was still loaded. He looked for the safety and found it. The ruck sack was still in the clearing. Even though it had some food, it was not disturbed.

As Ivan contemplated his next move there was a sound coming behind him on the trail. It was impossible that the tracker was already after him. It was one of the two men from the village running and carrying a sack.

Ivan stood up to receive the runner who ran up to Ivan and handed the sack to him. Ivan accepted it graciously. It was obviously full of food. He thanked the man the best he could and motioned to the bears down the trail. The man shook his head that he understood. Both men walked out to the trail.

The man pointed to Latko and to the bears. Ivan understood and said "Latko, go."

Guard dogs are not used to barking, their specialty is growling. However, Latko made an exception in this case, growling and barking. The bears taken by surprise leaped into the tangle of forest. Ivan ran past the torn body of Donbas still in its underwear.

The village man did not disturb the pile of clothes that Ivan had shed. When Ivan looked back, the man waved to him and started jogging back up the trail. Ivan wondered if the man would come back to retrieve the body or wait for the military to direct them. He hoped the man would wait for the military.

After treating Mishkov for an hour and feeding him, the villagers took him across to the camp. The guard who had seen the approach had summoned Sergeant Surgut who came running. The two waited on the shore and as the boat approached Surgut told the private to get Captain Yaroslav.

Yaroslav directed that Mishkov not be taken to the infirmary, but to one of the outbuildings of the camp. The doctor arrived and said that Mishkov needed hospital care that could not be given at the camp.

Yaroslav then sent a guard to Mikoyan who soon arrived.

Mishkov quickly related the story, honestly and truthfully. Mikoyan grimaced when he learned that Ivan had taken to flight.

Mikoyan gave orders to Yaroslav to get a statement from Mishkov, have him sign it and then have Mishkov taken to the army hospital at Krasnoyarsk where he is to be treated with dignity, since he is a hero. Yaroslav didn't understand the hero part, but he would obey the order.

Major Mikoyan then sent for Sergeant Vologda and told him to take the skiff, two prisoners, cross the river and bring back the body of Private Donbas. Once Vologda got back, he was to report the situation to his commanding officer, Major Mikoyan.

It was three hours later and near midnight when Vologda came back into camp with the body of Donbas. He reported to Mikoyan who was waiting in his office.

Vologda stated that the body was badly mauled by the bears and there were no signs of a gunshot wound in what was left of the body. He believed Mishkov's statement to be true in every detail.

Mikoyan thought for a while. "That leaves us with prisoner four forty one and his escape."

Vologda nodded. "When should I contact the tracker?"

Mikoyan said, "Get a good night's sleep and we will handle this in the morning. The tracker does not need much time. He is the best man at his job that I know."

That night the major slept on the couch in the sitting room. His wife noticed when he came in, but did not rise herself. In the morning Mikoyan left at six o'clock sharp. Sergeant Vologda was waiting for him at his office.

The major asked "Have you been thinking about how we should proceed?"

"Yes, I will write a letter to the family of Private Donbas and state that he was killed by a bear while he was bear hunting and then I will contact the tracker and have him go after Ivan, I mean prisoner number four forty one."

The major sniffed. "You understand my orders then. I don't have to tell you what to do."

"I understand major, would you like me to go over the orders with you, just in case I don't understand them?"

"Yes, I think you should do that.

Sergeant Vologda began. "I will contact the tracker. We will find a body about the size of prisoner four forty one and dress it in the clothes of prisoner four forty one that I now have in my possession, and bring it back to camp for viewing and burial in the camp cemetery."

"I am surprised at you sergeant."

"Why is that commander? Have I misjudged you?"

"You must put a purple tattoo on the right ear of the body."

"I would have remembered that. I will go out to contact the tracker and accompany him on his mission." He saluted and the major returned his salute.

That night, the major told Lorraine the details of the hunt. When the major said that the tracker was contacted, Lorraine held her hands in a praying movement. The major then told her about the scheme of Vologda and Lorraine picked up his hand and kissed it.

*   *   *

Ivan continued along the trail and found a fork in the road. He took the one to the right. At least now there was a fifty-fifty chance of delay in the chase. Of course, he was unaware that nobody would be after him, since Sergeant Vologda had set the escape plan in motion. Despite the lack of pursuit, the taiga was dangerous and had claimed many lives throughout history.

The sack that the villager had given Ivan contained bread, dried meat and a small bottle of brandy. There was also a small pack of safety matches. The air was cold and Ivan's breath escaped him in puffs of clouds. Even Latko's breath could be seen.

There was no direction in Ivan's plans except to go east and away if possible from populated places. When night came, there was a crescent moon which soon set. It was impossible to see the trail and Ivan made his way into the bushes with Latko at his side. Latko and Ivan enjoyed some dried meat and Ivan took a few sips of the brandy. The man and dog went into a fitful sleep that night. Ivan would have nightmares as the cold woke him up time and again.

Ivan was in the taiga north of the Angara River, which is one of three major Tunguska rivers that flow from the east into the Yenesey. The Angara region is the source of many of the logs that find their way to Igarka.

Travel though the taiga is very difficult. Fallen trees rot slowly, leaving a tangle of trees and undergrowth on the forest floor. This covers a mat of moss and lichens. Trees and downed trees have lichens over them. There are also vines which add to the difficulty. Where the old growth coniferous trees are removed, deciduous trees such as birch, aspen and poplar replace them.

One could fly over the taiga for hours and not see any signs of human development. Away from the few logging roads, clearings and fields are completely absent. Near the rivers and large tributaries, one may find a cart road. The hunter and trapper trails leading to settlements have been maintained over the centuries. The lesser trails often become part of the tangle of fallen trees after their main use has diminished.

Along a larger river, one might find a clearing with two or three log houses, mostly used as a way station by river travelers. These houses are built over logs laid directly on the earth. Thus, they rot from the ground up due to the continually damp earth beneath them. . Maintaining them over a long period of time is difficult. Where windows exist in these houses, they are usually patched with pieces of rare glass. In these houses the window cracks are often pasted over with newspapers coated with resin.

The rivers freeze in winter, and to get water, one must chop through thick ice. For these people, furs supply an income in winter and fish in summer. Those in the logging industry have employment for ten months of the year and are basically idle for the two months of summer.

On the second day of his journey Ivan did not run, but kept up a steady pace of walking. He paused every two hours. He could tell when the two hours were up, because he had the pocket watch of Donbas. He calculated he was making four miles per hour but what did it matter, he didn't have any destination in mind. His knowledge of the cities and villages in this area was nil. He didn't need any knowledge of the towns since they were extremely few.

Ivan thought about the legends of Yermak he read in grade school. Ivan the Terrible had given the Stroganovs permission to exploit and conquer Siberia. The Stroganovs were powerful merchants who had the market cornered on salt in the region of

Perm. They hired Yermak to lead a small army of three hundred soldiers into Siberia and conquer what he could. Yermak's group was very successful in conquering the main city of the Sibirs. Conquering the area after that was not much trouble, but Yermak's small army was fast losing numbers as every battle saw a drop in personnel.

In elementary school Ivan and his friends played Yermak and his army. They dressed in make believe skins and fought imaginary battles.

In one of the stories, Yermak is separated from his men during the month of January. He built a shelter by bending over small saplings and interweaving sticks into it and covering it with earth and moss. The shelter was big enough for him to crawl into. In the day, he set traps and captured ermine and sable. He lived this way for a month and even had the ability to sew the skins into a blanket by using spruce roots for thread.

Ivan thought this would be good if he had the time, but his main focus was on getting to some village, where he could convince them he was a soldier looking for an escaped prisoner. He would take it from there.

The food supply dwindled fast and the traveler thought to conserve it as much as he could. He finished the last of the cheese and bread. He still had the dried meat the villager had given him and some hard biscuits. He thought if he didn't feed Latko, the dog might catch something for his own dinner.

Back at the camp, Sergeant Vologda and the tracker had gone to Krasnoyarsk in the small truck used to transport prisoners. It could hold about twenty crowded men. They talked about the war and other situations.

The tracker had a bombshell for Vologda. He looked at the sergeant and squinted his eyes. "Do you know, you have a child from your union with the Evenki woman last year?"

Vologda gasped. "You're making a joke, aren't you? It is her husband's child."

"No, I do not joke. It is your child. Her husband has been dead for about three years. I saw the baby and it resembles you greatly. It is a boy. He is strong. When he cries, the entire village can hear him."

Vologda grinned. "How about that? I don't know what I can do for the child. I have nothing but a few rubles to offer."

The tracker smiled. "She does not need anything. The entire village is happy to have the baby. There were three babies born in the village this year. Two died and yours is the survivor. The village will treat your baby like it was a prince. Everyone in the village likes you and so they will honor your child."

"I'm glad you told me about that. I am in shock."

The trapper said "The mother of your child wishes you to come back and perhaps she could have another child by you."

Vologda reached into his upper pocket and produced a photograph of himself. It was one Ivan had taken when he was in charge of photographing new prisoners. He had called Vologda over and had him pose for the picture. The sergeant handed the picture to the tracker. "Here is a picture of me. Perhaps the mother would like the child to see what his father looked like. I hope I can go on a salt run this year and see the child."

The tracker was serious. "Maybe the mother and child will be coming down this way sometime and I could let you know and you can meet with them somewhere."

"I would like that very much."

Both men were silent for a long while. When they arrived at Krasnoyarsk, they went directly to a railroad siding and consulted with a yard man.

The railroad siding at Krasnoyarsk was used to organize trainloads of grain from the region, which would be sent west to the major cities of Russia. When the trains came back empty, there were transients on them, as well as people being exiled to Siberia. The transients usually hid under the cars, or on top of them, or in vacant grain cars. Sometimes the transients, or even the legitimate passengers, would be found dead when the yard man and his workers checked the cars. Sergeant Vologda knew this and had stored this information in his mind, in case it would come in handy some day. This was the day.

He asked the yard man if any people turned up dead this week. The yard man took him to four male bodies that were laid out near one track. Vologda and the tracker examined the bodies. Vologda pointed to one male body and said that this was the man they were looking for. The tracker pretended to examine the body and added his assurance.

"Take it," said the yard man. "I will be glad to get it off my hands."

The body was loaded into the back of the truck by the tracker. Vologda gave the yard man thirty rubles for capturing an escapee and told him to get himself a few bottles of vodka.

On the way back, the tracker remarked that this was the first time he had let an escaped prisoner go. Vologda assured him that Ivan was a special person. He told the tracker about the Evenki village experience and how the head man had given Ivan some sort of trinket that was respected by the Evenki. After the tracker asked for a description of the trinket, he assured Vologda it was no trinket.

The tracker knew that the head man had given his sacred amulet to a prisoner from the camp. He was just making certain that he knew the right man.

There was the usual ceremony at the compound with lights going on and all the prisoners called forth. Barracks Nine was now officially military and the prisoners with their numbered clothing sported a red armband. They were proud, and Penza had them marching to orders.

When everyone was permitted to go back to their bunks Rasputin lagged behind and asked Private Vilnius if he could talk to Sergeant Vologda. When Vologda was asked about this, he immediately went to Rasputin. "What can I do for you number six six six.?"

"I considered myself a friend of the dead man. Could I be on the burial detail tomorrow?"

Vologda broke his military stance. "Yes, of course, I considered myself a friend of the dead man also."

The next day, Private Vilnius drove the wagon with Rasputin, the dead man and one of the new prisoners to the cemetery. The prisoners dug a grave and when they were done, Rasputin told Vilnius they needed to rest. Vilnius said he was going to go up by that tree and take a piss and have a smoke. The men could rest a while before burying the dead man. He gave each man a cigarette and lit them.

When Vilnius was up at the tree Rasputin went to the corpse and withdrew a secret knife he always carried. He cut the sack around the face and looked inside. He grinned until he laughed out loud. Vilnius heard, but ignored the laugh.

The body was interred and covered with earth. A stake, with the number 441 painted on it, was driven into the ground. After another hour the burial detail headed back to Camp 193.

Meanwhile, back on the trail, there was an air of desperation, but also a need to relax. When Ivan sat down in a small camp clearing to rest, he would take off his boots and rub his feet. Latko would sit at his side. He was in the process of getting Latko to follow commands such as sit, get back which meant to heel, and go, which meant to charge forward. He would hold Latko by the shoulders, point him in a direction and say "go" and the dog would run forward. "Latko nyet" told the dog to stop in his tracks.

The clearings were about four miles apart if the conditions for clearing were good. As they approached one of the clearings there was a wolverine on one of the seat logs. Latko started toward it and Ivan yelled "Latko nyet."

Ivan didn't know if his knowledge of wolverines was complete or not. He had read that a wolverine could bring down a reindeer or caribou and was a fearsome foe of dogs. Many dogs had been killed by wolverines. Latko stopped and the wolverine disappeared into the brush. Ivan still had the rifle and perhaps could have shot the wolverine. At this time he was not thinking in these terms. Besides, he had never fired a gun.

At this clearing, he took off his shoes as usual and ran his feet over the fur of Latko. The dog lay on his side and enjoyed the foot rubbing. Ivan reached down and turned Latko over and rubbed his stomach. The dog was not used to affection and his reaction was one of uncertainty. When Ivan rolled him over again Latko leaped to his feet and approached Ivan with his face close to the ground. Latko yelped and actually grinned and swayed away from his master. He approached Ivan several times in this manner and Ivan knew that Latko was playing, probably something the dog had never done. They continued in this manner for about twenty minutes.

Night was coming on and the crescent moon was getting larger. In two weeks, there would be a full moon and traveling could be done at night. Ivan was not going to be caught in the cold as he was last night. He made his way about thirty feet into the brush and gathered moss. He put this in a hollow near the roots of a large tree and stomped it into place. He gathered more moss and stomped it until he had a bed of moss. He lay on it and curled up. Latko came and placed himself at Ivan's back. The two of them kept each other warm and there was a pleasant night's sleep. In the morning Ivan thought, if he only had something for a cover.

It was in the middle of the third day when someone approached Ivan on the trail. It was a trapper bent over with a heavy sack of furs. When they met, the trapper paused and put down his load. There was an exchange of greetings. The trapper knew the rudiments of Russian and a feeling of mutual survival was in the air.

Ivan reluctantly shared some of the dried meat with the trapper, who was sitting on his bundle of furs. The trapper pointed to his furs and pointed to Latko. He wanted to trade the furs for Latko. Ivan said "nyet." The trapper pointed to the rifle and the furs. Ivan again said "nyet." The trapper laughed and threw his hands in the air.

Donbas had been a heavy smoker and had a small bag of tobacco in his upper pocket and some cut squares of newspaper. Ivan handed the tobacco and a square of newspaper to the trapper who took it eagerly and rolled a cigarette and returned the rest to Ivan. . Ivan produced one of the precious matches and lit it for the man who puffed heavily.

When the cigarette was still burning Ivan bid the man goodbye and started down the trail. When he had gotten about thirty feet away, the man called out for Ivan and motioned him to come back. Ivan did. The trapper pulled a beaver pelt from the sack and handed it to Ivan. Ivan thanked him and took the pelt. In return Ivan gave him the rest of the tobacco, but not any of the matches.

That night Ivan had a cover. The beaver pelt was about thirty inches across in both directions. It was softened, so it made a fairly good cover for Ivan's upper torso. When Latko started chewing on the pelt Ivan had to stop him.

171

So it went. When the travelers came to a fork in the trail, they turned right. He was worried that he might go around in a circle and come back to where he started. But, he figured he started north of the Angara River and by turning right he would end up on one of the mud roads that paralleled the river. He was certain there would be a road along this important river which connected Irkutsk with western Siberia. The Trans-Siberian Railroad connected Irkutsk with Krasnoyarsk.

It was the beginning of November and one night it started to snow heavily. Ivan made his traditional bed of moss. This time, he cut some small branches from a spruce tree with the hunting knife. As he and Latko lay down, he pulled the beaver pelt over them and with a free arm covered his legs and the pelt with spruce branches.

In the morning, snow covered both dog and man in their hideout. The outer air had dropped to twenty below freezing, but both animals were warm in the burrow as the insulating snow kept the temperature around the freezing mark, while the body temperatures kept the burrow around sixty degrees. It was a warm night indeed. Ivan thought perhaps he should do that every night.

One night Ivan allowed himself the luxury of a fire. He quit his sojourn early and gathered twigs and branches and put them in the fire circle of a camp clearing. The wet wood would not burn and Ivan used up two of his matches. He then remembered the story of Yermak, how Yermak had shaved slivers of wood and took dried twigs directly from the tree and not from the ground. This worked and in a short while there was a nice fire going. A big gust of wind nearly scattered the fire into the brush, but it was saved and the wind no longer affected it. Ivan lay beside one of the seat logs. Latko lay beside him and they were both partially covered with the beaver pelt.

On the twenty-first night of the sojourn Ivan was awakened by Latko growling. There was something running on the trail. It sounded like a person but Ivan thought nobody could run on the trail at night, even with a light snow and a quarter moon. It must be a large animal. The sound of running passed and Ivan went back to sleep.

As the nomads made their way down the trail in the early morning a man jumped from the underbrush in front of them. He had a rifle at the ready position. Ivan stopped in his tracks. Latko moved in front of Ivan.

It was the tracker. "Hold your dog," he commanded:

"Get back." Ivan commanded and Latko got behind him.

The tracker asked, "Are you Ivan Ivanov?"

"No, I am Private Donbas chasing after an escaped prisoner."

The tracker grinned, "Follow me Ivan." He turned his back on Ivan and walked forward.

Ivan had a loaded rifle and a loaded pistol and he could have easily shot the tracker in the back. However, he wondered why the tracker had not disarmed him. The tracker must have known Ivan would not shoot him.

There was a rest after about ten miles and the tracker told Ivan the story of how Mishkov was declared a hero for some unknown reason, sending the remains of Donbas home and the burial of Ivan. He told of running into the trapper and getting a feel for the direction Ivan was heading. He was good at his job.

Ivan looked at the tracker. "Even though no one is after me, what am I to do? Why are you here? I still have to survive in Siberia."

Tracker ignored the questions. "There is a small village near here. Show your necklace and they will do most anything for you. I will go with you and help get things straightened out."

"What is the significance of the necklace?"

"The amulet is carved from a mammoth tusk which was found buried in the tundra. The man who gave it to you risked his life to save a group of Evenki who were stranded in a very desperate situation. He was a young man at the time. When he arrived with supplies and saved about thirty people the shaman of the tribe carved this amulet and gave it to him. Many miracles are attributed to the amulet and its picture can be found on many paintings on hides and on doors of the native peoples of Siberia. Supposedly, no one is allowed to duplicate the amulet. You are wearing a historic artifact."

The tracker went on. "I am here because you have within you, one of the spirits of my ancestors. In protecting you, I am protecting a very important ancestor." Ivan didn't want to give any argument about that thinking.

There was another ten miles of travel. Along the trail Latko had captured a Siberian squirrel. Ivan asked Latko why he hadn't thought to do that when they ran out of food three days ago. Latko never responded, but ate the squirrel completely.

The village consisted of four log houses built along a small stream where three small boats were moored. The tracker was welcomed by the small band of people which came to meet them. There were several children standing far off. A girl about twelve years old ran out to Latko and started petting him. The tracker warned her that it was a guard dog and to be careful. Apparently Latko had given up his guard dog status, for he relished the girl's affection.

Ivan and the tracker spent two nights at one of the log houses. They were offered a chance to sleep with women, but both refused. Meanwhile the twelve year old girl had taken over the care of Latko. It was November and one of the village bitches was in estrous and Latko took advantage of this situation by humping her continually. Ivan thought it funny that his dog didn't have his scruples.

Most of the people of the village had tattoos and the artist asked Ivan if he wanted his ear tattoo removed. Ivan agreed and there was a razor cutting of the ear and a flap of skin brought over the removed portion. The ear would be slightly disfigured but there would be no tattoo.

The tracker drew a crude map for Ivan. It had on it the location of the Angara River, the road along the Angara and the major villages he would encounter. He was to make it to Bratsk, which was about four hundred miles away. At Bratsk, he was to find the October Inn and ask for a Mister Simon Barishnakov, who would give him advice on what to do.

Ivan was to give up the rifle, but keep the pistol without the holster. He was told to not hesitate to shoot anyone who tried to take him prisoner. He was advised to keep the leash for Latko. This would be needed when he went into a town where there were chickens or other livestock animals. The tracker gave Ivan three hundred rubles to carry, a gift from Sergeant Vologda who had sent the tracker on this mission.

Ivan was given a new set of clothes altered by one of the village woman. The uniform was burned in the village burn pit. A boat would take Ivan to the gravel and mud road which paralleled the Angara. An identity card which had a picture of a bearded man was also given to Ivan. No one would be able to tell if it was Ivan or not.

Ivan gave the valuable beaver pelt to a man whom he thought was the oldest man in the village. In return, the man gave Ivan a large wool blanket and a leather thong with which to carry it.

On the day of departure, the twenty three people of the village came to see Ivan off. The little girl was still petting Latko and certainly would have welcomed him into her heart, but Ivan already had Latko in his heart. He didn't know how things would work out for him with Latko, but he wasn't about to give up the only visible emotional attachment he had. Besides, the village would be blessed with Latko's descendents next spring.

15. Trek to Bratsk

Two men of the village packed their boat with furs and fish and headed down stream with Ivan and Latko as passengers. After an hour of travel, they came to a wooden bridge over the stream. They indicated to Ivan that this was the road the tracker had identified for them. Ivan was to head east until he came to a crossroads and there take the road that went south. He would come to a better road which paralleled the Angara River. The Angara River eventually led to Bratsk. He was warned that a large dam site was being prepared by slave labor near Bratsk and he should be careful how he presented himself.

If Bratsk was four hundred miles away and Ivan made forty miles a day he would be in Bratsk by the end of November. He could find Simon Barishnakov at the October Inn and see what the future held for him.

The first day of his new journey was warm for the middle of November, with a temperature above freezing. As night came on, the temperature dropped considerably. Fortunately, there was no snow, but a constant low wind was uncomfortable.

As the daylight began to fade, Ivan again sought the underbrush, where he wrapped the large wool blanket around himself and Latko. By morning, he had also buried his head under the blanket. He could survive like this. The villagers had supplied him with dried fish, biscuits and dried meat, enough for about five days, if he didn't share it with Latko.

The new clothes were comfortable and a pocket to carry the pistol had been installed inside the back right side of the trousers. Padding hid it nicely. The fur cap was of Siberian design. Its flaps came well over the ears and could be tied beneath the chin. The jacket was well insulated and the felt boots were common Siberian footwear.

On the second day, Ivan found the cross roads and headed south. After a few miles on the road, he came across a camp of warmly dressed gypsies. They greeted each other and the gypsies offered him tea and bread which he accepted. One of their members spoke excellent Russian.

These gypsies were descendents of gypsies that had migrated from India. They had Indian brassware for cooking and they still made runs to India to renew family ties and get some supplies, such as tea and curry.

There were four chickens roasting on spits and Ivan was offered some chicken. Latko was given a bowl of boiled rice. Ivan procured one of the rubles from his pocket and offered it to the spokesman who refused it. After a while, Ivan offered it a second time and an old lady came over and took it saying that "They had to respect their guest's wishes."

The fires were warm and Ivan could have stayed with the gypsies, but he had to keep moving. There was a discussion about Latko and could he be obtained with barter of some goods. The spokesman pointed to his ear ring and said it was gold and he would give it to Ivan for Latko. Of course, Ivan refused and bade the camp farewell. Ivan had kept his amulet hidden from the gypsies.

Light snow glistened in the air, but there was not enough to be of concern. It was the night cold and wind that had to be overcome. With the gypsies, there was a loss of twenty miles from the designated distance that had to be covered each day. But, what did it matter, there was no where to go and no future yet outlined. Besides, the war with Germany was in full swing and in a city, he might be conscripted for military duty.

The main mud road to the Bratsk area was found; and, it was

no better than the road he had traveled to the Evenki village. It was certainly not in the condition of the road the prisoners of Camp 193 were building.

Ivan thought he missed the camp, but it was the kindness and friends he had made at the camp that made him nostalgic. Even in that desperate situation, he was able to triumph and overcome adversity by befriending some of the military and many of the prisoners. He wondered about Rasputin, Lev and Mishkov. He had a strange feeling toward Vologda, the major and Lorraine. He could not understand the feelings, but he could understand his feelings toward Milla and her image appeared many times in his mind during the cold nights when he snuggled with Latko under their makeshift shelters.

The road was not like the trails of the trappers and hunters in the Taiga. It had more traffic and, after the third day, an occasional truck with logs rumbled past. There were carts pulled by horses carrying hides or families. Ivan thought these families were people being sent into exile. He avoided talking to anybody, as much as possible, except to greet them with the traditional "Dobra dien, good day."

There were some scattered log houses along the way. He knew the Angara River was to the south and many small roads branched off the main road in that direction. For a time, he thought about going to the river and trying to hitch a boat ride to Bratsk, but thought the less contact he had with people the better off he would be. He felt at ease, since he knew he was not being pursued. However, there were always the thoughts that the police or the military would detain him.

It was on the seventh day that the main road took a direct turn south. He had made it to the big bend in the Angara. It came north out of Lake Baikal and turned west toward the Yenesey. The Angara had always been the main water route to eastern Siberia, since it was in the south where the temperatures, although not ideal, were moderate, compared to lands further north. The two other Tunguska Rivers further north led nowhere but to a dense Taiga. The Middle Tunguska was the site of a comet that leveled thousands of acres of forest. It took researchers two years to find the site even with accurate directions from the natives who lived near there.

Small villages became more numerous. Ivan bared his amulet when he entered the villages, and more often than not, he was offered food and drink. In one village, he was asked to spend the night and was given a bed which had a mattress stuffed with straw. An offer of a ruble was rejected. People were especially fond of Latko and ruffled his fur and gave him food. Children hugged the dog, who responded by licking their faces, probably to get the salt.

The first big town encountered was Ust Ilimsk about one hundred and thirty miles north of Bratsk. It was a bustling fishing, lumbering and trading port. Ore from as far away as Dudinka came by its facilities as it headed for Irkutsk. Ivan thought to pass through the town very quickly. He attempted to circumvent the main street which was the riverfront. He put Latko on a leash.

As Ivan came down a side street, two policemen met him. He pretended to limp. They told him they needed him to help load a military boat which was anchored in the harbor. There was no other labor available for this job. He had no choice but to follow.

When they approached the main street, Ivan saw an oriental lady standing near a doorway. He bared his neck piece. The lady stared at it. Ivan asked "Would you take care of my dog until I am finished with this job." She said she would.

The job was to load boxes of food onto a cargo ship. He was one of about twenty men conscripted for the work. Four policemen were among the conscripts and they worked hard at the job. The work took about four hours and when it was done Ivan headed back to find Latko and the lady. One of the policemen in charge of loading gave Ivan a small sack of flour, a tin of sardines, a loaf of bread and some tobacco. He thanked Ivan for being so cooperative. Ivan limped away.

Ivan found the lady in the street. She was brushing Latko with some sort of hairbrush and the dog liked it. Ivan thanked her. She invited Ivan to her room which was upstairs. Ivan begged off and said he had to get to his home as soon as possible. He gave the lady the sack of flour. She refused at first, but eventually took the sack.

This was a warning to Ivan. He now figured he better move through these towns at night and hole up somewhere during the day.

If he found lodgings, he would stay there until it got dark. It was already December. The night temperatures dropped precipitously as the sun neared the winter solstice.

Ivan had followed a road south and found himself in the village of Novaya Igirma. This was not one of the towns mentioned by the tracker and it was a good sized town with maybe as many as six thousand inhabitants.

There was an old man burning sticks in a used oil drum and Ivan approached him. He asked the man how far it was to Bratsk and the man said it was difficult since there was a major stream he had to cross. He was no longer on the Angara, but had followed a tributary. He cursed himself for not noticing the size of the river.

The town was northeast of Bratsk. The quickest way to get there would be to go south to Zhalesnogorsk and then head directly west. There was a bridge at Zhalesnogorsk.

It took Ivan another day to get to Zhalesnogorsk, but he was in the vicinity of Bratsk, which was now about eighty or ninety miles away. He had lost three days by taking the detour. Perhaps two days fast hiking would get him to Bratsk. But there was no need to hurry. He was apprehensive as to what awaited him.

The trip to Bratsk was not eventful. Ivan and Latko had obtained a ride on the back of a small truck with three other men. The driver must have figured that extra weight on the truck would help it over the icy road. The truck slipped and slid on the thin snow and ice surface. At one point, the four men gave the truck a push to get it away from ruts that it had created as it broke through the thinly frozen surface. It was a two hour ride and Ivan figured they had covered about forty miles. Ivan walked another fifteen miles and decided to hole up in a dilapidated shed near a log cabin. Its owner was unaware that Ivan and Latko were there. Ivan zipped back the lid of the sardine can and he and Latko shared its contents.

Bratsk was not the large city that Ivan had anticipated.. The town consisted mostly of men who were in the service trades of handling round logs, ore boats and farm produce. It was a place where products were taken to be loaded onto boats.

Ivan entered a tavern and ordered a meal. The waiter brought Latko some cow bones and fed him at the back door.

Ivan listened intently to the talk around him. There was talk about a big dam to be constructed near Bratsk and the hydroelectric power that would be generated would supply a new batch of cities that would spring up. A new railroad had been planned to short cut the Trans Siberian by going north of Lake Baikal. If this came to pass, it would include Bratsk. Up until this happened, Bratsk would be a dead city.

Ivan asked for directions to the October Inn and was told it was on the waterfront. There was a Red Star on a sign over the street entrance. He was told the food there was not as good as the food he was now eating, which was boiled cabbage, potatoes and horse meat.

At the October Inn, Ivan was told by the desk clerk that Mr. Simon Barishnakov would not be available until late evening. He and his nice dog could wait in the small room off from the desk, but it would be a long wait. An upstairs room could be had for one ruble and Ivan paid the price. He and Latko went to the room, which had a single bed. Ivan locked the door and both fell asleep immediately.

There was only about seven hours of daylight now and the sun went down early at this latitude in winter. But there was a long dusk and dawn, so the usable light lasted about eight hours. Most of Bratsk's inhabitants were in a state of semi-hibernation. They came out to work but immediately retreated to their lodgings once work was completed. There were few travelers using the few inns and restaurants of the city.

It was about eight o'clock in the evening when a knock came at the door. Ivan, who slept in his clothes, answered it. The desk clerk said that Simon Barishnokov would see him in his office which was downstairs.

They went downstairs. The clerk said to go right on in. Ivan and Latko entered. There was regular office furniture in the room. A man dressed for warmth with his hat on was seated at a desk with his head down as he looked at some papers. He mumbled in a low voice, "What can I do for you?"

Ivan answered hesitating, "I really don't know at this time. A man, whose name I do not know, told me to look you up if I could get to Bratsk. I have come over four hundred miles."

The man looked up. Ivan gulped, "Plushna, it's you. It is you

180

Plushna."

"No, I am Simon Barishnakov." He rose to his feet, came around the desk and embraced Ivan and said, "You look like someone I used to know very well."

Ivan sat in the chair near the desk and Simon returned to his chair behind the desk. He withdrew a bottle of whiskey and poured two glasses, giving one to Ivan. "Let us drink to the future and forget the past, it is dangerous to remember the past."

They toasted and Ivan blurted, "But I saw your ear, it was no mistaking it was your ear."

Simon removed his cap and showed that his right ear had been cut off. "When you have ears as big as mine, you only need one. It was a small trade for my life."

"Will you tell me how you got here and what it is you do?"

"I made a deal with the tracker. He even gave me his sister as a wife and we are very happy. You should take a native wife Ivan, they know how to treat a man, and they work hard."

"How do you make a living?"

"I am a businessman who deals in lumber. I buy logs and my mill turns them into boards. The business was given to me when the previous owners were taken into the military. I escaped the drag net by showing off my ear and saying it was shot off in a battle in Finland. Remember when the Finns resisted our take over."

"Yes I know about the war with Finland."

"I am Simon Barishnakov and have my discharge papers to prove it. I also have a medal that I earned in that war."

"How did you pull that off."

"You realize Ivan, if you tell anyone about this, I will have you killed."

"I suppose it is a risk for you to take me into your confidence."

Simon agreed it was a risk. He said his real business was changing identities of living people for those of dead people. He dealt mostly with bureaucrats that have gone out of favor and who wished to disappear. He had not been at this business very long, but there were others who organized the operation, who were still in charge, he merely worked for them.

Ivan asked about an identity for him and Simon said he would have to see what was available at this time. It was possible that Ivan might have to wait a long time for an identity. In the meantime, Ivan could work in the lumber mill stacking sawn boards to dry in the warehouse designed for that purpose. He could work from sunup to sundown which was less than eight hours and in return he could keep the room he occupied, and eat two meals in their dining hall.

Naturally Ivan accepted the offer. He reported to the lumber mill which was a small operation. Men fished logs from the gathering pond of the mill, hauled them up a ramp and fed them into a giant saw. The logs were cut into one, two and three inch thicknesses. It was Ivan's job to place the sawn timber, which was not cut to widths, into proper piles, inserting strips of wood between them to facilitate drying.

In the Angara River region, the valuable timber was mostly pine, whereas in the north it was spruce. Many of the pine trees, still available, were three feet in diameter. Large rafts of the valuable pine were constructed and floated as far as Igarka, down the Yenesey River.

Simon informed Ivan that America was now in the war and the Japanese were allies with the Germans. There was an unannounced agreement that Japan and the Soviets would not fight each other at this time.

Germans had captured most of the Crimea and were on their way to Moscow. Cold weather was hampering their movements and they seemed to be content to pull back a little and wait for the weather to improve, as well as replacing their expended supplies. A front existed from the Baltic Sea all the way to the Black Sea.

Ivan obtained another set of clothes. He even took a bath once in a while. His small beard was clipped with scissors. Since he went from the inn to the mill, he was not in contact with anyone except the people at the inn and the mill. Latko slept in the room with Ivan and accompanied him to the mill. Ivan carried the loaded pistol with him to the mill, just in case. He shared his lunch of bread and butter with Latko each day. Sometimes, he had white salted bacon, a favorite with the Russian peasantry.

The old year passed and it was 1942. There were no slack days at the mill, or in the office of Simon Barishnakov. An occasional stranger would be seen with Simon, but this was not a frequent occurrence. Simon poured over identities that had been garnered by his superiors. He was on the job because he was fluent in Russian and had some knowledge of Arabic.

It was January sixth, payday for the workers. Simon came to the mill and stayed on until closing time. He paid each of the workers and bid them good night. When Ivan prepared to leave, Simon asked him to stay. There was a man looking for Simon at the inn, and he was dangerous. He, Ivan and Latko would stay in the mill that night. There was a small room there which was well insulated. Simon brought the key to the padlock that was on the door. They could light the kerosene lamp for warmth. Simon brought food for their suppers.

Simon explained that when they changed an identity, the person involved had to pay a large sum of money. After all, it usually meant his life. In this case, the man objected to the sum which was actually taken from the effects of the dead man. The man in question thought that the money of the dead man would be his. So the controversy continued. The man lived in Irkutsk and traveled to Bratsk by river, and Simon's associates, who were unknown to the man, had spotted him in Bratsk and warned Simon.

Simon figured the man was busy and could only stay around a day or two, at most, and had to return to Irkutsk. Simon would spend the night here and go to his home in an undisclosed location tomorrow. He did not have time to leave town this night. He didn't want Ivan at the inn, in case there was trouble.

Ivan thanked him for his concern. What they didn't know was that the man in question had beaten the desk clerk until his nose and mouth were bloody and one eye was damaged. He was on his way to the mill.

The Irkutsk man saw the light of the room through the cracks of the door. He asked Simon to come out and talk to him. Simon and Ivan emerged locking Latko in the room. Simon assured the man, he had no call to harass him. If Simon had known he was a hot head, then Simon would not have helped him. Simon said that they couldn't take these risks without some monetary reward.

The man retorted that the reward was excessive and he didn't have any money to live on. He had a job, but it was not enough to keep him in his previous lifestyle. The man got angrier as time passed and the argument continued. Ivan sat on some boards and didn't say a word.

Eventually the man punched Simon. He then picked up a slat of board and went to hit Simon. Ivan leaped to his feet to intercept the man and was slapped across the head with the slat. Ivan slumped to the dirt floor with a gash across the side of his head which bled freely since the head region bleeds more profusely than other parts of the body.

The Irkutsk man went after Simon who had picked up a slat of his own. Simon was no match for the big man and his slat. Simon's slat was knocked away and Simon was hit on the head. He too slumped to the earth. The Irkutsk man continued to hit Simon with the slat.

Ivan had regained his senses and tried to get to the door to release Latko, but the man blocked him and hit him on the other side of his head sending him again to the floor. He went back to hitting Simon.

Ivan lay on his left side. He reached into his secret pocket and removed the pistol. He aimed it at the Irkutsk man and said "I have a gun, put down the stick."

The man turned and stopped with the slat upraised. He was about to speak when the gun went off hitting him in the forehead, killing him instantly.

Ivan lay awhile before he went to Simon, who was moaning. Blood covered most of Simon's face. Blood also ran down both sides of Ivan's head and there was much pain in his head.

Latko was released and ran from man to man. He licked Ivan's face removing some of the blood. Ivan smiled, "Don't get too used to that blood my buddy, it would not be good for either of us."

After being bathed with ice water from a bucket Simon was able to sit up. Ivan told Simon that he had to shoot the Irkutsk man. Had he been able to get to Latko, the outcome of the battle might have been different. Simon said he did not know Ivan had a gun in his possession.

Simon got to his feet. He was shaking, but seemed to have his senses about him. He turned to Ivan. "This will be a long night. Let us hide the body for this night. We will go back to the inn and see if anyone there is still alive. We will get medical help and you will come back here before work time and tell everyone there will be no work this day. Tell them to go home and come back the next day. Ivan understood.

Ivan's face was cleaned with the same cloth Ivan used to clean Simon. The men sat awhile and finished drinking the small flask of brandy that Simon had brought with him. They dragged the body to the room where they were to spend the night. Simon put the lock back on and pocketed the key.

At the inn, the native cook was tending to the injured desk clerk. When she saw the condition of Simon and Ivan she nodded her head. The two men sat and waited for their turn at sterilization and bandaging. Ivan had gashes on each side of his head. Simon had a cut forehead and his head had several lumps on it. But he would recover without permanent damage. Ivan's head would have to be sewn and the native woman was already getting out black thread and a needle. The men could sleep at the inn now.

Ivan rose two hours before sunrise just to make certain he would be at the mill before any of the workers. He had taken an ample breakfast of hard boiled eggs, bread and butter and tea with him. He heated the tea over a small pot bellied stove as the men came by and were told to go home. The men were happy to have the break and there were no complaints. They considered Simon to be a hard task master. The mill foreman wanted to know if he should stick around, since during the day, the mill was his responsibility. Ivan told him that he was to go home also.

Later that day, Simon arrived with a helper. Simon's face was swollen and his head had a bandage on it. Ivan's head also had a bandage which was hidden under his fur cap with ear lugs. Underneath the bandage, most of his hair had been trimmed from the site of the wounds.

Simon told Ivan to go back to the inn and rest and he would talk to him in the evening. Ivan and Latko made their way back to the inn.

It was after supper when Simon arrived back at the inn. "What a day," he huffed.

"We just picked up another identity for our use, but we will have to figure out how to move the new man out of Irkutsk. My associates are used to that."

Ivan worked at the mill all through January when Simon said he finally had the right identity for Ivan. He had gone through about fifty male identities and was sure he had the correct one, Yuri Bulganin.

Yuri was a war hero. His plane came down in northern China, south of the Amur River. Although the Soviets were not at war with China there was constant shooting on both sides of the Amur. Yuri's plane was surrounded by Chinese who occupied the area. With machine pistol's, Yuri and the crew of four fought their way back to north of the Amur. All five were severely wounded and by the time it was all over Yuri had been the only survivor.

Yuri spent two months in a hospital at Chita where he recovered from his head and leg wounds. It was determined that he could never stay in the military because of the damage to his head and leg and he was discharged. His fate was now in his own hands.

Yuri was the son of the famous General Lazlo Bulganin, hero of the German assault into the Baltic region. General Bulganin was in the first line of defense. He ordered his men not to be captured and to fight on. They did and all but a few of them were wiped out. He is a "hero of the people" but he is dead.

Yuri has no other close living relatives who might recognize Ivan. Besides, Ivan looked a little like him. Ivan had the head wounds and his hair would never grow back in a few spots. Something would have to be done about the leg wounds.

Pictures of Yuri appeared in Pravda, but they were all distorted. With his wounds and bandages, Yuri's picture looked like anybody. A short biography indicated that he had graduated from the Institute of Kolomna with a degree in technical engineering. He had been an excellent student and captain of the soccer team. He took flight lessons at Nizhni Novgorod and volunteered for the Far East. It was not known whether the Chinese shot down the plane or it failed on its own. The plane remains in China.

Ivan hesitated to ask. "How did you get the body?"

"It's no mystery. Yuri headed west on the T-S-R and just after passing Ulan Ude he died. His body was removed from the train and he and his identification papers fell into our hands."

"Do you think I could pass it off?"

186

"Certainly, there is no one west of Ulan Ude who knows what he looks like. His mother and father are dead and as far as we know there are no relatives who have associated with him. He will claim his father's wealth and you will turn more than half of it over to us."

"I agree."

Simon said, "You can quit working at the mill. We will have the papers here tomorrow. Continue to stay at the inn. The native lady will disfigure your lower left leg muscle to coincide with the wounds of Yuri. You already have the head wounds which will be evident to anyone who looks at your head. Maybe you should thank the man from Irkutsk?"

"Where is he, I would like to thank him."

Simon laughed, "We cremate all bodies, so there is no trace whatsoever. Well Yuri, you will be able to move in society at will."

Yuri thought, "You say the man graduated from the Institute of Kolomna and took flying lessons at Nizhni Novgorod. Then it is possible, I can get employment in some technical industry."

"Yes he has impeccable credentials. You could even rise high in government circles if you wanted to. By the way, you are now twenty nine years old. You also get a military pension. Not too bad a deal."

"Twenty nine is a good age." Simon nodded. Yuri went on. "I don't think I want to get into any public arena. These are dangerous times."

Simon told another story of Yuri Bulganin. In July and August 1939 Soviet forces faced Japanese forces in a major confrontation on the Manchurian border with Mongolia. Yuri Bulganin was a pilot. In that conflict, his light bomber plane destroyed a Japanese troop train. After several other setbacks, the Japanese retreated back to the interior of Manchuria.

When the war with Finland broke out in 1939, Yuri was set to transfer to that theater of operations. The Soviets wanted territory from Finland, since Finland was less than twenty miles from the second largest Soviet city, Leningrad. The Finns turned out to be a better foe than expected, but were finally defeated.

It was decided that Yuri and his crew should stay in the Far East and patrol the Amur River where Japanese were fighting small bands of Chinese. It was in this location that Yuri further distinguished himself.

Ivan assumed the identity of Yuri Bulganin. The lady surgeon made several cuts in Yuri's left leg and rubbed some herbs into the cuts. This made convincing battle scars. After a week these as well as his head wounds were healing nicely.

A small item was leaked to agents of Pravda that Yuri had amnesia after leaving Chita. He wandered around Ulan Ude for a couple of days before he was recognized. While he recovers from his wounds, the impetuous young man would live in a government apartment in Irkutsk with his faithful dog. One of

Simon's associates had made the arrangements in Irkutsk as well as getting the news release. It was obvious that the anonymous associates of Simon had connections.

16. Rehabilitation

Simon had arranged boat passage to Irkutsk for Yuri. He had also arranged for government housing. Yuri had two furnished rooms in an apartment complex. These were a small kitchen, a combination sitting and bedroom and a shared bath. There was a sofa by day which opened to a bed at night, or one could simply sleep on the large sofa. The apartment was heated with natural gas. The manager of the complex was pleased to have such an honored tenant.

Latko was billed as an assist dog, trained to help rehabilitate people and assist those handicapped. Yuri explained to the manager that when he collapsed on a side street in Ulan Ude, it was his assist dog that saved him by calling attention to his location. Yuri said he owed his life to that dog and he was speaking the truth.

Irkutsk is located about forty miles from the "Blue Pearl of Siberia," Lake Baikal. It is on the Angara River which flows out of the lake and the only outlet of the lake. Although a tributary of the Yenesey, the Angara is over one thousand miles long.

When Yuri arrived in Irkutsk, it was a bustling metropolis with half a million inhabitants. They were caught up in the war effort and manufactured aircraft and small armored vehicles. Food processing was a major industry, utilizing grain and sugar beets from the region. There was also a sizable dairy industry in the surrounding area. Much of the milk was turned into butter and cheese before shipment to the west.

Irkutsk had always been a favorite place of exile for the Czars. One of their most famous residents was Vladimir Lenin, who, in exile, lived a comfortable life here. The dissident leaders known as The Decembrists were also exiled to this city. They were intellectuals, who had been military leaders when Napoleon was chased back to Paris. Since they had connections, the Czar executed only five of their leaders and sent the rest to Irkutsk. These Decembrists built an opera house, ballet theater, museum and founded a university.

During the fight between the Red Army of the Bolsheviks and the White Army supporting Czar Nicolas II, Irkutsk became an important battle area. Most of the White Army was located in the region.

Once the Trans-Siberian Railroad was completed, the city grew rapidly. Moscow was only four days away by rail as trade between southern Siberia and the western populated areas of that region was enhanced.

It was February and Irkutsk was cold. The average temperature in this month is zero degrees Fahrenheit. Needless to say, most people stayed indoors and an outdoor adventure was a quick dash out of one's rooms for food and supplies.

The communist government did not permit inheritance, but it did recognize ownership of personal property and inheritance of such. The manager of the housing complex had registered Yuri with the local police and the administrator of the military district. The police supervisor interviewed Yuri to find what he needed in his new capacity as a civilian. Yuri needed an internal passport. This was a document that had an updated photograph and the life history of the individual. It was to be presented upon request from authority. No one questioned Yuri, his head wounds were testimony to his identify. The police supervisor had sent to Kolomna for Yuri's vital statistics and an internal passport was issued with a photo of Ivan on it.

The police supervisor questioned Yuri about his experiences and Yuri filled in the blank spots with his imagination. He had been awarded Hero of the Soviet Union, as well as several other medals. These were delivered to Yuri by the local commander of the Red Army. Yuri kept bottles of Armenian wine handy for such visits. One of Yuri's exploits was to carry a comrade from the plane to a safe village, even though Yuri himself had a leg wound and severe head wounds. The comrade died a short time after arrival.

The police supervisor asked Yuri how far he had carried the man. Yuri thought about how he had carried Mishkov and answered, "I think it was six miles."

Once the location of Yuri was received in Kolomna the effects of his father General Bulganin, along with his medals, were delivered to Yuri's apartment. The valuables included a dozen small gold objects, weighing between two and four ounces each. Apparently the old man had melted gold and made it into cashable trinkets.

Yuri also enjoyed a pension for wounded veterans and a bonus for his Hero of the Soviet Union award. He could live comfortably on this income.

Near the end of February, a visitor came to Yuri. He mentioned that he was a friend of Simon Barishnakov and that Yuri owed Simon some money. The code word was "apricot." Yuri said he had little money, but he did have some gold objects which were convertible to any currency. The envoy accepted ten of the gold trinkets and left Yuri with two. Gold was valued at thirty two dollars an ounce and the ten trinkets weighed at least twenty ounces. That was a considerable amount of money.

"I send my regards and affection to Simon." said Yuri as the envoy was leaving.

It was against the code to speak of the personal lives of any of the inner circle, but the envoy said that Simon was in his glory, since his wife was about to have a baby. He had recovered from his wounds and thanked Yuri for saving his life.

On February twenty-eighth Yuri had another visitor who introduced himself as Commander Federov. Yuri thought that this must be a local military commander, but it turned out that the suburb of Irkutsk, newly named Sverdlovsky, had no less than nine research institutes of the Siberian Branch of the Academy of Sciences. Commander Federov was the coordinator for this group. He asked about Yuri's health and if Yuri thought he was up to working on some research projects within the institute. Yuri said that he might check this out, but he had to think about it for several days.

The commander said that the institute was hurting for legitimate scientists, since most of their top people had been conscripted into the military. They discussed what news there was about the war. Yuri read Pravda regularly now, but the news in it was slanted and gossip was more reliable. The commander had connections and filled Yuri in on the war effort.

On the front lines, the Soviets had made some gains into the Caucasus and Ukraine. However, these were probably lulls as the Germans were not prepared for the harsh Russian winter. German armies had pulled back to await reinforcements and supplies. The German Field Marshall von Reichenau died of a stroke. This was a set back in leadership.

In January, there were several Red Army paratroopers dropped south of Smolensk and these were actively training people in guerilla warfare. Their first efforts were successful and much publicized. Hitler had ordered any partisan captured, to be shot immediately.

Commander Federov returned a few days later. He made small talk about the weather. The average temperature in Irkutsk in March was fifteen degrees Fahrenheit, still seventeen degrees below freezing.

The Commander had contacted the Kolomna Institute and the air school at Nizhni Novgorod and obtained Yuri's scholastic record which he handed to Yuri to survey to see if it was complete. Yuri took the documents and poured over them. Apparently he had been an outstanding academician. He said that everything seemed in order.

Yuri noticed that there were several German language courses emphasizing science in the mix. He was comfortable with this, since he had studied German and knew how to use the language, but he was not an expert. He could brush up on German if he had to.

The conversation centered on the duties he might have before him. One of them would be teaching local college students the basics of science. Most of these would be girls, since the healthy boys and young men were involved in some war effort.

Sometimes we are visited by flashes of brilliance when we least expect it. Yuri had such a visit and could hardly contain himself. He made an attempt at controlling his enthusiasm when he spoke.

Yuri grimaced. "I am too well known around here. I would like to go somewhere off the beaten path for a year and then see what I can contribute to the war effort. People are coming to see me almost every day and I need some more rehabilitation."

"I understand," said the commander, "I had been wounded in Finland and needed at least a year of settled down before I had my wits about me." This was an exaggeration, but so what, it was good conversation between war heroes.

Yuri went on with his brilliant scheme. "I understand there is a research program at the University of Tomsk which engages young people in the study of languages and science. Perhaps I could do something there? What do you think?"

Ivan expected the commander to be upset but instead he was elated. "I know Major Georg Volosky who is in charge of the very program I think you mean. They selected twenty or thirty students out of hundreds who took a test. Some of our kids were selected, since all the contestants were from Siberia. Major Volosky and I go way back to before our university days. We are working the same side of the street."

Yuri said, "Maybe I can get into the program somehow."

"You can probably be a lecturer. There is a shortage of teachers everywhere. However, I think this program has top government priority and they are probably well staffed."
Yuri thought, "Maybe I could be one of the students, after all, I am only twenty-nine years old and there is a life yet to live."

The commander beamed. "I'll contact Major Volosky and see what I can do for you. I'll come back as soon as I hear from him. "

The commander returned in two days. "I have some good news for you Yuri. Major Volosky said that he would be happy to consider your credentials. He is worried about your head wounds and wonders if they have affected your brains to the point where you are erratic. He needs people who have all their wits about them."

"I think I am not erratic. Perhaps a mind doctor can verify that."

The commander still beaming said "Major Volosky is coming to Irkutsk to interview you. He expects to be here on Saturday. I will entertain him then and we will visit you on Sunday. Don't make any dumb Lithuanian jokes, since the major is Lithuanian by birth. Yuri could hardly wait.

Around one o'clock on Sunday there was a knock on Yuri's door. Yuri let in the Commander and a man in a major's uniform. Latko went over to the major and sniffed his trousers and then went back to his rug in the sitting bedroom. After introductions, Yuri motioned for the men to sit down.

Major Volosky said that he was impressed with Yuri's record and then the conversation shifted to Yuri's health and mental state. Yuri said that he thought his mental state was normal and made a maniacal face. Both guests laughed loudly.

Yuri started to make tea for the men, but changed his mind, and brought out a bottle of wine. "This is imported from Armenia, said to be the best wine in the world."

The commander laughed. "It is difficult to tell since I just gulp it down."

Major Volosky put his arm around his old friend. "You must learn to pause and appreciate the fine things of life. Sip life slowly. We might not be around tomorrow. Live every day as if it might be your last. Who knows, in the present circumstances each day might be our last."

This sobered up the conversation and Yuri asked about the purpose of Volosky's institute. It had to do with preparation of a research team of young people. The exact research could not be disclosed, even to a war hero, and the commander of the local institutes.

Yuri said that he would like to be a part of some project that would go on for a long length of time, especially if it had to do with the future of the Soviet Union. What could he do to convince Major Volosky to give him the opportunity?

The major said that the students had taken a test of two hundred questions and perhaps Yuri could take the test. If he did well he might be placed among the students. The commander said that he thought with Yuri's academic record Yuri would qualify as a lecturer. The major said that this was not a research project based on favoritism and that Yuri would have to qualify. He said that his reputation was at stake and the project had to have the best minds available.

Yuri asked, "Did you bring a copy of the test with you?"

The major answered that he did. Yuri then asked if he could take the test.

Volosky said that he would give Yuri a book to prepare for the test and he would be back tomorrow.

Yuri thought the hell with it, he didn't want to wait. "Give me the test and I'll take it now. If I don't pass, then you will know my knowledge is limited." Yuri was counting on his tutoring of Milla to pull him through. Her every answer was fresh in his mind. Everything she ever said to him was fresh in his mind.

The major hesitated. He liked this brash young man. "Very well, you can take the test. The commander and I will go out for something to eat while you take the test."

Yuri thought to himself that the major was giving him a chance to cheat and get a higher score. "No major, I would like you and the commander to stay here and observe that I took the test without the aid of any references. I have another bottle of wine and if you want, there is food in the cupboards."

The test and pencils were given to Yuri who dug in immediately. The major and the commander went to the kitchen where the major took out a deck of cards and the two men played a game which involved keeping score.

It took almost two hours for Yuri to complete the test. By now the commander and major were eager to get out of there and organize social events for the evening. The major took the test and put it back in its leather container.

"I will check this test later tonight and have the results and my decisions for you tomorrow. I hope you did well."

Yuri saw them to the door saying that he would take Latko for a walk to get some fresh air. The temperature outside had risen above freezing and was considered a balmy day at thirty four degrees.

At the commander's apartment the two leaders and their wives had supper. The wives knew each other from the university days. They were four fast friends. Their children were all in boarding school at this time.

After supper, the major settled at the cleaned off kitchen table and began to check the answers on the test. He would say "wow" every once in a while. This would get the attention of the other three people in the apartment who assumed that the major was impressed with the test.

When the checking was all finished the major turned to the commander. "This man has made a perfect score. He must be brilliant beyond imagination. I will offer him a position as lecturer."

The major's wife chimed in. "He can have Major Ulavek's apartment since the major has been called to Moscow." She turned to the other wife. "It has three rooms and is very comfortable. Anyone would be glad to have it."

"Yes, we could arrange that. I will have to talk to Yuri and we can probably make arrangements for him to come in June. By then, I can supply him with textbooks and reading material."

The major's wife used the term "called to Moscow" which had not yet had the fatal connotations that it would soon have.

The next day Yuri was told of his score on the test and the offer of a lecture position with the University of Tomsk. His salary was discussed and the best feature was that he could keep his military pension. It was March and by the first of June Major Volosky would have his living arrangements finalized and register him with the university, police and the military leadership.

Near the end of March, a list of the students in the project and a short bibliography of each was sent to Yuri. He noted with pleasure the name of Ludmilla Mikoyanova on the list. He remembered her nude body rotating in the window. But that seemed like an eternity ago. She probably wouldn't even remember him. Then he thought, she certainly would remember him.

Major Volosky visited Yuri again in April. The weather was considerably warmer now and the two of them, along with Latko, walked along the Angara River front. The major told Yuri that the students had three weeks off at the beginning of June. They could visit home if they wanted or their parents could come to Tomsk, but they had to leave the dormitory. When they got back to Tomsk they had one week to get settled again and classes would start in July. They could not leave anything in the dormitory, but could store their possessions in a safety room on campus.

The major also informed Yuri that he might be asked to teach a regular class at the university, since there was a shortage of teaching staff. The assignment would be in his science field and probably his choice from the catalog of university offerings. Yuri liked that idea.

Yuri mentioned casually that he thought he might know one of the students, Ludmilla Mikoyanova. Her father, Major Mikoyan and his father General Bulganin, were once assigned to the same outfit. He remembered Ludmilla as a little girl who followed him around like a silly goose. He would shoo her away, but she kept after him. He said he was about sixteen at the time and she must have been around six or seven.

Volosky had a laugh at that. "She probably wouldn't remember you. Every child grows up so fast. I thought my own daughter was twelve years old, but my wife informed me that I had missed two years somewhere and she was fourteen." Yuri laughed at that.

When Major Volosky again visited in the first week of May he had something else in his bag for Yuri. He said that he understood Yuri had knowledge of German. Yuri begged off, saying his knowledge was limited. However, the major said he had confidence in Yuri and that is why he was going to give him some captured classified German documents to read over..

Yuri looked at the documents. He knew they were beyond his abilities. A few days after Major Volosky left for Tomsk, Yuri called on his friend the commander of the institutes. He wanted to know if there was anyone doing research that had a Class A clearance and knew German fluently.

The commander said he had a man, Dieter Loesch, who was descended from the Germans who lived along the southern Volga River. This group had been imported from Germany by Katherine the Great, sometime around 1790. They were loyal to Russia, but unfortunately, Stalin didn't think so, and sent many of them into exile in Siberia. Dieter ended up in Irkutsk. He had a Class A clearance, despite his heritage.

Dieter met with Yuri over the next several days and translated the documents with him. Yuri made many notes and by the time the sessions were over, he was able to translate much of the material himself.

The Germans had a large number of rocket types in service against the Soviets and British. The material given to Yuri concerned the 21 cm Wurfgranaten 42. It carried 22 pounds of high explosives. It was spin-stabilized by the thrust shot out through various vents. Various frames, both mobile and static, were employed in launching the rockets

Yuri would memorize the entire packet of documents and pass himself off as an expert on this particular subject. If he knew all the material, he would be able to discuss it with authority.

The students left for their homes or to do some war effort duty in their cities. Yuri took the Trans-Siberian Railroad to Kemerovo and the railroad to Tomsk where Major Volosky and his wife waited to greet him. He was immediately shown to his apartment and enjoyed a dinner at the Volosky's.

Tomsk was the largest city in Siberia until the construction of the TSR by-passed it. The cities on the TSR increased in population while the population of Tomsk remained steady at about a half million. The University of Tomsk was the oldest university in Siberia, founded in 1880. Tomsk was also a great cultural center with a dance troop and classical orchestra that toured all of the Soviet Union to entertain troops.

Located on the Tom River, a tributary of the Ob, the city produced ball bearings, machine tools and electric motors for the war effort. There was also a flourishing chemical and petrochemical complex. Much machinery from the war zone cities had been moved to Tomsk and other Siberian cities to secure them against the invaders.

When Yuri arrived in June, the German army had made tremendous advances since their winter pull back. They had crossed the Don River and moved their lines closer to the Volga River. The

Soviet Sixth Army was being encircled near Donets. The city of Voronezh would probably fall any day and Yuri was pained with the thought that his family would become victims of war.

During the three week wait for the students, Yuri got to know the other teachers involved with the special project students. They were a pleasant lot and serious about their duties. There were eleven of them, seven were women. Yuri felt a couple of the women were watching him a little too closely for comfort.

The students were coming back in two days and Yuri approached Major Volosky about a plan. He wanted to meet with each of the thirty students in the week before classes. His office, which he didn't have to share, was between that of Major Volosky and Lazlo Lugosi. The secretary could draw up a time schedule and he would allow a half hour for each student. He would meet ten students each day for three days.

When the students returned, they were greeted by Major Volosky. He said he would like to introduce the staff, but they were all at a meeting. There was a new man on the faculty, Yuri Bulganin, who was a pilot and a war hero. They will meet him individually on the following schedule which would be posted on the bulletin board. The major concluded by saying that Bulganin's office was next to his so the students would not have any trouble finding it.

Yuri had the student's dormitory assignments. It was the end of June and the sun set late at this latitude. He donned a dark outfit and left Latko in the apartment. Then he made his way across the campus and watched the dormitory that housed Ludmilla. She was nowhere around.

He waited in a secure place near some shrubbery and continued to watch. Here at last came Ludmilla, walking down the sidewalk, holding hands with a young man. Yuri's heart sank. How could he try to interfere with this? He followed them as they walked along. When they got to the dormitory they quit holding hands and stood talking. After about five minutes, a blonde girl came from the dormitory, threw her arms around the young man and they walked off together as Ludmilla said goodbye to them and for them "to have a good time." Yuri breathed easier, but he still didn't know what was going on.

It was Tuesday and the first ten students had filed through Yuri's office. He questioned them intently and had their records before him. They liked his manner and were very pleased that he seemed to have a personal interest in their welfare. Most of their teachers treated them as if they were machines.

When Olga, Ludmilla's room mate came back from her meeting with Yuri she was asked about the new teacher. Olga answered, "He can have my body any time he wants it."

Ludmilla was shocked at this and mentioned Olga's boyfriend. All Olga could say was, "Wait until you meet him."

On Wednesday, Ludmilla would be the third to enter Yuri's office. Major Volosky had asked him how the meeting with students was coming along and was Ludmilla the little girl that he had mentioned. He said he hadn't met her yet and maybe she wasn't the girl he thought she was. The major went to his office.

The first two students were announced by the secretary as it was her duty. When it was Ludmilla's turn she came to the door with Ludmilla and said "Mr. Bulganin, I would like to introduce Ludmilla Mikoyanova." Then she closed the door behind Ludmilla.

Yuri waved to the chair and said, "Please sit down Ludmilla." His voice had a familiar ring to it, but she didn't recognize it. When Ivan had been tutoring her, he always had a short beard, so he was not easily recognized by her.

Yuri got up from his desk and walked around to Ludmilla. She looked up, screamed loudly and leaped to her feet and hugged him around the upper arms.

In the outer office, the secretary hearing the scream started for the office of Yuri. She was met in the hall by Major Volosky who waved her off. He entered Yuri's office to see Ludmilla hugging Yuri with tears flowing from her eyes.

Yuri looked at the major. "She remembered me."

The major smiled a wide toothed grin. "I see, carry on with your interview." He turned and exited the office, closing the door behind him.

Yuri wasted no time in kissing Milla. She nearly wrenched his neck with hugging and kissing. A while later, Yuri looked at his watch and said it was time to meet another new student. He would be in contact with Milla soon and they can pick up where they left off. He noted that Milla was wearing his triangle piece of jade which she had set into a necklace ornament. She said, "When you give someone a piece of jade you give them a piece of your soul. You have always had a piece of my soul." She walked out the door.

Ivan and Milla have found each other and in the well worn phrase they have pledged themselves to each other until death do they part. In this time of history in Russia, death was a common visitor.

Few people in their lifetime are fortunate to experience the delirious euphoria of true love. One may have a sexual relationship with an acquaintance or someone they feel strongly about, but the experience of sex with a true love is beyond description and mere words could never capture that exhalation. When each person is totally committed to the other, there is no holding back or reservation. There is an elevation of spirit and the true meaning of life becomes evident.

17. The University

Despite trying to live in secrecy, Yuri and Milla became a recognized couple. It was difficult for faculty members to hold parties and invite Yuri without inviting Ludmilla.

The couple decided to not take any chances of pregnancy, since that would have a negative effect on both their lives and careers. They had intercourse only on safe days and, even then, used condoms. Russian condoms were not top quality items and were the subject of many jokes.

It was in November when Major Volosky approached Yuri about his association with Ludmilla. He said that he approved whole heartedly and hoped they would get married. If they were married and Ludmilla finished the program, he would be in a position to assign them both to the same project, regardless of location. Once the program study was completed, all the graduates would be assigned research somewhere other than Tomsk. Maybe they could go to Irkutsk where the social life was pleasant. The other young scientists were going to be assistant researchers on special projects that were now in the planning stage. .

Yuri said that he would not marry Ludmilla until he met her parents and they approved of the marriage. Major Volosky thought that was old fashioned and perhaps foolish, considering the war and the social upheaval of the country before the war.

Yuri continued his German studies. When he had a week off, he took newly captured German documents concerning rockets to Irkutsk and met with Dieter Loesch to discuss the translations. At Irkutsk, he had a chance to renew friendships with the commander and his wife and usually stayed in their apartment. The commander's wife had heard about Ludmilla from the major's wife and was anxious to meet the young woman who had won the heart of Yuri. They all started considering Yuri as part of their families.

When Ludmilla visited her parents at semester break the previous June she was told that Ivan had been killed and buried in the camp cemetery. Ludmilla collapsed and it took about fifteen minutes to revive her. Lorraine begged her husband to tell their daughter the truth, which he did. Ludmilla was much relieved and concerned that her father did not trust her. The father said that she would probably never see Ivan again and he thought that way she would get him out of her mind. At that time, she said that Ivan was a part of her and she would never forget him. The mother understood.

Ludmilla wrote to her parents in December saying she had found a man she might consider marrying. He was Yuri Bulganin, son of General Bulganin, who was killed two years ago. She told of Yuri as a teacher and about his war wounds and how everyone liked him. She was certain she had a future with him.

Her mother, Lorraine, wrote back with a hundred questions about Yuri. She and her husband discussed Milla's letters. In her heart, Lorraine thought that Milla belonged to Ivan, but he was a thing of the past.

In her letters, Milla told all about Yuri. She said that Yuri and she talked about marriage, but Yuri said he would never marry her without the consent of her parents. He was old fashioned that way. Her parents would have to wait until next year to meet Yuri and, at that time, could consider their approval.

At the beginning of November, the Germans had taken Voronezh and Ivan followed these developments with great concern. He was told that the Germans usually left the civilian population

201

alone, if the population left them alone. However, if an SS officer was with the conquerors, then Jews were executed for no other reason than they were Jews.

In November, the Germans had also advanced within nine miles of Moscow. For some unknown reason, this advance was halted. Perhaps the cost of victory here would be too high. German army units concentrated on Stalingrad. Hitler had decided to embarrass Stalin by taking the city that bore his name. Hitler also figured it was a good place for his armies to cross the Volga.

The Battle for Stalingrad was one of the greatest battles of history. It began as skirmishes and amassing of troops in November 1942 and ended with the surrender of the German remnants on February 2, 1943. An entire German army had been destroyed. A contingent of 280,000 German troops had been surrounded in the city. About 40,000 of these, mostly wounded, had been evacuated. Almost all of the rest were destroyed and 90,000 prisoners taken. Less than 5,000 of these would ever see Germany again.

The Soviets announced, in their inventory after the battle, that 147,000 German and 47,000 Soviet bodies had been removed from the site. The credit for victory at Stalingrad went to General Chuikov.

As the war progressed, thousands of prisoners were taken on both sides. The Soviets often caught up with the Soviet prisoners as they were being taken toward Germany. These were liberated and many of them were sent directly to work camps within the Soviet Union. The German prisoners taken by the Soviets were sent to work camps around the cities. The Russian prisoners were usually put to farm work since most Russians were considered peasants by the Germans. The German prisoners were treated harshly and the death rate was high for this group.

The road projects and the big dam projects of Siberia were abandoned after Stalingrad and many of the prisoners on these projects were taken into the Soviet army and used as cannon fodder. Another large number of them were assigned to farming. Records were kept and many of them would have to return to finish their sentences after the war.

The Yenesey road project was one of the casualties and Major Mikoyan was assigned to operate a prison camp near

Magnitogorsk involving captured Germans. The prisoners were put to work mining iron ore at Magnitaya Mountain. The major's orders are to keep them alive long enough to work, but, eventually work them until they die.

Magnitogorsk was an open area until magnetite ore was discovered near there. The city was ordered built in 1929 by Stalin. Hundreds of laborers were conscripted for the project. These included engineers as well as common laborers. There was a huge contingent of volunteers who were happy to get out of their situations at that time. By 1931 the city and its first steel mills were completed. Coal for manufacturing steel was procured from mines near Karaganda in Kazakhstan. Much of the coal was produced by political prisoners of that area. One could say without contradiction, that the industrial might of the Soviet Union before the war, and its progress, was based on conscripted labor.

When Camp 193 was given the order to dislocate and relocate, there was a considerable amount of paper shuffling and verifying the prisoners and their new assignments. Major Mikoyan thought it would be useful to have Lev Lefkovich stay with him. Despite the flagrant disregard of written laws, he was a useful interpreter of bureaucratic documents.

Lev's association with the camp officers permitted him to meet the vivacious Magda whom he courted intensely. When the camp dissolved, Lev and Madga were officially married by the post commander Major Mikoyan who had obtained a letter of amnesty from General Frunze for both of them. Lev and the officers involved were not sure about the legality of the entire affair, but they were willing to do it. Mikoyan had convinced Frunze that Lev was a valuable asset to them both.

However, when Judge Vishinsky was informed that one of his gifted students at Moscow University had been incarcerated, he asked for an investigation of the matter. The investigators traced Lev to Camp 193 and to the major's headquarters at Magnitogorsk Prison. Lev was summoned to Moscow where he told his story to Vishinsky.

Judge Vishinsky sent an official complimentary letter to Major Mikoyan and General Frunze thanking them for preserving and freeing such a valuable member of Soviet

Society. The judge who had sent Lev to prison was subjected to several harsh days of torture in prison and then executed. In sentencing him, Vishinsky said, "We cannot have arbitrary judges who act immorally as agents of the Soviet people. We are a nation of laws and procedures which must be observed."

In November 1942, the Germans had taken Voronezh. Ivan's sister Tanya had taken over her husband's job at the shipyard. Her husband, Dimitri Stepanovich and their neighbor Igor Mikovich were both in the army. They had volunteered to join a division organized at Voronezh. Igor Mikovich became the political officer for the corps. He managed to get Dimitri Stepanovich the rank of sergeant in the quartermaster unit which he assumed would be far from combat..

Ilych, the son of Tanya and Dimitri, was fourteen years old. He worked along with his mother in the shipyard. They worked a twelve hour shift and ate in the cafeteria.

The steel plate making apparatus of the shipyard had been converted to stamping out and shaping tank turrets and other parts. These were shipped by rail to Kuibyshev, just off the Volga, where the tanks were assembled. Much of the government organization was now in Kuibyshev, formerly known as Samara. The area was considered the gateway to Siberia, and unless the Germans were highly successful, safe from invasion.

Anya, the fourteen year old daughter of Igor, worked in the local hospital. Like every other hospital worker, she put in a twelve hour day. On some days, she put in sixteen to twenty hours. She often slept at the hospital. Like all workers, she ate in the hospital cafeteria. .She was in a position to bring food home, which she often did. The food that was nonperishable, such as tins of sardines was stored in various compartments in the two apartments.

Gemma, Anya's grandmother, and Olga, Ilya's grandmother continued to live in their assigned apartments. Gemma took care of both apartments, hers and Tanya's

As German prisoners were processed, those with special talents and knowledge were set aside. Those that were scientists were given the choice of helping the Soviets or death. Several chose death.

Scientists and soldiers with special knowledge of rockets were sent to Tomsk University where they were interviewed by

Yuri, whose ability in the German language was considerably improved from the time he first started at Tomsk.

Yuri soon found that slight errors in translation could prove disastrous to lab workers. He put in a request to Irkutsk Institutes for the transfer of Dieter Loesch to come and work with translations at Tomsk.

Dieter did not have the same tolerance toward the Germans as Yuri and when prisoners proved to have nothing to offer, he didn't hesitate to transfer them to work camps. He once said to Yuri, "Remember, whether we approve or disapprove of our government's policies, these bastards are invaders of our Motherland and must be punished for their transgressions. It turns my stomach to think that we have to put up with any of them. Sure, they have technology we can use, but once we capture their equipment, we can determine if we should make changes in our own."

Yuri responded, "But, these people can give us a shortcut to technology. It might take us years to discover what these guys can tell us in a couple of days. I would like to get my hands on the guys who are sending the rockets over to London."

18. The Battle for Voronezh
(an eye-witness account from a German and a Russian)

Voronezh is located on the river of that name. It is a navigable tributary of the Don River. The city was founded in 1586 as a fortress against the Crimean Tatars. It became a ship building center under Peter the Great. From this port, he launched a military campaign to the Sea of Azov. The city was largely destroyed in World War II. It has a large university, an 18th Century Potemkin Palace and the famous Nikolsk Church.

The city is directly east from the plains of Kursk, which was the site of the biggest tank battle in history. The German military command calculated that by taking Voronezh, a staging ground could be maintained which could take them all the way to the Volga River and mastery of the rich farmlands between the northern Don and the Volga.

The German Army introduced the Nebelwerfer rocket propelled gun as they approached the Don River, just west of

Voronezh. It was the prototype of a weapon to be introduced six months later. The rapid detonations of the Nebelwerfer barrage created variations in air pressure which caused the enemy soldiers extensive lung damage and killed many of them, simply by changes in air pressure. The explosions created huge depressions in the earth and killed everything in the vicinity.

When the German Army South approached the Don River and put the Nebelwerfer (fog maker) into action, many of the Soviet soldiers threw down their guns and ran screaming, discarding equipment as they ran. When the Germans advanced, they found many Soviet soldiers collapsed or crying in spasms as they lay on the ground.

The purpose of the big gun was not to produce shrapnel, but to create the blast effect. "Craters were created in the snow and the mounds around them were streaked with black and yellow earth." The shell casings of the projectiles were thin and the explosive charge within them was quite heavy.

When the thrust east had begun in earnest, the mud of spring slowed the advancing army. But once summer was in full swing, the mud dried and the roads became thick clouds of dust as the Germans advanced eastward.

The Germans were appalled at the Soviet contempt for the life of their soldiers as they sent wave after wave of them into deadly enemy fire. The line of Soviet soldiers stretched from horizon to horizon and advanced as robots. The Germans were frightened by this ancient method of warfare. It was as if they were fighting an army from another planet.

When the Germans moved through rural Ukraine, they were amazed at the houses with no electricity and no toilets of any kind. It was a modern army going to fight in a medieval landscape. People lighted their strange huts with candles. The sun determined the length of the working day. Many of the huts had roofs covered with straw where moss grew abundantly.

When the first German forces moved through the steppes of the Ukraine they were greeted by peasants offering them pails of water or milk. They looked upon the Germans as liberators. Once the SS got to them and inflicted brutal torture and death, the peasantry gave up the idea of collaboration and began a system of guerrilla warfare never before experienced by an army. The army had to contend with the enemy before them and the enemy within their midst.

Bridges over streams had to be rebuilt by the advancing army. The old bridges were designed to carry horses and carts and could not hold up under the weight of heavy machinery.

Despite the German army and its abundant modern weapons, they still had two and a half million horses in service. In much of the terrain, the horses were more useful than armored vehicles which stuck in mud. However, the German horses died by the thousands in that first winter of battle.

At the beginning of World War II, the British army was the only mechanized army in the world completely free of horse dependency. Every other army had horse brigades. Estimates of the German army were that eighty percent of its materials were transported by horse power. Approximately, eight hundred thousand horses were used in the opening battles of Barbarossa which was the German code name for the invasion of Russia.

In the second summer, the Germans confiscated as many of the Russian panje horses as they could. Most of the German horses died when the temperature reached five below freezing while the Russian panje could withstand working conditions as low as fifteen degrees below freezing.

In the summer of 1942, several hundred Russian Cossacks united with the Germans to fight the Soviets. These were excellent horsemen. Most of the Cossacks were employed in the battle for the Caucasus, but many were later captured at Voronezh.

The Kalmuks along the Caspian Sea was another group of horsemen who volunteered to fight with the Germans. Of the Soviet citizens, the Kalmuks were considered the group most loyal to the Germans. Stalin had the Kalmuks exiled to Siberia and the central Asian deserts by the thousands.

The Cossacks loyal to the Soviet Union proved to be troublemakers for the Germans who were often attacked behind their lines by corps of cavalry. In the first rush of Barbarossa, the Soviet army relied more on their horse power than on their tanks and armored vehicles. After each battle, the field was strewn, not only with dead soldiers, but with the carcasses of thousands of horses. After each battle in the Ukraine, the local peasantry whose houses and property were destroyed, relied on horse meat for sustenance. The tactic used by the Germans as they advanced toward Voronezh was to advance, halt, fire, advance, halt, and fire. Red armor usually attacked when the army was in the halt position. This proved not to be the best move, since the German SP guns fired best from a halt position. These were powerful guns placed on a platform. They could destroy a tank with one shot.

Generally, the Reds sent in tanks in waves. The Germans could expect a lull between waves of tanks and could reload and refit their heavy weapons during this lull. In one skirmish, on the way to Voronezh, the SP guns destroyed forty one Soviet tanks.

It was General Hoth's 4th Panzer Army that had been sent to capture Voronezh, a strategically important town. Once on the outskirts of the city, the Germans engaged in heavy bombardment with conventional heavy weapons, as well as the fog maker. After four hours of bombardment, the town was shrouded in smoke and dust.

Not all the Soviet defenders were killed or captured. Many of them had moved their weapons into position to attack the advancing infantry. Once these pockets of resistance were discovered, many of the German big gun crews gave up their heavy pieces and took up small arms to clean out the nests of resistance.

As the infantry advanced toward town, they encountered the houses on the outskirts. From one house, a machine gun would open fire. Then another from the opposite side of the street joined in. Then a third burst of fire came from a house further down the street.

The big gun groups could not abandon the big guns altogether, since they could not advance beyond the machine guns. An SP gun would be brought up and put into position. It would soon blast large holes in the houses holding the machine gunners. They were soon buried in a hail of bricks and mortar. From other doorways, Soviet soldiers would emerge carrying white leaflets that had been dropped the day before telling them how to surrender by waving the leaflets in the air. These were a passport to prison, but at least they were alive. However, they all faced retribution when the war ended.

A resident recalled; "From out of the chaos, a Soviet tank appeared and roared down the rubble strewn street. It stopped to aim. Before it could get off a shot it was hit by an SP shell which had such force the explosion hurled its turret hundreds of feet into the air."

Since the sniper and machine gun fire was intense when the Germans moved into the main city, the Nebelwerfer was brought in. It proceeded to blast away several large buildings and create craters when it didn't hit a building. The smoke and dust was immense.

"Many of the buildings were now burning and the air was full of hot ashes. Everywhere, there were buildings on fire. It was as if a volcano had formed within the city. The vehicles which followed the infantry had to go over rubble and maneuver around the craters in the main street of advance."

Soviet resistance folded and the town was now in German hands. Defense measures were taken. A perimeter of heavy antitank guns and land mines were laid in various locations around the city. This was no light task as the city was quite large and there were roads and railroads leading in every direction.

Colonel Klein was in charge of managing the city. He created six zones of occupation with a major under control of each zone. They were given the task of examining buildings in their zone for soldiers and whatever food could be confiscated from the citizens who chose to remain in the city. .

Citizen men, women and able children were employed in clearing the streets of rubble. The water supply was put back in limited operation. Huge stockpiles of ammunition and gasoline were stored in various areas of the city.

German soldiers within each section were free to find sleeping quarters wherever they could. Colonel Klein made it very clear that any soldier raping a civilian woman was to be executed. He wanted the soldiers to concentrate on their duties at hand. Many soldiers used their canned food rations to gain favors from city women. This did not violate the rape order.

The rules for civilians were conventional and strictly enforced. Curfew was from 9 p.m. to 6 a.m. except for hospital workers. Anyone caught out during those times without official papers would be shot. Any Soviet soldier in civilian clothes would be shot. Display of the Soviet flag was forbidden. No one was to leave the city without permission. Absolutely no fraternization between Germans and Soviets would be permitted. The citizens were to report any mistreatment by Germans to the nearest commander.

There were immediate reports of mistreatment given to the captains who transferred these to their majors. Soldiers accused of mistreatment were given warnings. Some soldiers shot civilians and defended their actions by saying they thought the civilians were hiding hand grenades under their clothing. Many soldiers simply kicked civilians that were in their way.

Voronezh fell on July 7, 1942 and was occupied for the rest of the year. On December 20 the Soviets had cut the railroad from Rostov na Donu to Voronezh. This was the main supply line for the Germans. Without their main supply line, it was just a matter of time before they had to either advance or leave the city.

The Voronezh Front for the Soviets was the responsibility of General Golikov. He was operating with limited man power and supplies, since the main supplies and man power were diverted to Stalingrad to the south. Stalingrad was located where the big bend of the Don River approached the Volga River. This closest distance between the rivers was about eighty miles.

On January 23, 1943 General Golikov's Voronezh Front Army attacked the city inflicting heavy damage to the occupying troops as well as the civilian population. On January 28 the Soviets captured Kastornoye a small city east of Voronezh. With this news, the Germans prepared to leave the city and retreat west.

As the German Army retreated west, they left behind heavy mortar and machine gun units in order to halt the advancing Soviets. There was also considerable anti-tank and anti-personnel land mines laid almost everywhere.

When the Soviets advanced, they deployed lines of humans to walk forward through the mine fields and clear a path for their tanks and artillery. These people consisted of military officers who failed to take their objectives, soldiers who had thrown down their weapons and civilian collaborators. These units became known as punishment brigades. Many of the civilians had simply been rounded up and pressed into service without hearings of any sort. The military officers in charge were thinking of expediency and it was every citizen's duty to do what one could for the war effort.

The punishment brigade would walk along with small space between individuals. When a land mine exploded, bodies around it were thrown into the air. The gap in the line was quickly closed as it continued forward. Behind the explosions, armored vehicles moved slowly forward. After the armored vehicles, came the tanks laden with infantry soldiers ready to dismount and engage in combat.

When the Germans made a counter attack they captured many members of the punishment brigade. The interrogator of one of General Hoth's units was appalled at the docile acceptance of the punishment unit members. They thought their punishment was justified and somehow it was their fate. The officers did not think that perhaps the objective they had to take was impossible under the circumstances. Nor did they think the punishment was unfair. The civilians in the punishment units thought it was their duty to help in the fight for their Motherland, even by sacrificing their lives.

About seventy miles west of Voronezh, the Soviets encircled a large number of the enemy. They captured about 50,000 soldiers. Of these, only about 2,500 were actual Germans. Many of those captured were former Soviet citizens living in the Caucasus and Ukraine. The Germans took care of their own by transporting them on vehicles while the non-Germans had to travel on foot.

These prisoners were put to work on burial details. Dead humans and horses lay everywhere. For every dead German, they found six dead Soviets. Since the capture was made a week after the initial engagement the smell of putrefied flesh was ghastly. Many of the prisoners worked with bandanas tied around their faces.

Since it was winter, the armies were dressed in heavy gear. Many of the burial details were instructed to take the heavy coats, hats and felt boots, valenki, from the dead Soviets. Piles of boots, hats and coats were put on carts and sent toward Voronezh.

It was the dead of winter, and as the Red infantry units advanced, they had to seek shelter in the night. Even though they were better equipped than the Germans to fight in cold weather, they still could not stand the bitter cold of the nights with its paralyzing effect, not only on the body, but on the human spirit.

The Soviets would send an advance party to the next village and see how many chimneys was producing smoke, indicating occupation. Then they would head for that village and try to eradicate the Germans in that village and in those houses. The fighting was often fierce, not only to remove the enemy from the village, but to have a place to stay out of the howling winds.

In one village, between the Don River and Voronezh Rivers, there was intense fighting for the right to occupy the village at night. A diary, later captured had recorded the event.

The Red assaults were all driven back and the Soviets had to spend the night in temperatures thirty degrees below zero. That is sixty two degrees below freezing. Even their wool coats, fur caps and felt boots were useless in that temperature. The hot soup kitchens had not come up to give them at least hot liquids to stave off the cold. The leading troops of the offensive had outrun their supply lines and could not go back to meet them, since to retreat was often punishable by death.

When light appeared the next day, the small, but well armed, Germans could see the dark coats of hundreds of Soviets surrounding the village. They picked up their arms to move through the Soviets and met no resistance. The Reds had been numbed and bewildered by the cold. The Germans fired no shots and made no attempt to kill the Soviet troops who were standing as if frozen or lying on the ground. The Red soldiers were shivering and misery was on every face. No shots were fired because this might awaken senses in the shivering enemy and call him to action.

Further back in the lines, behind the infantry, was the motorized division. In that thirty below zero temperature it was difficult to get any motor running. Many of the engines were thawed by filling empty tin ration cans with earth and pouring gasoline on it. These were set on fire and put under the engine and under the differential. The vehicles were often under cover of a canvas tarpaulin. The canvas gave the men some protection from the wind and it also hid the light of the fires from planes that came in the night dropping anti-personnel bombs.

By the time daylight appeared, the motors were running and when daylight did come, the convoy moved out onto icy and rutted roads. Vehicles skidded from one side of the highway to the other. The vehicles which started before daylight, moved without their blackout lights, using the reflections of the ice and snow to guide them.

Many vehicles would run into ditches. Cables would be attached and the rescue vehicle would have to pull slowly, or it too would end up in the ditch.

Once the motorized vehicles got under way, they moved slowly from village to village. Most of these small areas had been liberated by the advancing infantry. When the infantry was pinned down on the flat land, the motor vehicles with their machine guns and mortar crews would go into action. Generally, the Germans were in full retreat and only skirmish groups were left behind to delay the Voronezh Front Army.

19. The Home Front

The Germans had crossed the Don River in the autumn of 1942 and were on their way to the Voronezh River and the main city. Voronezh had a population of slightly more than half a million people. When news of the German advance spread through the city, those who could flee did so. They moved on foot, by horse cart and by train. Although the train came under German air attacks, it still managed to get people out. About half of the population was evacuated by the time the city was first attacked. This was slightly less than three hundred thousand citizens.

When the attack started, Soviet soldiers in retreat set up machine gun and other barriers to halt the enemy advance. Germans moved up heavy artillery and blasted away buildings and the machine gun nests in them. About half the city was on fire and the air was choked with dust and smoke.

When news of the impending attack spread, Tanya and her son Ulya rushed to the grandmother's apartment and told her to pack up and come and live with them. The grandmother refused to leave her chutchkies behind, but Tanya insisted and they went out into the street and started moving the six blocks to Tanya's building. There was a large basement there and they would presumably be safe from attack.

Shelling started and the grandmother moved slowly. Tanya insisted that the old lady move faster, but she couldn't. By the time they had moved two blocks, the shelling had increased. The Germans were getting closer. A large explosion occurred to their left and half a building tumbled down.

Tanya noticed an abandoned wheelbarrow where new cement had been recently laid down. She sent Ilya to fetch it. The wheelbarrow was of construction size. With the aid of Tanya and Ilya, the grandmother got into it. Tanya picked it up and started wheeling as the shells exploded throughout the city. After a block, Ilya took over. He was not tall, but he was a strong fourteen year old. It seemed like an eternity, but it was less than half an hour when they reached the apartment building and the safety of the underground shelter.

. .There were about a hundred people in the shelter, most of them lived in the apartment building. They were there for two days while the shelling continued. People had brought food and water which they generously shared with each other. Most of the people in the shelter did not know each other. There were a few close families, such as Tanya's and Igor's.

Most of the people in the shelter were woman and children. Except for some old men and young boys, the males had gone off to war. They worried about the impending food and water shortage and wondered how the Germans, if successful, would treat them.

After two days, the battle was over. Most of the Soviet soldiers had retreated toward the east. People in all parts of the city emerged from their shelters. What they saw was a city half in ruins. Fires seemed to be burning in every direction.

One end of the five story apartment complex behind Tanya's had a section of apartments shot away on the fourth floor. The fifth floor hung over it like a balcony. The floors beneath the missing area were intact. Materials from destroyed buildings were quickly used to shore up the overhanging rooms. The apartment building of Tanya's was untouched.

To be sure, there would be a housing shortage. However, considering that half the city population had fled, and assuming half the apartments had been destroyed, then it would be about the same occupancy as before the attack. Since the apartment complex of Tanya was intact, they could expect the occupants to start bringing in their less fortunate relatives and friends.

Once the defenders had evacuated the city, the enemy sent in dozers to clear a path through the rubble on the main street and then the side streets. The Germans entered Voronezh in the manner of a military parade. Tanks and soldiers moved down the main streets. Weary soldiers put on their best front by marching upright. The city was soon surrounded by anti-aircraft cannon, mortars and tanks.

On the second day of occupation, German soldiers started checking buildings for remnant Soviet soldiers. Those that did not surrender were soon killed.

While ferreting out the soldiers, the Germans conscripted civilians to start organizing more of the rubble in the streets and making room for heavy equipment to move through. A corridor of mortars and machine gun emplacements was erected around the streets leading from the town.

When it became an effort to round up able bodied citizens, the Germans started offering food as an incentive. The water system was somewhat repaired and since most of the infrastructure of the system was damaged, piping was laid along the streets and faucets were in place. To get water, people would have to bring containers to the faucets. As time passed, more faucets were added, and the soldiers as well as civilians had a supply of drinking water.

The city council, which was put in power by one candidate elections, acted responsibly and cooperated with the Germans. By the end of September, many of the apartment buildings had gas service restored. If this held up, there would be little freezing during the winter.

Food was another problem. The council was given permission to meet potato and flour suppliers at certain checkpoints. No one was allowed to leave the city completely and none of the suppliers were allowed into the city. There was no exchange of money of any kind by the buyers and suppliers. The Soviet government made the supplies available and volunteers brought it to the city. Volunteers picked up the supplies. Ilya was one of the volunteers.

When the supplies reached the city, the city council had

organized several distribution centers. By September, they knew the pockets of settlement and were able to ration the supplies with only a minimum of skimming for their own uses.

People in the damaged buildings soon gathered material from the rubble and were able to make minimum repairs. As each day progressed they settled into a lifestyle of deprivation, but were able to survive. Large posts were put under the apartments on the fifth floor that had the lower apartment removed by the Nebelwerfer. These stretched from the third floor to the fifth, a distance of about twelve feet. People living in the overhanging apartments now felt secure.

A big problem had been sewage disposal. Most of the sewer system had been destroyed by the big blasts of the Nebelwerfer. People kept shebels, a pot designed as a toilet, in their apartments. Each day they carried the shebels to designated shell craters around the city and dumped it in.

The toilets of Tanya's apartment worked but there was no water. During some days, Tanya and Anya would go to the river with two buckets each and bring back water which was used to flush the toilet. They were in luxury compared to most dwellers of the ravaged city. Where the flushed toilet contents ended was of no concern to Tanya.

The precious drinking and cooking water was not used to flush toilets. Gemma and Olga, the babushkas, would go out each day and bring back their allotment of one bucket of drinking water.

There was an active barter exchange going on between the citizens. Tanya traded some of Dimitri and Igor's clothing for candles. She figured, if the gas supply was cut, they could probably huddle in one room and heat it with candles. In September, people thought about the coming winter and how they would fare. Those who had lost most of their belongings were eager to get the clothing.

Occupation life settled into a routine of official rationing and self-imposed rationing. How long would it last?

Ilya brought home food supplies by working at street jobs for the Germans. Practically all male residents worked at these jobs. Ilya often traded his German bread for fresh eggs from a family he made contact with early in the occupation. They kept chickens in their apartment on the edge of the city. They wondered how long it would

216

be before the Germans decided to have some chicken dinners. Until then, they bartered their eggs and when a hen stopped laying eggs, they had chicken meat to eat, or barter.

At the end of November there were several raids in the city made by partisans who came in and blew up several German vehicles. These did not do much damage physically, but had a psychological affect on the occupiers.

What was left of the city council was summoned and given orders that would minimize guerrilla activities. Reward and warning leaflets were posted everywhere in the city, along with the regular curfew leaflets.

Tanya had taken over the job of caring for the neighbor's daughter Anya and the grandmother Gemma. They all lived in the same apartment complex and Tanya's word was law and had to be obeyed.

When the German's moved into the city, she ordered all of her charges to stay indoors as much as possible. She would go out to procure food for them. They had food hidden behind various walls in their two apartments, as well as in their shared bathroom. Most of this was canned goods. The potato harvest that summer had been fair and everyone's bed was underlain with sacks of potatoes. Before the men left for war, they had pilfered army rations which were also stored among the booty.

It was an unfortunate turn of events in early December when a partisan unit came into the city and blew up part of the railroad station. Twenty two German soldiers were killed, including two officers. The Germans put out an all-points bulletin and offered rewards for information about the partisans. After three days and no results, the Germans asked the city council members to produce one hundred citizens for execution. The council refused and they were hanged in the main square. Their bodies were left hanging for over a week. This changed the complexion of the occupation from tolerant to brutal.

After this hanging, one hundred citizens were dragged from homes, marched to the square, lined up against a wall and shot. When they were about to be executed many of them fell to their knees or flattened themselves on the cement They were still shot and a German officer examined each body and pumped an extra pistol shot into many of them. He had to reload his pistol many times.

An announcement was posted that relatives could come and claim the bodies of those executed. Many came to look at the corpses, but only about thirty bodies were claimed. The rest were piled into horse drawn carts and taken to a small ravine outside of the city and dumped into it.

The guerrilla activity was stopped when their leaders were contacted by their family members who lived in the city. It was explained that an offensive was planned outside of town and the reserve battalion should be able to drive the Germans out, since the Germans had outrun their supply lines.

Colonel Klein, in charge of the Voronezh occupation, sent out word to each of the district leaders to bring in some important people to hold as hostages in case there were more guerrilla incursions. They had no idea who was in the first batch that was shot. This time, he wanted to hold people important in public life, perhaps performers, university professors, school teachers, restaurant managers, in short, people who were recognizable.

At this time, word had spread through the apartment complex that there was fresh meat available at the packing house. When it looked like the Germans were going to advance into the city all the animals at the packing house were slaughtered and put in the ice room. The ice had been cut from the river the previous winter. The Germans had missed the building in their searches, since the building was run down and looked vacant.

Tanya knew it might be dangerous, but she wanted to preserve their stashed food supply as long as possible. She didn't know how long the Germans would be in charge. Since citizens were allowed on the streets, it was worth the risk. She bundled herself against the December weather. She put on an extra heavy sweater, her long coat, hat with ear flaps and felt boots. She folded her shopping bag into one coat pocket and headed for the packing house.

The soldiers along the way ignored her and she found herself in the packing house along with about thirty other people who had heard the rumor. It was true. There was meat to be had and many people were walking out with bags of meat. Tanya got at the end of the line. Two other women quickly moved in behind her. If she had to pay something for the meat, she had money which might be worthless, but still it was money.

Someone had tipped off the Germans. Perhaps it was someone who was stopped with a bag of fresh meat.

Three German infantrymen burst through the door with rifle ready. Everyone stopped what they were doing.

The three soldiers kept everyone from moving. There was only a moments pause until a German captain walked in and said in Russian, "All of you follow me."

The captain, along with the three soldiers, marched the contingent of about thirty individuals to a building which was the former headquarters of the Young Pioneers. They were put in the gymnasium.

The Young Pioneer Building had a gymnasium, shower room and kitchen on the first floor. There were sleeping rooms and an office on the second floor.

Major Hans Schneider occupied the office. He had two assistants whose job it was to bring each arrested citizen before him. The major would go over the internal passports and decide which people to hold as hostage. The hostages would be separated from the general group in the gymnasium and the others were free to go home.

The major hurried through the passports and told his two henchmen to put this person in the A group to be held or the B group to be set free. It was a situation that the soldiers were used to handling, since they occupied cities off and on for two years.

The major came to Tanya when about half the group had been processed. She was not impressive in her drab clothes and cloth cap with the ear flaps down. However, she appeared young when compared to the other women.

The major told his two assistants to take a break, go down in the gymnasium and have a smoke, he needed a moment of relaxation. "Come back in an hour." Tanya understood the meaning, even, if she didn't have complete understanding of the language.

Tanya was told by the major that he had been on the battlefield for two years now and he needed to have sex with a woman. Tanya said that she read the documents around the city which stated if a woman was raped by a German soldier; it was to be reported immediately. She had heard that a soldier was executed by the commander for such a crime.

The major was blunt. He told Tanya that if she cooperated it would not be rape and it was in her best interest to cooperate. Without her cooperation, she might be kept in confinement for several days and whoever she lived with would not know her whereabouts. She might even be executed, because they were making up a group of hostages. Even if she wasn't executed, she might be taken along with the army, if they had to move out. Besides, as hard as he was, it should only take about five minutes.

Tanya weighed her options and agreed to the deal. Major Schneider then took her to the next sleeping room and told her to take off her clothes as he was taking off his. Tanya put her long coat and hat on a chair in the room. Tanya said she was too cold, couldn't she just take off her underpants and lift her skirt.

"In the interest of time that would be acceptable." said the major. He continued to undress until he was completely naked. .

Tanya removed her boots, but not her stockings. She then took off her underpants which were heavy cotton and knee length. She lay back on the bed awaiting the major who was completely nude and sporting an erection. She pulled her skirt up to a roll around her waist.

Tanya moved down until she was flat on the bed and the major with penis in hand moved to her. Tanya moved her knees up and toward her head to receive the thrust. The instant the penis was against her it deflated to a limp finger. The major tried to push it in, but it wouldn't go.

The concerned major breathed deep. "There is something wrong. I can't get in. Help me out."

Tanya reached down to her pubic area and held the sides to the entrance of her vagina open in order to ease the entry. She held and squeezed the penis until there was a response. The major was reasonably hard and moved in again toward her. Again it went limp as it touched her.

The major got off his knees and sat on the edge of the cot and muttered to himself. Tanya was afraid he might blame the situation on her, and there is no telling what could happen. She moved to assist him again.

As the major sat there looking at the floor the door burst open. It was one of his assistants. "Major, Colonel Klein has ordered all senior officers to headquarters immediately. All soldiers are to report to their alert stations."

The major started to dress. Tanya, stood up, put on her boots without lacing them and headed for the door. She picked up her hat and coat on the way out. Neither the major nor the assistant tried to stop her.

On her way down the stairs, she stuffed her underpants into one sleeve. She didn't want any of the others to see her carrying her underpants or she might have been considered a collaborator. That would have been an unfortunate designation. No one saw her since all the detainees had fled the building.

Heavy bombardment of the city had started by the time Tanya reached her apartment. All the occupants were huddled in the basement, but Tanya went upstairs.

Tanya still had on her unlaced boots which she kicked off. She removed the underpants from her sleeve and put them on. She then went over to the sofa, laid on her back and stared at the ceiling. She would lay awake and stare at the ceiling throughout the night. The shelling lasted for two hours. There was the sound of heavy motors moving about. Most of the sounds were receding. Someone in the basement yelled loudly, "The Germans are pulling out."

It was another two hours before people left the basement and returned to their apartments. The main street was visible from the window in the Mikovich apartment and the two children and their grandmothers went there to view the activities. From that position, they could see Soviet soldiers moving in the street.

While the main action was at Stalingrad, the Voronezh Battalion had its hands full south of Moscow. Five of the seven divisions of the Third Romanian Army had surrendered and were being funneled through their ranks.

Tanya's husband, Dimitri was put in charge of verifying that one section of the new prisoners was unarmed and marched eastward toward the Volga River. He was always advised by the battalion political officer, his friend Igor.

Dimitri rode in and occasionally drove a military car while

the prisoners and their guards walked along. He would race to the head of the line, which was easy, since the ground was frozen and then he would leisurely make his way to the back of the line. He wanted to stay as long at the head as possible, since there might be an attack at the rear.

The entire time they were marching the prisoners, Soviet artillery was shooting over their heads. They had to wend their way through a scattered Soviet artillery group who were well equipped. Dimitri rushed ahead to tell the artillery group they were coming with several thousand prisoners.

When he got to the group, he was greeted by a captain of artillery who took him into his tent. The captain asked the distance of the marchers.

Dimitri answered, "About three miles, it only took me five minutes to get here but it should take them at least an hour."

The captain said, "Then you have time for some Russian tea my comrade. Please sit." He then went out to a sergeant and told him the situation. Firing at this point ceased, but continued down the line.

The captain looked at Dimitri. "So you are from the Voronezh Battalion. What is your name?"

"I am Sergeant Stepanovich and I actually live in Voronezh. I was working in the shipyard there when I got this job. I like the hours and the pay scale."

The captain laughed. "I knew a man from Voronezh in my last assignment. Perhaps you know him. His name is Ivan Ivanov."

Dimitri gulped his Russian tea which was straight whiskey. "I am not certain, it is a common name in Voronezh. How do you know him?"

"We were instructors in a school together. I really liked this intellectual fellow. He was a graduate of Voronezh University. He stayed behind when I got this assignment."

"How long ago was that?"

The captain laughed again. "Believe it or not, it was only four months ago."

"Then this Ivan is well. You say his name is Ivanov. When I go back to Voronezh I might try to find his family and tell them that he is well."

"They might be hard to find. His only sibling is a sister who is married and has a different name, which I do not know. They have a son named Ilya. He also has a grandmother which may have the same name. I don't know. We had a chance to talk while we were teachers, but we didn't give too many details of our private lives."

Dimitri finished his Russian tea. "Thanks for the drink. I needed that. I'll have to get back to supervising the prisoners. There is a pile of them, ten thousand at least, maybe more, all of them Romanians."

For two days, the Romanian prisoners filed past the artillery post. Some dropped out of line and were shot immediately. The line was a giant centipede moving over the landscape of light snow. Eventually, the last of the prisoners moved past the artillery position which started firing again.

Dimitri came back to the end of the line in his squad car and was greeted by Igor who stopped him. Igor blurted, "We have orders to stay with this artillery unit, so run up the line and tell the guards at the end to come back here. The line will continue in its mission without so many soldiers guarding it."

Dimitri did as ordered. When he got back, the artillery unit was packing up and heading west. Dimitri, eager to learn more about Ivan, maneuvered toward the unit with the former friend of Ivan's who said his name was Alexander.

The unit was moving rapidly. The Germans were in full retreat. Alexander said the boss told him the Germans were either retreating or advancing to help the encircled army at Stalingrad. The battle for Stalingrad had started in earnest in September and was now almost to its conclusion with the German army surrounded there. This unit of Germans heading, perhaps in that direction, had to be stopped.

If one had to pick one word to describe the battles and action on the steppes of Russia it would be "encirclement." Groups and units were trapped and surrounded by the enemy on this great plain. Almost every great battle had its encirclement.

So it was that the artillery battalion found itself encircled. The German army had retreated to be sure, but only long enough for the Soviet artillery battalion to come forward and find itself flanked on all sides. Another German unit was moving in behind them.

Thus, the news came to Dimitri, Alexander and Igor. They would become prisoners of war in about three days unless some miracle happened.

Dimitri was in Alexander's tent discussing the situation. Alexander was a tactician and knew the score. He said to Dimitri, "If you are taken prisoner, just go along with it. As long as you are in a military uniform they will let you alone. However, your friend Igor will be shot immediately, since he is a commissar. We shoot all SS officers immediately and they shoot all partisans and commissars immediately upon capture. If you get a chance, you might warn him about that."

Dimitri paused, "I don't know where he is and don't know how to find him."

Alexander continued, "Another thing, if you do happen to escape and get back to our lines, don't tell them you had been captured. Tell them you hid out and managed to get back to our lines."

"Why not tell them the truth, they might find out anyway."

"Maybe so, but it would be better not to tell them you were captured and escaped. They won't believe you. They will think you made a deal with the Germans. You might be executed immediately, or sent to some military prison for questioning. Worse yet, you might be put in some punishment battalion and get blown up walking over land mines. Pick up a gun if you escape and pretend it's yours. If asked for its serial number, just give them any ten digit number, nobody will be checking it."

It was just about an hour when the commander of the artillery units sent word that they had surrendered and everyone was to head toward the flares that were being sent into the air at ten minute intervals. Dimitri and Alexander joined others as they headed for the flares.

There were dead soldiers from both sides along the road the group was taking. No German guards were evident at this time. Alexander noted that no guards were needed, since they were completely surrounded and it would be difficult to get through the lines.

When they passed the body of a German officer Dimitri said to Alexander, "This is where I get off." Alexander looked at him through weary eyes and wished him luck.

Dimitri took the helmet and cloth under hat of the dead officer, a captain, as well as his military coat. There was a machine pistol with the body and he also took that. He shed his own coat and hat.

As he walked through the crowd of captured Soviets, he noticed them stepping out of his way. Soon he was out of the lines which were forming, and out on the open plain. The snow swirled about in ghostlike images adding to the surrealistic atmosphere..

After he had walked about two miles, Dimitri came to the German lines which were moving forward slowly. A squad car stopped to pick him up. It was occupied by two soldiers, a sergeant and a private. Dimitri got in the back seat and asked, "Vo ist de commandant?"

The sergeant answered, but his rapid German was incomprehensible to Dimitri, who only knew a few phrases that he learned from a handbook given to non   commissioned officers. It had essential phrases concerned with capturing and holding prisoners and asking directions. He had practiced his accent, but spoke in a low voice.

The sergeant assuming that the captain wanted to go to the commander got out of the car and told the driver to take the captain to the rear. The driver said something like "Ya vowl" and headed back into the advancing ranks.

As the main group of soldiers were passed, Dimitri said to the driver, "Gehen sie links." Go to the left. The driver obeyed. Then "Gehen sie recht."

When it looked like a clear path to the east Dimiti told the driver to halt, which he did. He took out the machine pistol and told the driver to get out and start walking back to the German lines. The driver realizing that Dimitri was a Russian fumbled for his pistol and Dimitri shot him in the chest. The driver was able to get his pistol clear and managed to shoot Dimitri in the right upper chest. The bullet went just below the collar bone. Another shot by Dimitri and the driver was dead.

Dimitri was able to drive the squad car, but had a lot of

trouble with double clutching, which was a feature of the German gear system. Once he had mastered the clutch, he headed east. Eventually he saw a light in a house. It was an isolated house on the steppe.

Dimitri abandoned the squad car, the helmet and under hat and the coat and walked forward. With machine pistol in hand, he burst through the door. Inside huddled around a small stove were three women and an old man. He asked if there were any soldiers about and they answered in the negative. One middle aged woman said there was a Russian unit about five miles away and they sent patrols in this direction about every two hours.

Dimitri was freezing and went to the fire. Eventually the patrol came by. The patrol of five wanted to make a stretcher out of a blanket and poles for Dimitri, but he said he thought he could make it for five miles. They sent two men back with him while the other three continued their patrol. They took the machine pistol with them. It was a fine weapon and they were glad to get it. The three would eventually find the squad car, which they never connected with Dimitri, and demolish it.

About a mile from the field hospital Dimitri collapsed and the two escorts took turns carrying him. He had regained his senses when brought into the warmth of the hospital, which was more of a first aid station. A field doctor came over to him and removed his jacket and shirt. He looked at the wound and said it was just a little hole and wouldn't take much of a bandage.

The hole was an entrance wound. Dimitri turned around and showed the exit wound which was a gaping hole of torn flesh which was still oozing blood. They immediately bundled Dimitri in warm blankets, gave him some hot tea and put him in the cab of a small truck and transported him further east to a better hospital facility.

At the hospital, he was treated with antibiotics and given a hot meal of boiled potatoes. He was interrogated by a captain who wanted to know why he hadn't surrendered with the artillery unit. Dimitri said he wanted to fight those bastards until his last breath and he didn't know how many he had killed in order to get back to his group. When he got to the place where the group was supposed to be, they had already moved out and he didn't know they had surrendered.

Dimitri said he came across a dead captain with a machine pistol. He took it and killed about six or seven Germans which were blocking his way. One of them shot him. He eventually made his way to the isolated farm house which turned out to be a disguised Soviet observation post.

When the three men who had finished the patrol returned, they said they had found five dead Germans in one group. The captain assumed these were men killed by Dimitri. Since the story of Dimitri was "verified" the captain filled out a report indicating that Dimitri had killed sixteen Germans single handedly. He was recommended for two combat medals. He also indicated that Dimitri was ready to go back to the front, but the captain was giving him at least two months to recuperate and then would make a decision about his next assignment.

20 Yuri Meets the Family

The annual June break for the Tomsk students was approaching. It was 1943. The Germans had been defeated at Stalingrad and driven out of Voronezh. A dispatch by General Stroop, the SS commander in Poland, is monitored. In it, he states that the synagogue in Warsaw has been blown up. More than 14,000 Jews had been killed in the ghetto and another 40,000 have been sent to Treblinka to be exterminated. In other dispatches, it was mentioned that the Jews in Kiev had been rounded up with the aid of the local Ukrainians. Executions near Kiev had not yet been made public.

Yuri knew the most intimate details of the lives of his special student's. He had other students but these were not in the special class. He was particularly interested in one Lazlo Gregorov who was originally from Voronezh. He called Lazlo in for an interview.

After several small talk remarks, Yuri asked, "Will you be going home to Voronezh on your break?"

"Yes, I plan to go to Voronezh and visit my grandmother, if she is still alive. My parents say she is, and, since I can get a special rail pass in my status as student I can go. My parents live in Kemerovo, where they supervise a textile mill, making uniforms for the military. My mother can't get permission to see her mother, my babushka."

Yuri went on. "The reason I asked if you were going to Voronezh was because I have friends there, from my childhood, and I wonder how they made out during the occupation of the city. I wonder if you could make a side trip and find out for me."

"It would be my pleasure, sir. Just give me the details and I'll see what I can do."

"Come back at noon in two days and I'll give you the details and maybe have a present you can give to my old friends."

In two days, Lazlo came back as requested. Yuri gave him a small packet containing one of the remaining gold trinkets that he had inherited from his new father. Along with it, he put in a note "Take this to Mr. Saperstein, he will know its value and buy it from you in an honest deal. If Mr. Saperstein is not available, then perhaps his son is. If not, then hang on to this memento." Mr. Saperstein was a friend of Olga's and a little known jeweler in Voronezh. He kept a low profile.

Lazlo was told to look up Tatanya Stepanovich on Petro Street, apartment 3C. There should also be a young boy there, her son Ilya. Lazlo should find out all he can about their condition and give Tatanya the package.

Yuri said, "It is just a small gift to let the family know I remember them."

Lazlo began to get friendly. "How do you know these people?"

"When I was a little boy I lived near this family. The mother and I were about the same age and used to play in the playground together. Her mother used to come out to the playground and give us cookies and milk. Her mother used to call me her little flower petal."

"Crazy, I can't imagine you as a little flower petal."

"I was more of a weed than a flower. Anyway, I loved that old lady. Be sure to ask about her. I think she lives in a different apartment than my friend and her husband. Probably, the husband is off somewhere in the war."

It was the end of June 1943 and the annual break for the Tomsk students. Ludmilla stayed with Yuri. Her parents were not able to come to her because of her father's new assignment. There would have to be a meeting between Yuri and her parents at a later time, perhaps in the new year. The program of young scientists had one more year to go before the students would be sent off to their permanent assignments. Yuri was not sure what his fate would be. He could stay on as a teacher at the university, if he so wanted, but he wanted to be with Milla, forever..

Lazlo went to Voronezh and finding his grandmother coping nicely, he went to visit Tanya. When he got to apartment 3C on Petro Street he was told by Olga that everyone, but she, was working. Tatanya and Ilya would return sometime around six o'clock in the evening. "Come back then."

Lazlo had to cool his heels for two more hours. He walked down to the river and watched reconstruction on the port. A man in a black uniform with gold braid asked why he wasn't in the military and asked to see his identification papers. Lazlo didn't want to challenge the man who looked like he had some kind of authority. He gave the man his internal passport and his Special Highest Grade railroad pass. Anyone holding this pass could travel anywhere that railroads traveled.

The man smiled, "So, you are somebody special. I am the commissar for Voronezh region. If I can help you in any way while you are visiting, please don't hesitate to ask."

Lazlo told him about his grandmother and her apartment conditions. The man said he would look in on her and see what he could do for her.

When Lazlo returned to Apartment 3C he was brought into the sitting room by day and bedroom by night. Tanya and Ilya had returned from work. Ilya was in the sitting room and Tanya was bathing. Olga gave Lazlo a cup of tea and apologized for not having any cream to put in it.

Lazlo smiled, "I like it without cream. I am so used to cutting out frills that now I have trouble drinking tea with cream."

Ilya asked Lazlo why he wasn't in the army like his father. Lazlo said he would answer that when he met Tatanya. Ilya said his mother went by the name Tanya.

Soon Tanya appeared and welcomed her guest. "And to what do we owe this visit from such a handsome young man."

Lazlo blushed. "I am a student at Tomsk University, studying science. One of my professors said to look in on you and find out how your family is doing."

Tanya looked skeptical. "And what is your professor's name?"

"It is Yuri Bulganin."

"I don't think I know anyone by that name. At least, I can't recall it in my memory." Olga shook her head in agreement.

"He said you and he used to play together as children, and your mother used to bring milk and cookies to the playground."

Olga butted in. "I used to bring milk and cookies to the playground to all of Tanya's friends. I can't recall this Yuri Bulganin either."

Ilya blurted, "I suppose I wasn't even born at that time, so I don't remember him either."

Lazlo was at a loss. "Could you at least tell me how all of you are doing and I can report back to him. He has given me this package to give to Tatanya."

He handed the well wrapped package to Tanya. She accepted it with apprehension.

"Well, thank him for the package, perhaps you have the wrong apartment."

"No, I have the correct address and the correct people. He said you had a son about fourteen years old and his description was accurate. I know I am not mistaken. He said that your mother used to call him her little flower petal."

Tanya gasped. There was a pause. "I do know this man now that you mention it." She fought to control her emotions.

Olga started crying profusely. She put her hands together in prayer. "Thank you God."

Tanya said. "My mother remembers him too. Please tell us all you can about him."

Lazlo went on with what he knew about Yuri. He was a brilliant professor who had two scars, one on each side of his head. He was practically living with, and was about to marry the daughter of Major Mikoyan. Everybody liked this professor and he, as well as other students, would do anything for him. The professor was a hero of war against the Japanese in the skirmishes of the Far East. His father was General Bulganin who was killed in the early stages of the war."

Lazlo was given some of the stew Olga had prepared for supper. He was pumped for more information, and when he had no more information, he was told to repeat what he had said. He couldn't understand the intense interest in his professor.

Tanya said, "We know where this man's relatives live, and when we contact them, they will want to know everything about this man. They had lost touch with him when his father was killed. The name just was lost in my memory."

Lazlo nodded, "I understand. Times are so unsettled now it's a wonder any of us has brains, let alone memory in those brains. I will leave now, since I want to spend as much time with my babushka as possible."

Tanya told Lazlo to wait while she wrote a letter to Yuri. He agreed to wait.

In the letter Tanya did not address it to anyone. She merely started in with how she was well and so were her son and her mother. They all sent their love. They had survived the occupation of the city. Her husband was a quartermaster sergeant and was wounded in action. He would be able to come home soon, and they would exchange stories. Her husband's best friend was captured by the Germans and executed. (It would obviously be Igor and Yuri, nee Ivan, would surely know whom she meant.) They would all be anxious to see him again, and she remembered the happy days of their childhood together.

If this letter should fall into hostile hands it was of such a nature that it could have been written to anyone and would not tie the writer and its receiver together in any way that could be verified. Fear dominated the average Soviet mind.

Lazlo took the letter, put it in his back pocket, and bade the family farewell. Olga and Tanya hugged him and Ilya shook his hand. Olga gave him two hard biscuits for his journey.

After Lazlo left, Ilya said he would like to meet Yuri Bulganin. Tanya assured him that he would meet Yuri sometime in the future.

It was November when Dimitri was permitted to come home from the hospital. His wounds had healed and except for some muscle problems in his right arm he was fine.

When he arrived at the railroad station, there was a tremendous homecoming and Tatanya and Ilya were given a day off work to welcome him and the other veterans. A train finally arrived carrying many soldiers. A band played military music as the veterans stepped down. Further down the platform, where few could observe, boxes containing the bodies of dead soldiers were being unloaded. There were hundreds of these.

The time off for Tanya and Ilya was a one day affair. They had to go back to work the next day. They were working seven days a week and any time off had to be by application and approved by the shipyard supervisor.

Dimitri carried a crutch with him and he used it to get sympathy and better seating when the opportunity arose. Before he left the hospital, one of the nurses gave Dimitri a chocolate candy bar which had been taken, along with other food stuffs, from captured German stores. His family could share it..

There were several medals on Dimitri 's chest and Ilya wanted to know what they were for and all about his father's adventures. Dimitri obliged. He didn't have to exaggerate because his true experiences were better than fiction.

Ilya told his story about getting his grandmother into a wheelbarrow during the bombardment and the race through the streets. Ilya told about the big gun of the Germans and how it created craters all over the city. Most of the craters had been filled with rubble from destroyed buildings. The water system was working once again. Sewage disposal was a problem. The city merely adjusted the pipes so they ran out into the river and most of the city sewage went downstream toward Rostov na Donu. The city would fix the system, as soon as it could.

Olga told how she and Gemma carried water under the watchful eyes of the German soldiers. Tanya did not mention her detainment by the Germans and the incidents of the evening before the Soviets came back to the city.

Dimitri told them about the artillery officer who knew Ivan and was a teacher with him. Tanya then told the story of Lazlo and how there was no longer any Ivan, but there was Yuri Bulganin, and we all must call him that when we see him. Yuri was safe across the

232

Urals in the city of Tomsk. They were sure he would visit as soon as opportunities arose. Ilya wondered why his mother had not told him that Yuri was the new name of his Uncle Ivan.

Anya and Gemma came over and wanted to know all about Igor and his execution. They cried most of the time, as Dimitri told about the leadership qualities of their man. Dimiti said the Germans got Igor, but he got at least sixteen of them. However, this did not make Anya and Gemma feel any better.

The leave lasted five days and Ilya and the four women saw Dimitri off at the railroad station. The band was there, as usual, to play for the daily arrivals and departures. Troops boarding this train didn't know if they would ever return.

Dimitri was sent to the Minsk front where he was given duties in a supply unit behind the lines. The commander in charge was General Timko. Here he met Captain Penza who had been a guard at Camp 193 north of Krasnoyarsk. Dimitri thought it wise not to ask any questions about the camp, and if Penza was in a talkative mood, he would give out information.

The Soviets entered Gomel, Belorussia which was along a Dneiper River tributary and northeast of the Pripyat Marshes, which had kept the Germans from massing troops for a northern assault on Moscow. If the westward advance continued, Timko's army and Penza's division would soon be in Poland.

One of Dimitri's duties was to prepare bodies of Soviet soldiers for shipment home. There was no embalming in this procedure. The bodies were merely wrapped in canvas and tied with strings. These were put in a wooden crate. The name was painted on the crate, as well as its destination. Since it was winter, there would be no odor of decaying bodies until the spring thaw. By that time, the bodies should have been buried.

After each battle, there were hundreds of bodies to be shipped east. The crate makers worked feverishly to keep ahead of the demand. At this time, in every area of operations, Soviet soldiers were being killed by the thousands.

People who survived in Gomel lived in basements and in make shift dwellings. The Soviet soldiers entering the city of Gomel had little restrictions on them. They looted and raped freely. Belorussians were their kinsman but, hell, this was war, and you never knew when the next bullet had your name on it.

Sergeant Dimitri and Private Cherkas had finished packing a truck with frozen carcasses of cattle and sheep which was being sent to the front. There were pipes built inside the covered truck and the hind feet of the animals were tied together and tied onto the pipes. When they finished packing, there was little room for anything else on the truck. Dimitri closed the door and put a lock into the opening for it. However, he did not close the lock, in case they had to add something more to it.

    The two then went to a pile of coats, hats and boots they had removed from the dead soldiers under their care. Before wrapping the soldiers in canvas, they removed hats, coats and boots if they had them. These were thrown on a huge pile which was eventually packed into trucks and sent to a massing center for new soldiers.

    The sergeant and the private began packing coats in a second covered truck. Except for the two of them the street was empty.

    It was January 10, 1944 and the night temperature was only twenty degrees below freezing. During the short day, the temperature had risen to ten degrees below freezing and Private Cherkas said if it got any warmer he would have to take off his coat and hat. Dimitri laughed at that.

    When the truck was packed about two feet high, Private Cherkas said he was going to take a smoke break. Dimitri agreed. Cherkas lit a cigarette and Dimitri lit the pipe which he carried with him.

    As the soldiers lolled beside the truck a woman came down the street. Cherkas told Dimiitri he needed some sex and this might be an opportunity for them. Dimitri puffed at the pipe, "Not for me, do whatever you want. We have plenty of time."

    When the woman, a young girl, got to them Cherkas spoke up. "Beautiful woman, how would you like to please a Soviet soldier who is fighting for your country?"

    It was a young girl. "I have already done my duty comrade. Do you have any food you could give to me. I haven't eaten anything for four days and I have come out of my basement home to search for food. There is no food in January."

Cherkas laughed. "If you have sex with me in the truck, I will give you food."

The girl responded. "If you are a true humanitarian, you would give me the food without the demand."

Cherkas again laughed. "You know, I could throw you into this truck, on this pile of coats and get sex without any strings attached."

The girl said. "Then you will have to do that. I do not want to give my body to you, even if you had food, which you appear not to have."

Cherkas reached for his rifle with the bayonet and pointed at the girl. "Get in the truck and take off your bottoms, so that I can shove it to you."

The girl hesitated and Cherkas whacked her on the arm with the side of the bayonet. The girl let out a muted shriek and got in the back of the truck and did as she was told. Cherkas was on her immediately, and as he stated, soon shoved it into her.

Dimitri was an observer of the situation. He did not interfere because rape was a standard procedure in the Soviet occupied territories. Even though Belorussia was a part of the Soviet Union, they were not true Russians. Dimitri did not want to offend Cherkas, whom he might have to rely on for support some day. He went over to the meat truck.

When Cherkas was done, he called out to Dimitri. "It's your turn now."

Dimitri lifted himself into the truck. He was carrying a pair of small felt boots. Cherkas lit another cigarette and moved away from the truck.

The girl was sobbing. Dimitri climbed into the back of the truck and said, "Don't cry little one. I do not want to have sex with you."

"Why not, all the soldiers want sex. The Germans were better than the Russians. They left us alone and carried on the war. I hope they come back and kill all of you bastards."

"I don't blame you for thinking that. Are you all right now?"

"No, I'm not all right. This is the fourth soldier who has raped me in two days. My grandmother told me not to leave the cellar, but we are hungry, and haven't eaten for four days."

Dimitri reached in his pocket and took out a hard biscuit. "Here, eat this." She grabbed it and furiously chewed on it. "I guess you are very hungry."

The girl gulped. "Yesterday, I went out to search for food. A Soviet soldier grabbed me in a doorway and put me on the steps. He told me to take off my underpants. When I tried to get my underpants off, he couldn't wait and took his bayonet and cut them enough to get it into me. That was the first time I had sex with any man. I was a virgin until yesterday."

"That is horrible."

"Then this morning, I went into an office where two soldiers were working on papers. At least it was warm in there. They bent me over the table they were working on. One held my arms forward while the other ripped off my underpants and raped me from behind. When the first man was done, he exchanged places with the second man. My only two pairs of underpants have been ruined."

Dimitri patted her arm. "Look, I brought you a pair of small boots. But something more important, I loaded both boots with meat which I cut from some storage animals we have in the other truck.

"Thank you, kind sir."

"Where do you live? Perhaps I can walk you to your basement and protect you."

"About three blocks from here. I'm not sure I can walk just yet. After all, I have been raped four times in two days and I am not used to it."

Dimitri walked the girl to her basement dwelling. When they arrived there he asked, "How old are you anyway?"

The girl looked directly at him. "I had my fourteenth birthday last week."

Dimitri said. "I have a fourteen year old daughter. Maybe she's fifteen, I don't remember. My mind is not quite right. With the execution of Igor, Dimitri assumed that Anya was now his daughter."

The girl disappeared into the basement carrying the two felt boots loaded with meat. Dimitri walked down the street. After a block he began sobbing. He waited until he was through sobbing and in control of his emotions before he went back to work with Cherkas.

February 1944 and the long awaited meeting between Yuri and the parents of Milla was planned. Milla would be graduating from the special class in June and would receive a new assignment. Commander Volosky said that he would see that she and Yuri would receive an assignment together. Volosky hinted at their new assignment. Yuri could stay on at the university, if he wished, but he would be more useful to society in another capacity that Volosky didn't want to discuss at the moment.

The meeting was set for one o'clock, February 14 at Yuri's apartment. Milla met her parents at the railroad station. They had taken a train from Magnitogorsk to Chelyabinsk and another to Kemorovo and then on to Tomsk. The trip had taken two days and they wanted to freshen up before meeting their potential son-in-law.

Milla asked if they needed more time. Lorraine said they didn't have more time, since they would have to head back to their new camp duties as soon as possible. She wanted to wash and change into the special outfit she had brought for the occasion. Major Mikoyan merely brushed off his hat and military jacket and put on his great coat.

They walked the four blocks to Yuri's apartment. Yuri saw them coming and put Latko outside the apartment. Latko took his usual place beside the door. Yuri went back and sat on the sofa.

When the party got to the apartment, Latko went to Milla. She bent down and patted him on the side. Mikoyan looked at the dog as if he had seen such an animal before. Milla then opened the door and asked if everything was ready and Yuri said it was. The three entered the room and Yuri rose to his feet.

Milla spoke, "Mother and father, I would like to introduce my Yuri Bulganin to you."

Lorraine said, "It is my pleasure to meet you." Then she took a good look at Yuri and a lump came to her throat. Her mouth went slightly open and she put her hands to her mouth. Her hands were lowered slowly to her breast and then clasped together. She fell to her knees and bent over with her hands on the floor, and with her face in her hands. She let out small screams and cried.

Major Mikoyan had not seen what Lorraine had seen and he

assumed his wife was in shock from meeting her daughter's future husband. He bent over and said, "Mother, please, get up."

Lorraine stopped making noises, but kept on the floor with her head in her hands. The major turned to Yuri to apologize for his wife's behavior. Then it hit him. "Ivan, it's you."

The major stood frozen, just staring at Yuri. Lorraine lifted her head from her hands and was still on her knees.

Yuri spoke, "No, I am Yuri Bulganin, teacher at Voronezh University Institute. Perhaps, I look like someone you once knew." The major helped Lorraine to her feet. Lorraine rushed over to Yuri and clasped him to her. After a couple of seconds of holding him she released her hands from around him and pulled his face to her. She kissed him profusely, over and over, until Yuri took her hands down and put his around her and kissed her several times on the cheeks before releasing her.

Major Mikoyan came over to Yuri and held his hands on Yuri's cheeks and kissed him on the mouth.

Yuri smiled, "I take this to mean that you approve of my marrying your daughter."

Lorraine continued crying and couldn't answer. The major just stood there grinning.

Once the initial shock was over, the party settled down and all found seats. Yuri served Armenian red wine to everyone. They sat there just looking at each other.

The Mikoyan's wanted to know all about Ivan's metamorphosis, but he refused to divulge any information. He repeated that he was the son of General Bulgarian and had trained at Kolomna and Nizhni Novgorod. He had been on assignment in the Far East for four years. He was now considered an expert on rocket engines and was involved with interrogating captured German scientists.

Major Mikoyan described his new duties as commander of the German prisoner-of-war camp. He also described his past duties as commander of the camp north of Krasnoyarsk. He said he had made friends with a lot of the prisoners and mentioned several of them. Gregor Mishkov recovered from his wound enough to work and was rehabilitated. He was sent to Kazakhstan to supervise a collective horse farm. Animals raised there would be furnished to the army.

The major added that he and the captains knew that Mishkov was a casual informer for Frunze. When Frunze's man came up from Krasnoyarsk, he usually went to the stables which was a tip off. The general sent Mishkov food parcels once a month. So when Mishkov had his unfortunate accident, we called him a hero and sent him to the hospital in Krasnoyarsk. Frunze wanted to reward the man who carried Mishkov six or seven miles to the river, but we had to tell him that the man was killed. We didn't mind rewarding Mishkov, since he gave us good reports. He is an honest man.

Lev Lefkowich had his record expunged by Vishinsky himself. He married a woman prisoner named Magda, and they went to live somewhere near Moscow. When the major mentioned Magda, Milla shot a glance and smile in Yuri's direction.

Yuri wanted to know about Rasputin, but didn't want to give up the charade. He also wanted to know about the captains and Sergeant Vologda. Finally, he asked about them. Rasputin was released and went to live with the Evenki somewhere in the north. He was considered a powerful medicine man. The captains and the sergeants were still with the major and it may not be in Yuri's best interest for him to visit Magnitogorsk and have them see him. Yuri agreed.

Major Mikoyan asked how Yuri got the head wound. Yuri explained that he was wounded in a clash on the Manchurian border. Then he admitted, a man tried to kill him, but he managed to thwart the attacker. However, he was in bad shape for a couple of months.

Mikoyan said that the dog outside the apartment was a fine looking animal and wondered how long Yuri had had him. Yuri said the dog's name was Latko and had saved his life once, and got him out of ticklish situations several times. The dog would protect him and Milla as long as it remained healthy.

Yuri said he had a surprise for Milla. He and Milla would be assigned to a new project called "Sputnik." He wasn't sure what it was, but, he would work on the project and Milla would translate documents from English into Russian. They might eventually be sent to Bakinor in Kazakhstan where rocket launching facilities were being built.

Lorraine produced a photo album from her large hand bag.

"Milla asked me to bring my family photo album, to show you our family."

Lorraine sat in the middle of the sofa with Milla on one side and Yuri on the other. They went through picture by picture. When they came to a picture of a small girl with long white hair Yuri asked, "Who is this yellow haired little girl?"

Lorraine beamed, "That's Milla. When she was little, her hair was like golden sunshine. Everyone remarked about it. Just to look at her, and her hair, made everyone smile."

And they lived happily ever after. Anyway, as happily as one could under the Soviet system.

The End: To be continued.

Other books of this nature by the author: The Incident at Natasovo and the Battle of Poltava- Emeral Mountain, The Identity Thief -

The Home Grown Terrorist - The Witches of Leone Manor - and the five books in the Detective Ann Morgan Series

Printed in Great Britain
by Amazon

20192922R00139